THE ETERNAL CHAMBER: AN ARCHAEOLOGICAL THRILLER

THE RELICS OF THE DEATHLESS SOULS, BOOK 1

TOM HUNTER

ONE

The incessant thunder of the helicopter's blades made it difficult for Samuel McCarthy to focus; the relentless pounding causing him to lose his train of thought yet again. He forced himself to tune out the repetitive thumping as he examined the dry, dusty map in his hand, comparing it to the satellite image of the region on his lap.

"Have you figured it out yet?" the voice of the stocky pilot, Josh Bradley, crackled through the headsets they all wore.

The sandy-haired archaeologist in the rear of the helicopter frowned, causing the lines on his forehead to deepen, as he closely examined the two documents he was holding. Clinging onto the overhead handle for support, he leaned out of the open door, looking for confirmation that the parched desert below matched the map.

"All the signs suggest that my comparison should be correct this time. If I'm right, whatever secret this map is hiding, it should be just beneath us."

"If," Josh snorted. "You said that the last time. Might I remind you that we've been flying around this sector for twenty minutes now and we've only got the one back-up fuel tank. We're getting dangerously close to the point of no turning back, and I'd really rather not be stranded out in the middle of nowhere because you've got your north and south confused again."

"Hey!" protested Samuel. "I only did that the once and in my defense, I was more than a little hungover at the time thanks to a certain pilot deciding that he needed to drown his sorrows the night before."

"Yeah, yeah." Josh shook his head. "A bad archaeologist always blames his team."

The olive-skinned Nafty, the third passenger in the helicopter, listened in silent bemusement as the two old friends exchanged quips. Such unprofessionalism would not be tolerated if he were in charge of this mission. You only had to look at McCarthy to see that the man clearly didn't care about standards. Was it really too much to ask that someone shave before coming to work?

"You're going to need to tell me where to set down soon or I'll have no choice but to turn back," Josh warned.

"I know, I know." Samuel ran his hand through his sandy hair in exasperation. "Just give me a minute, okay? I'm close to pinning it down."

He opened his notebook, skimming through his notes. Flicking through the pages, he quickly scanned through insights that had hit him as he translated the comments written on the map in faded ink. It would have been helpful if the person making the notes had written them in English in a more permanent pen, but when was archaeology ever that easy?

A few geographical landmarks had been annotated, which Samuel had initially hoped would make it easy to identify them. Unfortunately, it turned out that the region was nothing but the same landscape repeated over and over, so he'd had to refer back to the 'days traveled' noted on the map, and dotted lines not drawn to scale, to dead reckon the distance to their objective.

Comparing his notes to the map, he wished that he could figure out what the ancient explorer had meant when they wrote 'Confirm that I am not dead before the door and be welcomed into the chamber beyond.' He hadn't told Josh about that comment, knowing the kind of reaction it would provoke. For some reason, the pilot had issues about any suggestion that they might die in their quest for relics.

"We should be right on top of the cave now," he announced. "Give or take a quarter mile."

"Give or take?" echoed Josh. "A quarter mile is still quite the circumference. This is hopeless. We're looking for a needle in a haystack here."

"I know, but I'm positive we're in the right ballpark now," Samuel told him. "The limestone, rain, and river survey I got from the Ministry would suggest that this is roughly where a cave would develop if one were to form in this area."

"Suggest? Why can't you ever be more specific?" Josh sighed, turning the helicopter to go for another sweep over the area. "You're going to need to figure this out, stat, or this will be yet another wasted trip."

"Do you need any help looking over the map?" Nafty broke his silence to offer his support. "I might not have your level of archaeological expertise, but I've done my fair share of map reading and I do know this region better than either of you. What's the point in bringing me along as your guide if you won't let me guide you?" He undid his seatbelt to come over to Samuel's side, trying to get a closer look at the map.

"Don't worry," Samuel assured him. "You'll get your chance to be helpful when we hit the ground. But I was incredibly lucky to get hold of this map. It's an irreplaceable ancient artifact. I can't hand it over to just anyone."

"I'm not just anyone," Nafty pointed out. "Come on. Let me have a look. A second pair of eyes might spot something new. I could find that missing piece of the puzzle and save us all a lot of work."

"No offence, Nafty, but this is the original document and as the chief of the excavation, I have a professional duty to keep it safe. Maybe I'm being over protective... Imagine if you lost your grip and it fell out of the 'helicopter? It might be lost forever, along with all its secrets. No, this map stays in my possession. If we don't find the cave on this final sweep, maybe I'll be able to make you a simplified copy back at camp, but that's the best I can do."

Nafty opened his mouth to protest, but the firm set of Samuel's jaw told him that he'd be wasting his time, so he decided against pushing it.

"All right, guys." Josh interrupted their discussion. "Since we still haven't found what we're looking for, I'm going to turn us around rather than risk going into our extra fuel reserves. I've still got to get us back to a refueling station and while I appreciate your enthusiasm, Samuel, you're not the only one with a professional duty here. It's my job to keep you both safe, so I'm making a judgment call to take us back in."

"Why don't you just land?" Samuel suggested. "I'd like to look things over on foot and it'll give Nafty a chance to show off his skills."

"All right. It's your funeral," shrugged Josh, looking around for a suitable site to touch down. Spotting a clearing, he began to lower the chopper.

"Now we just have to hope that the Bruard haven't gotten there before us," muttered Samuel. "Knowing my luck, we'll be in the right place, but they'll have already got their filthy mitts on it and another precious artifact will be lost forever."

Nafty's eye twitched, his hand clenching into a fist at the mention of the brutal regime that had attempted to conquer the entirety of Europe in the middle of the 21st century. Although they'd been fought back, it was only a matter of time before they attempted world domination again.

"Is something wrong?" Samuel asked.

"You should not say that name," warned Nafty. "Even mentioning that organization is a bad omen. It is said in my culture that to name someone is to attract their attention to you. You don't want their attention upon you, do you?"

Samuel sighed. "I'm sorry. You're right. The longer we can keep this secret, the better. I'd hate for the Br- for *them* to steal something that belongs to the world. We need to recover whatever it is this map is concealing and get it safely to a museum, so historians the world over can study it for the benefit of everyone. Knowledge should never be confined to a select, privileged few."

"We're just coming into land now," Josh announced. "I'd like to thank you all for traveling with Josh Bradley airlines and- WOAH!"

The helicopter suddenly jerked to the side as Josh yanked the control stick to the right to narrowly avoid a rock face that had abruptly appeared out of nowhere. As the helicopter lurched away from the stone, the rotor blades missed the rock by inches, and the sudden movement sent Nafty tumbling out of his seat and out of the open door.

"Help!" he screamed, as Samuel threw off his seatbelt to dive after him. Their fingers brushed against each other, the contact coming just too late, as Samuel braced himself against the doorframe, making one final desperate lunge to save his colleague. Somehow, he managed to grab hold of Nafty's hand.

"Climb back up!" Samuel urged. "I've got you."

Nafty kicked his legs, desperately trying to get enough momentum to pull himself into the helicopter, but despite his best efforts, his other hand flailed about uselessly, unable to find anything within reach.

Samuel's eyes widened in shock and fear as he felt Nafty slowly but surely slip out of his grasp.

TWO

A single, bare lightbulb slowly swung from side to side, suspended from the ceiling by a cable. Its glaring brilliance illuminated the small room, exposing the run down space for the slum that it was, as shadows rolled like waves with the movement of the light. The sound of a television in a nearby room filtered through the walls, an inane infomercial extolling the virtues of the latest must-have fitness accessory to anyone who would listen.

There was little furniture, the walls bare and unadorned apart from a board hanging next to the door with an impressive array of tools mounted on it. In stark contrast to the peeling paper and poorly maintained room, the tools were brand new, gleaming with the promise of a job well done.

The only other visible item was a chair nailed to the floor in the middle of the room, an unconscious man firmly lashed down to it. His head hanging low, he started to blink his eyes, slowly coming around. Moaning, the first thing he was aware of was the throbbing headache that overwhelmed him.

As he attempted to lift his hand to brush his hair out of his face, the Egyptian realized for the first time that he was bound. Desperately trying to break free of the ropes restraining him, he thrashed his body around, but despite his best efforts, he couldn't even move the chair, much less slip out of the ropes.

Raising his head, he got his first glimpse of the room around him, his blood running cold when he spotted the tools hanging on the wall. Panic made him fight even harder against the ropes, every instinct in his body screaming at him to get as far away as he could, but all he succeeded in doing was scrape away the skin where he was tied down.

"Help! Somebody! Anybody!" The gag around his mouth muffled his shouts. Nevertheless, despite the noise of the television, it appeared that someone heard him. The sound shut off abruptly, giving way to footsteps getting louder as an unseen person made their way towards the prisoner.

The man held his breath as if his silence would render him invisible, regretting calling out. Whoever was coming, they were probably not there to set him free.

He racked his brains, trying to figure out how he had ended up in this place. All he could remember was leaving work and heading towards his car. Then... nothing. The way his head was throbbing, all he could assume was that someone had hit him from behind to knock him out and kidnap him, but why? What on earth could anyone want with him?

The door in front of him opened, and the light from the corridor was blocked by the giant outline of the man who walked through, stooping to avoid knocking his head against the doorframe. His custom-tailored shirt defined his muscular physique.

Holding the door for the man following him, he stood to attention as his boss strode in. Although he was half the size of his henchman, there was a whiff of evil from the small, bald man that told the captive that *this* man was the one he should be afraid of. Sharply dressed, he wore a dark navy tailored suit that fit his body perfectly, coordinating his polka dotted white handkerchief with his perfectly knotted tie. Yet, his dark brown leather gloves were a strange affectation that jarred against the rest of his outfit.

Coming to a stop in front of the bound man, he leaned forward so that the two of them were almost touching noses. Instinctively, his captive held his breath, craning his neck to escape the intense scrutiny, but he was so tightly bound he could barely move. The only act of rebellion open to him was to close his eyes and pretend that he was anywhere but here.

Taking his time to examine every inch of his prisoner's face, the suited man finally gave a tiny nod and stepped back. Gesturing to his henchman that he should give their prisoner a little freedom, the gorilla stepped forward and pulled the gag away.

"Let me introduce myself. My name is Pin Nam-Gi and this fine gentleman is Gord," the small man began, before his captive could get a word out. His voice was cultured, suggesting a high level of education or years spent socializing with aristocrats. "Perhaps you've heard of me? No? No matter. By the time I've finished with you, my name will be permanently emblazoned on your memory. I take it you are Haisam, Director of the Ministry of State for Antiquities?"

Haisam opened his mouth to lie, but Pin tutted and shook his head.

"Don't say anything. It was a rhetorical question," Pin said. "I already know exactly who you are, but I do so like to observe all the formalities. Just because we have some unpleasant business to attend to doesn't mean that we have to act like savages, does it? I like to put my business acquaintances at ease while we deal with the matter at hand."

"What do you want with me?" Haisam demanded. "Why am I tied up like this? If you know who I am, you know that if anything happens to me, you'll have the Egyptian government to deal with. Set me free immediately!"

"I'm sorry, but I'm afraid that won't be possible, much as I will give your warning the respect it merits." Pin projected genuine remorse, but the twinkle in his eye ruined the effect. "And let me make one thing quite clear. I am the one who asks the questions here. Your job is to answer them honestly and completely. If we stick to our roles, this will be so much better for both of us."

"Ask as many questions as you like. I'm not telling you anything," Haisam spat.

"Oh, I think you will," Pin smirked. "In fact, I can guarantee that by the time I'm finished with you, you'll be begging for permission to tell me your entire life story."

Haisam cast an anxious glance at the tools hanging on the wall. "Do your worst," he said bravely, doing his best to keep the tremor from his voice.

"Oh, I will," Pin assured him. "You see, I'm one of those lucky individuals who happens to love his work. When I'm tasked with retrieving information, I leave no stone unturned in uncovering all the little details. I'm the best in the business. And business is good."

Haisam blinked several times.

Pin started to pace up and down the room, his hands clasped behind his back as he took slow, measured steps, looking as relaxed as if he were going for a walk in the park instead of preparing to torture someone.

"You see, it has come to my attention that a recent expedition carried out under the auspices of the Ministry has come into possession of a unique map. Although so far the secrets of the map remain elusive, if it is what I believe it to be, this map would provide the missing elements to some research that my employers have been doing, and answer a few questions that have been puzzling us for quite some time. Of course, there's always the chance that this is another dead end, but something tells me that this map will prove to be a useful lead. If it is, there's no way that I can risk letting it fall into the wrong hands. That being the case, I have decided that Director Haisam Ganem needs to personally oversee the further investigations to control the flow of information. Details of this map need to be kept on a strictly need-to-know basis and you will ensure that the map stays with those who will appreciate it for what it is."

"You're mad if you think that I'm going to do anything to help you," Haisam sneered.

"Oh, I'm sorry. There must be some confusion. Did you think that I was actually going to send *you* along?" Pin reached into a pocket inside his blazer, pulling out a small, cylindrical device. His bodyguard chuckled as Pin started tapping at buttons on the machine.

"Do you know what this is?" Pin asked, not waiting for a reply. "It's a holographic emitter. Maybe you've heard rumors of their existence? They're still very experimental and not available on the open market, but for those with the right connections, they are remarkably useful. You see, I could undergo plastic surgery to recreate your features. There are even some very talented makeup artists around who could do an exceptional job of making me appear to look like you, but, as I'm sure you'll agree, both of those methods are flawed and carry a high risk of failure. I refuse to leave anything to chance. That's why the talented Bruard scientists developed something to allow me to take on your precise appearance with absolutely no chance of revealing my true identity."

"The Bruard?" gasped Haisam, the full enormity of what he was facing finally hitting him.

"Who else?" smiled Pin. "Now, Gord here has already scanned your body while you were unconscious, so the physical part of the process has already been done. However, as I'm sure you'll appreciate, there's more involved in impersonating a Director of the Ministry than mere looks. The slightest quirk can raise suspicions if I'm not behaving exactly like you in every way. In the past, I would have been forced to observe you over a few weeks, build up a profile of your behavior to try and pre-empt any potential situation, but if I were to attempt to do that now, it would take time I don't have and even then, there's no guarantee that I'd learn everything I needed about you to keep my story straight. Fortunately for me, those same Bruard scientists have also developed a feature to this device that will hypnotize you, placing you into numerous different scenarios so that I can create a complete psych-profile.

"Once it's finished doing its work, there's nothing I won't know about you, no secret that won't be mine to exploit as I see fit, no matter what the situation. Even your own wife won't be able to tell the difference between us."

"You're a monster!" cried Haisam.

"No, I'm you," Pin corrected. "Gord?" The brute stepped forward, clasping Haisam's head in his hands, to hold it steady as Pin took long plastic ties from his pocket and started to strap it in place.

"I really would advise you not to fight against this," Pin told Haisam. "Don't get me wrong. I give you this advice not out of altruism. It is of no consequence to me what ultimately happens to you. However, due to its experimental nature, use of the device has been fatal on occasion, especially if the user has a weak heart, so the more relaxed you can be, the longer you'll survive. It really would be most inconvenient if you were to die before I gathered all the data I need. You see, it measures your response to the full range of emotions, including both pleasure and pain."

Gord snorted with laughter as Pin stepped back, critically eyeing his handiwork to ensure that the brain scanning device, roughly the size of an alarm clock, was properly fitted.

"Don't worry, Mr Ganem," he said. "I'll be sure to read your children a bedtime story when I tuck them up to sleep tonight."

He took a remote control out of his pocket, handing it to Gord, before turning and leaving the room. The henchman grinned cruelly as he flicked the switch.

All Haisam could do was scream.

THREE

"Don't let go, Nafty!" yelled Samuel, as the dangling man desperately reached out with his other hand, doing his best to grab hold of Samuel, the helicopter, anything that would save him from falling to his inevitable doom.

The helicopter's engine whined as it began to rise.

"What are you doing?" screamed Nafty, barely audible over the engine noise, fruitlessly kicking his legs about to try and propel himself upwards as Samuel yelled at Josh to bring the aircraft back down.

"There might be another invisible hazard down there," countered Josh. "Going lower won't do any of us any good if I fly into another hidden rock. I can't risk crashing. It'll kill us all. You'll just have to hold on until I find a safe space to land."

"Are you kidding me?" Nafty screeched. "Get me down right now!"

"I'm doing the best I can," Josh yelled back, ignoring Nafty's anxious cries. "I want to save *all* our lives and right now, I don't know if any of us are safe."

"I promise you, there won't be any more unexpected surprises," Samuel told the pilot. "The map would say if there was."

"Yeah, it did *such* a great job with that camouflaged cave," Josh grunted. "Nuh-uh. I'm not taking the risk, not unless you've checked and double checked that we are where you think we are. And do you want to be the one to explain to Nafty that you had to let go of him to consult the map that got him into this mess?"

"The map flew out the door," Samuel protested. "But I've got it memorized, so I'd know if there were any other hidden obstacles. Now please, Josh. Just take us down. Do you really want Nafty's death on your conscience? I know you. You'd never forgive yourself."

"I'd rather not have *my* death on my conscience," muttered Josh, but he did as he was told, lowering the helicopter as slowly as he dared in case another rock outcrop came looming up out of nowhere.

"Hold on, Nafty," urged Samuel. "We're almost there."

Nafty closed his eyes, swallowing as he tried to keep hold of Samuel's hand, which was becoming increasingly slippery with sweat.

Looking out across the approaching ground, Samuel noticed something flapping about the rear back strut supporting the helicopter's landing bars.

"The map!" he gasped, watching as the wind whipped the ancient paper around, so far keeping it in place by wrapping it around the strut. Glancing down at Nafty, Samuel mentally calculated whether he could angle himself around to recover the map before it was lost--for good, this time. If he could just wedge his foot under the seat to anchor himself, it might give him enough reach to grab it as long as Nafty could hold on with one hand while Samuel lunged out.

If... if... if...

A little part of Samuel died as he watched a gust of wind catch at the map, tearing it away and sending it fluttering off into the sands to be lost for a few more centuries. He felt a brief moment of madness, the urge to throw himself after it in case by some miracle he could save the precious document, Nafty, and himself, but self-preservation won out and Samuel put all thoughts of the map to the back of his mind as he fought to keep Nafty safe.

"Don't let me go! Please don't let me go," pleaded Nafty as Josh took what seemed like an eternity to land the helicopter.

"Don't worry, buddy," Samuel reassured him. "You're going to be fine. Now in a moment, we're going to be low enough for you to let go. You need to fall and then get away as fast as you can so Josh can bring this thing down without landing on your head. Are you ready?"

"No, no!" Nafty shook his head, eyes wide in panic. "I can't let go. Not until my feet feel the ground beneath me."

"Trust me," soothed Samuel. "I've kept you alive so far, haven't I? I wouldn't go to all that trouble to lose you now. When I count three, I'm going to let go. You need to drop, roll, and run. Okay?"

"No! No!" Nafty protested as Samuel started counting.

"One... two... THREE!" True to his word, Samuel let go. Without Samuel to help him, Nafty lost his tenuous grip on the other man's hand. Screaming, he fell, only to have his cries abruptly cut off a second later as he hit the ground, all the breath knocked out of his body by the sudden impact.

"Get back!" Samuel made a shooing motion with his hands, urging Nafty to get away as the man rolled around, his arms up in front of his face to protect his eyes from the artificial sandstorm created by the aircraft. Still clawing at his face, Nafty scrambled away from the descending helicopter, well out of reach of its deadly whirling blades.

There was a slight jolt, and finally they were all safely back on solid ground. Samuel climbed out of the helicopter, looking mournfully in the direction he'd last seen the map.

"Thank you, my friend. Thank you. I am forever in your debt." Nafty threw himself at Samuel's feet as Samuel tried to get him to stand up.

"You'd have done the same for me," Samuel told him. "I just wish that I could have found a way to save you *and* the map."

Nafty sat up, scowling. "What do you mean, save the map?"

"It was blown out of the door and got wrapped around the landing bars," Samuel shook his head, running his hand through his hair in exasperation and gazing out across the desert, as if hoping to catch a glimpse of the lost document. "Believe me, I did my best to get it back, but it was too risky."

"What do you mean, too risky? Do you know what that map is worth?" Nafty pulled himself to his feet, all his gratitude wiped out by the news. "How could you let it go just like that?"

"You're welcome for saving your life," shrugged Samuel.

"We could have followed the map to endless treasure, relics, antiquities," Nafty raged. "Now they'll all be lost forever and it's all your fault."

"I guess I'll just have to live with the guilt," deadpanned Samuel. "Next time you're falling out of a helicopter, I'll remember to save all the ancient documents before I help you."

"Er... Guys?" Josh's voice broke through their argument. "I hate to interrupt a lover's tiff, but that cave that we almost crashed into? It's gone again."

Nafty gasped, as he and Samuel scrambled over to where Josh was standing. Sure enough, there was nothing to see but billowing sand dunes, no sign of a rocky outcrop anywhere.

"I couldn't have imagined it, could I?" Josh shook his head, as if to shake free any hallucination.

"Nope." Samuel smiled smugly. "The cave's there all right. We all saw it. We're just outside of whatever illusion it was that blocked it from view. I told you, the map was right!"

He strode forward. Josh and Nafty watched in astonishment as Samuel suddenly vanished. A few seconds later he reappeared, walking backwards. Stopping to gaze up in admiration at the invisible shield for a moment, he walked forward once more, performing another incredible disappearance as if he were part of a magician's stage act.

Josh and Nafty stood in stunned silence as this time, just

Samuel's grinning face reappeared as he leaned forward through the invisible wall. "So are you two going to follow me here or are you just going to stand around catching flies all afternoon?"

His words broke the spell that had fallen over Josh and Nafty as they hurried forward to join him.

"This is weird, man." Josh shook his head as the cave suddenly appeared without warning, just as it had when he'd flown over it. "I've never seen anything like it. And you say that it was an *ancient* map that brought us here? How?"

"I don't know, but I'm going to find out," Samuel replied, heading towards the cave mouth.

"If this is a taste of what's to come, just think what else that map could have shown us," moaned Nafty, as he hurried to keep up with the archaeologist.

FOUR

"See you later, Malik."

"Have a good weekend."

Workers at the Ministry of State for Antiquities started to switch off their computers and finish up their work, winding down for the night as they looked forward to a couple days' rest after another long, hard week. One cubicle bore the nameplate Shafira Khouri. In it, a woman of around thirty, attractive and olive-skinned with her long hair all brushed over to one side, opened yet another email. She clicked on the attachments it contained to examine a series of holoimaging snapshots of a dig site out in the wilds of Egypt.

Printing out the email and attachments so she could examine them more carefully, Shafira swiveled in her chair to collect the images from the drawer of the printer next to her desk. Laying them out in front of her for comparison, she read the accompanying text again. Thankfully, the foreman who had filed this report was meticulous about detail, so she wasn't going to have to chase him for more information about whether they'd followed protocol every step of the way or cut corners.

Sighing, Shafira picked up an image that showed a group of

beaming archaeologists, the man in the middle proudly holding up an ancient vase. Even in the grainy printout, it was obvious that the vase was in excellent condition, its decoration almost as fresh as it must have been when it was first painted. Sitting back in her chair, she wondered what it would be like to be there with them instead of stuck in an office, living vicariously through reports from in the field. What must it feel like to be the first person to see an artifact after thousands of years? Sure, eventually it would be on display in one of Egypt's museums for crowds of tourists to coo over, that is, if it were deemed worthy, but it wouldn't be the same as seeing it *in situ*.

She sighed again, as she moved onto the next email in her never ending backlog. There were more attachments this time, so after she sent them off to print, she decided that now was the perfect time to take a break while her antiquated printer churned out the detailed color images.

Stepping out into the main office, Shafira crossed over to the kitchen area where the budget coffeemaker sat, still half-filled with coffee. Pouring some of the steaming beverage into her favorite mug, she added enough sugar and cream to make it drinkable and turned to go back to her desk, almost running into Faroukh, the clerk who worked a couple cubicles away from her. It was only her quick reactions and some nifty footwork that saved him from wearing her drink.

"More coffee? At this hour?" he remarked. "Don't tell me you're still working? Surely a young woman like you would want to be anywhere but here."

"I'd love to go home," Shafira replied, "but if you saw the size of my inbox, you'd understand. I want to get a few more emails done so I won't be freaking out over the weekend about how much stuff'll be waiting for me on Monday."

"I must say that I've always admired your work ethic," Faroukh told her, "but take some advice from one who knows." He leaned forward as if sharing a great secret. "*The paperwork never ends!*" He leaned back, smiling and nodding, as though he'd uncovered the deepest mystery in the universe. "If you're sensible, you'll do what you can while you're on the clock and leave the second your hours are over. You'll only burn yourself out otherwise."

"Thanks, Faroukh," Shafira replied, wearily. "I'll bear that in mind."

"Of course, if you're stuck for somewhere to go and you want some company..." Faroukh raised an eyebrow suggestively.

"*Thanks, Faroukh,*" Shafira repeated forcefully, turning to go back to her cubicle.

"You know where to find me if you change your mind." Faroukh's voice followed her. "Remember what I said. Don't give this place more than you have to. It'll only sap your soul!"

"I'm fully aware of that," Shafira muttered, as she slipped back into her seat, picking up the printouts to work through before letting them drop back onto the desk. Idly swiveling her chair as she sipped at her coffee, she wondered whether this was going to be it for the rest of her life. She remembered how excited she was when she received her acceptance letter from the Ministry, naively believing that if she worked hard enough, she'd quickly climb the ladder.

It wasn't long before she realized how mistaken she'd been, but there weren't many other openings out there for a non-graduate history fanatic that allowed her to get this close to Egypt's ancient heritage. She was lucky to have this job. She knew that. But still. There were only so many photographs you could examine before going cross eyed.

Looking at a shot of some archaeologists busy uncovering some stone slabs, she was struck by how much one of them looked like her older brother, Yusuf, when he was her age. The thought that Yusuf would ever been caught dead at a dig site made her snort her coffee. Back then, he would have been too busy getting into trouble at wild parties to even find his way to an excavation, let alone do any work there.

"But then, that's why you're at the Ministry and Yusuf is banned from half the bars in Cairo," she reminded herself, moving onto the next image.

Shafira soon fell into a rhythm, the routine of opening emails, printing them, and checking the details, and routing to one of many automated business processes. Slowly but surely, her backlog became smaller and smaller until she felt that the end was finally–finally!–in sight. Two more emails and she could get out of here.

Someone cleared their throat behind her. "Miss Khouri?"

Shafira jumped, not having heard anyone approach, and swiveled round in her chair. She gulped when she realized that none other than Director Haisam was standing in front of her.

"Sir." She jumped up to stand, smoothing down her jacket.

"Please. Call me Haisam," her superior smiled. "There's no need for all that formality when you're talking to me."

"Of course... Haisam." Shafira inclined her head a little in agreement, despite her discomfort at the notion of being so familiar with someone who held such an important position. "I'm sorry. I didn't realize you were standing there. I thought I was on my own in the office."

"You very nearly are," the Director informed her. "In fact, that's one of the reasons why I'm here. You're one of the very few people in your department who hasn't raced for the door the minute the clock turned 5:30. That kind of dedication will take you far."

"Thank you, sir...Haisam."

"I have a little project for you," Haisam announced. "Well, when I say 'little', what I actually mean is that it's really rather important, although I don't think it will impact too much on your other duties. Indeed, if at all possible, I'll need you to finish it this evening, but a woman like you should be more than capable of getting the job done. What do you say? Do you have time to do a small favor for your Director?"

Shafira's heart sank. The subtle emphasis on his position didn't escape her. She didn't need a last minute job when she was surviving on caffeine fumes and sheer stubborn determination, but making a good impression on the Director could mean a huge difference to her career. Maybe she'd finally get out of this cubicle and onto more challenging work.

"Of course," she told him, hiding her irritation.

"Excellent!" The Director beamed, clapping his hands together. "Just what I was hoping to hear. Now, then. I've heard mention that the Bruard have been active in the region you are responsible for monitoring, so I will need to personally double check all your reports before you send them to the records department for annotation and publishing. I will need you to gather together everything that you've worked on for this past week in date order, sorted by area code and relic type."

Shafira kept her expression passive, but inside she was screaming. Did he have any idea how long that was going to take? And he waited until *what* time on a Friday night?

"No problem, Haisam," was her smooth reply. "Are there any type of relics in particular that you think may be of interest to the Bruard?"

"I'm not sure," the Director said. "However, I do know that the cases you're in charge of have been flagged as being of interest. I'll know what I'm looking for when I see it."

"Of course. I'll get straight onto it."

"One more thing." Haisam stepped forward, placing his hands on her shoulders, gazing intently into her eyes. "I'm sure I don't need to point it out to you, but since the Bruard could be involved, this project may well be a matter of national security. As a consequence, the only person you may discuss it with is me. Under no circumstances should you mention what you are doing to anyone else."

Shafira squirmed uncomfortably, but Haisam only tightened his grip on her, wanting to be sure that she understood the import of what he was telling her.

"Am I clear?"

"Of course, Sir." Shafira nodded soberly. "I won't tell a soul until you give me the all clear to mention it."

"Excellent, excellent. I'd hate to think that I couldn't trust you."

At last, Haisam released her shoulders. "I'll expect the report on my desk tonight."

He turned and left her cubicle. Shafira shook her head, rolling her shoulders to release the sensation of the Director's hands on her. She reached out to take a large swig of coffee, but discovered that her mug was empty.

There's no way I'm going to be able to survive this without more *caffeine*, Shafira thought, getting up to fetch a refill. Heading towards the kitchen area, she saw the Director at the basin where they got the water for the coffeemaker. Deciding to ask whether he wanted the reports bound or loose, as she drew nearer, she could see that he was frantically scrubbing at his hands, muttering angrily to himself. Unlike his earlier calm demeanor, he didn't look the slightest bit approachable.

I'll get that coffee later, she decided, tiptoeing back to her desk to start the mammoth task of collating the requested reports.

FIVE

"Okay, let me just start recording..." Samuel adjusted the settings on his holorecorder so he could capture every moment of their initial investigation. "And... action!"

Josh rolled his eyes and shook his head as Samuel slowly turned in a circle, taking a sweeping shot of the desert to show that there was no sign of any cave formation.

"We're at an unspecified location that was marked out on an ancient map as being a site of special archaeological interest," he explained for the benefit of anyone who'd watch the film. "Unfortunately, the map was lost during a dramatic landing, caused by the sudden appearance of a cave that went something like this."

He moved forward, keeping the camera facing the spot where the cave would suddenly materialize once they got past the camo-cloak. He kept the view panoramic to capture every aspect of its unexpected appearance.

"As you can see," Samuel continued when he'd entered the camouflage field, "there's a very significant rock formation here, which includes a cave network. We have not yet had a chance to examine this, so this film will document our first approach to this incredible new discovery."

He kept the camera steady as he slowly moved towards the main entrance, Josh and Nafty following close behind, wanting to learn more about their discovery.

"The cave is unremarkable in appearance," Samuel noted, "and... wait a minute."

He zoomed the camera in to focus on some marks on either side of the cave mouth. Having filmed them in close-up, he stepped forward to take a better look. He ran his hand over them, turning excitedly to his companions.

"These etchings are Roman!" Samuel gasped. He peered closer, trying to make out the words. "We're going to have to get an expert to examine these. They're too worn away for me to translate them reliably without someone who can make an educated attempt at filling in the blanks. But this is a definite sign that we're on the right track–and that whatever it is we're going to find inside a cave that someone took the trouble to hide like this could well rewrite history. Come on!"

He went to enter the cave, but Josh held him back.

"I think we should leave," he advised. "I agree that there's something weird going on here, but I'm not convinced that it's got anything to do with ancient Romans. Think about it, man. There's no way that the Romans could have mastered camo tech to this level of sophistication. For all we know, they came here, defaced the caves, and left without burying any artifacts. That inscription could be the only Roman thing about this place. Smugglers or drug dealers could be responsible for setting up that cloaking shield. I'm not going in there without a weapon, not when we don't know who's waiting inside."

"Look at the sand." Samuel gestured to the ground. "Do you see any footprints or vehicle tracks?"

"They'd have been blown away in one gust of wind," Josh countered.

"Come on, Josh," sighed Samuel. "Nobody's been here for a long time. I promise you that there's no-one lurking in the cave. And since *someone* couldn't fly a helicopter straight, we lost the map. We might not be able to find this spot again if we leave now. I have to know if it's worth the trouble of sending out a full team to investigate before we go back to camp."

"I thought you said you'd memorized the map?" Josh pointed out.

Samuel blushed, scuffing at the sand to mask his discomfort.

"Listen to your friend," urged Nafty. "He's right. What if there are smugglers inside? You saved my life once already today. Don't make me any more in your debt."

"If there are any smugglers, I'll take the bullet for you both," Samuel promised. "But I'm telling you that there's no one inside that cave. We'd see the signs if there were. Besides, the distance from the shield to the cave is so small, only the smallest of groups would be able to get in unseen. We can take down a handful of men between us. I've seen you in action, remember Josh?"

"Bar brawls don't count," muttered the pilot.

"This is the find of the century," Samuel said. "We're the first people to see this for who knows how long. Even if it is 'just' a smuggler's den, the only people who could have set it up would be the Bruard."

Nafty frowned. "What makes you say that?" he said sharply.

"Well, it's just that you always read about the dangers of Bruard super-science," Samuel pointed out. "I never paid much attention before, figured it was just the media exaggerating again. Given how sophisticated that cloaking device is, they're the most obvious candidates for setting it up. And if they *are* behind it, then that means that the other stories about them are likely to be true too."

"That's sorted then." Josh folded his arms. "There's no way you're getting me in there, not if there's a bunch of Bruard thugs lying in wait."

"There aren't any Bruard thugs in the cave." Samuel made one final attempt to persuade Josh and Nafty to come exploring with him, but it was clear he was wasting his time.

"All right," he sighed. "How's this for a compromise? The pair of you keep watch and shout if you see anyone coming. I want to take a brief peek inside before we leave. It would be stupid to have come all this way and go through everything we've suffered just to turn back now."

"All right. If you must. But be quick," warned Josh. "This place gives me the creeps."

"Don't worry, I will be. Promise." Samuel pulled out a Maglite, switching it on and clipping it to his shirt pocket. Taking out a small notebook, he turned and headed into the cave mouth.

Out of the glaring sun, the temperature quickly dropped and Samuel felt his skin break out in goosebumps, although whether it was a result of the cold or his nerves showing, he couldn't tell.

The cave proved to be smaller than expected, the roughhewn corridor coming to a sudden stop at an unnaturally smooth, flat, stone wall. Samuel shone his Maglite across the wall, looking for any sign of a hidden door. Nothing.

"Hmm." He frowned and tutted, thinking back to what his research had told him about the cave site. When he'd uncovered the map, there'd been other documents accompanying it filled with strange riddles and verses. Perhaps the answer to the way forward lay among them.

Flicking back through his notebook, he found the page where he'd jotted down his rough translations. Among descriptions of strange rituals, there was one comment that stood out as being relevant. He read it aloud, translating it as he went.

Spelunca est unus solus frustra custos inter dunes. Priusquam iter unius calculo sisteretur praesidio. Et fac orationem magna mater est quod confirmat inter vivos adhuc stare et Phelethi legiones ex parte vias ejus ad te. The cave stands alone, a solitary sentinel amidst the empty dunes. Journey forward until your path is stopped by the stone guard. Offer a prayer to the Great Mothers that confirms you still stand among the living and the guard shall part ways for thee.

He looked up at the wall. "This must be the stone guard." He flung his arms out dramatically. "All right, Great Mothers. I'm still alive! *I et adhuc tota!*"

Nothing happened.

"Open sesame, Great Mothers?" Samuel chuckled to himself.

"Maybe it's not a literal prayer," he mused, turning his attention to the other cave walls. Sweeping the Maglite beam around the chamber, he felt about the cave surface, patting down the stone walls looking for a hidden latch, or at least a clue to the next step.

"A-ha!" In the middle of the cavern, he found a shallow dip in the ground that was too smooth to be natural. Falling to his hands and knees, he brushed away the sand surrounding it. At last, his fingers felt something. Bringing the light closer, he could make out more letters.

"M... A... G... Magna Matres–the Great Mothers!" Underneath the words were two arrows, one pointing towards the groove, the other indicating the blank wall.

Hands shaking, Samuel fumbled through his notebook again, his jottings finally starting to make sense. If he'd correctly interpreted the comments scribbled on the map, a bowl was to be placed in the sacred space and then filled with a blood offering while a ritual prayer was recited.

"What a shame I left my bowl and sacrificial goat at home today," Samuel muttered, his mind racing to come up with suitable alternatives.

Scrambling to his feet, he hurried out to where Josh and Nafty were waiting impatiently.

"Great. We can go now, yes?" asked Nafty.

"No." Samuel shook his head. "Josh, do you have anything to eat in the helicopter?"

"Really?" Josh rolled his eyes. "We're out in the middle of nowhere, Nafty and I are getting burned to a crisp by the sun and all you can think about is your stomach?"

"It's not for me. It's for the Great Mothers!" Samuel raced over to the helicopter and started to rummage around, looking for something that could serve as a bowl.

"Can you *not* destroy my craft?" sighed Josh. "Just because you like living in a pigsty doesn't mean that I'm happy dealing with your mess. Get out of the way. Tell me what you want and I'll find it for you."

Soon Samuel was back in the cave carrying a small plastic bowl filled with beef jerky. Kneeling down next to the groove, he placed his notebook on the ground opened to the page where he'd written the translation of the ritual. Clearing his throat, he began to perform the sacred ceremony.

"*Magna matres, aperi ostium mihi.* Great Mothers, open your doors for me." He held the bowl up high, as if showing it to the goddesses.

"*Ego sum non mortuus est.* I am not dead." He placed the bowl in the groove, hoping that it would be heavy enough to register.

"*Testor ego tueri arcana.* I call to witness, I shall protect the secret sources." He sat back on his knees, looking around expectantly. At first, nothing happened, but then he heard an almost imperceptible *click*! The bowl started to move towards the blank wall, pulled along by some unseen mechanism.

As it hit the stone, it disappeared, but Samuel had no time to wonder what had happened to it. The entire cave started to shake, a loud rumbling noise sounding as if it were about to collapse.

Jumping up, Samuel was about to run outside when the noise stopped and the wall in front of him shimmered, suddenly transforming. Whatever cloaking device had been in place had been deactivated by the ritual.

Samuel was standing in front of a massive Roman-style double door twice his height and three times his width. On the left side was a carving of Seshat, the Egyptian Goddess of accounting and astrology, while on the right was Moneta, the Roman goddess of memory.

For a moment, he stood there, paralyzed by this new apparition.

"You have got to be kidding me," Samuel breathed when he

finally found himself. He gazed up at the carvings, trying to take in every little detail despite the poor lighting.

Pulling out a pair of gloves, he tugged them on, his hands fumbling as he continued to stare at the doors, unable to tear himself away. At last, he managed to get the gloves on to protect the doors as he reached out to touch the carvings. However, before his hand could connect with the doors, they swung open, moving as smoothly as if they'd been recently installed, revealing an inner chamber.

Switching on the holorecorder, Samuel began to record.

SIX

Three hundred miles away, the sweltering sun beat down on the archaeological team beavering away at unearthing a newly discovered burial site adjacent to Samuel's original dig site. Makeshift shelters offered shade, but little respite from the heat as everyone rushed to get as much work done as possible before the temperatures became unbearable.

One team focused on carefully cutting through hard-packed stone to reveal more of the burial site, while others carried out scrolls and maps from the already excavated chambers, packing them carefully in crates for the Ministry for more in-depth study by off-site experts.

A man climbed up the ladder that led out of the burial site, his arms so full of documents he could barely move them to cling to the rungs. Using his chin to keep the top papers in place, he pulled himself out onto safe ground, but as he turned to move towards the crates, he stumbled, dropping one of the documents. Reaching out for it, he almost lost his grip on the rest of the scrolls, forcing him to clutch onto them. He could only watch in horror as the precious artifact tumbled towards the ground...

...to be saved by Chief Engineer Basile Rossignol. Hurling himself towards the falling scroll, he fell to the ground, juggling the parchment as he attempted to stop it hitting the dirt, finally coming to a halt centimeters away from the edge of the pit, holding the document triumphantly aloft.

"*Voila!*" he crowed, looking around to see if anyone had seen his brilliant save before clumsily pulling his tall frame back to a standing position when he realized that everyone was too focused on their work to notice. His bushy eyebrows made a V over his large nose, as he frowned.

"I am so sorry, *Monsieur* Rossignol," the man carrying the scrolls apologized, extending his hand to retrieve the scroll.

"What were you thinking, trying to carry so much at once?" Basile scolded. "Don't you know that it's considered terrible bad luck for these scrolls to touch the ground? Not to mention the damage the sand could do to them when they've been preserved in an airtight chamber for centuries? We have no idea what secrets are inscribed on these parchments. Ancient knowledge could have been lost forever due to your clumsiness."

"I'm sorry," the man repeated. "It's just that it's so hot. I thought that if I could get more scrolls that we could finish sooner. I really didn't think I was carrying too much. Of course I would never have deliberately risked such a treasure."

"Hot?" Basile kept tight hold of the scroll he'd rescued as he walked next to the man to place it safely in storage in one of the crates. "This is nothing. Why, when I was on a dig in the Amazon, this is what we woke up to every morning and it only got worse as the day wore on. And it was a damn sight more humid, too. None of us complained. We just got on with the job."

"Still, *Monsieur*," the man continued. "Don't you think it would be a good idea if we took a break for a little while? I'd hate to see anyone else make a mistake like mine."

"Did someone say break?" Another worker's ears picked up. "It's about time. We've been at this for hours."

"No one's having a break." Basile held up his hands, as the men loading crates gathered round him.

"Please, *Monsieur*," begged another man. "We would all be faster if we had a moment to rest and refresh ourselves."

Basile shook his head. "All right," he relented. "You can all take five. I'll gather up another team to take up your slack. But when I say five minutes, I mean five minutes and no more. We're on a tight deadline here, especially with having a new section to investigate."

"Thank you, *Monsieur*. Thank you, thank you."

The men scurried away to seek shade, as Basile checked his watch.

"What are they complaining about?" he muttered to himself. "They've only been going for two and a half hours. In my day, we wouldn't even have been thinking about taking a break until the sun was fully overhead. You'd think they'd be used to it, living 'round here."

He wiped the sweat away from his forehead. It *was* hot, but Basile knew better than most the importance of getting the job done as quickly as possible. He'd been on too many digs that had seen precious artifacts destroyed, their secrets lost forever because someone had taken too long to retrieve them after they had been exposed to the moisture in the air after untold centuries locked away.

Not for the first time, he wished that Samuel were here. Basile didn't like being in charge of digs. That kind of responsibility was better left to the experts so he could focus on his own field of expertise: making sure that all the structures were safe so they didn't lose anyone to a collapsing shaft or tunnel.

Basile would never forget the time he was trapped underground on one of his first digs after the Chief Engineer on the excavation had failed to notice that an important support was cracking. The claustrophobic sensation of knowing that there were tons of dirt above his head, only held up by a few planks of wood that might fail at any moment, burying him alive, was something that still haunted his dreams. He'd sworn then and there that no one would ever go through what he had and so far, no one on any of his digs ever had.

Shaking his head to wipe out bad memories, Basile decided to do a circuit of the camp and make sure that everyone was observing the appropriate safety protocols. Maybe he was just a superstitious old fool, but you could never be too careful. If his Chief Engineer had been as cautious, his accident would never have happened.

He headed over to where archaeologists were uncovering a new section of the burial network.

"No need to stop what you're doing," he told them. "I'm just here to observe."

They'd already uncovered what looked like the entrance to a completely new tomb and were working to secure it before entering the tunnel that led into an underground network. There were statues and carvings dotted around the entrance. Although the writing had been worn away by the sand and was no longer legible, the design of the statues alone revealed plenty about who might have been interred here. It looked like they were dealing with a member of the nobility. With any luck, their final resting place would contain a wealth of treasure that would have academics salivating the world over.

"Make sure you put up support as you go," he advised. "See that section over there?"

The team looked at where Basile was indicating. "As you're digging, you can see pieces of dirt falling through," he told them. "That's a sign that you haven't shored it up properly. Add a few more crosspieces before you dig any deeper otherwise you could be in trouble later."

"Will do," nodded the team leader, motioning to a couple of men to follow Basile's suggestion.

Basile waited for a few minutes until he was satisfied that the section was safe before moving on to another group. As he made his way through the extensive camp, he was glad to see that there were minimal issues to advise on. It was always good when your team paid attention to you.

However, Basile missed the thrill of being the first to break through the dirt in a brand new chamber. He'd never forget the moment he'd broken through into the tomb of a cousin of Pharaoh Amanineteyerike. Nothing can quite describe the smell that emanates from an ancient Egyptian sepulcher as fresh air hits the mummified remains of animals and servants placed there to accompany the dead King when he enters the afterlife.

Maybe when Samuel was back to relieve him of his leadership duties, Basile could take his turn in unearthing some of the tomb. This site was one of the most extensive he'd ever worked on. They were likely to be here for some months yet, if not years. He only hoped the Ministry would be willing to continue funding when they ran over schedule. It wouldn't be first time a site had been damaged because work had stopped when money had dried up. Given the quality of what they'd already uncovered, it would be a shame if that happened here.

He walked towards the section of the site set aside for the grunts, the unqualified camp supporters who did all the donkey work, loading and carrying equipment to support the archaeologists. The work was poorly paid and heavy going, so Basile always made a point of letting the men know how much he appreciated what they did. Without them, his job would be infinitely harder.

"Ah, Basile! Just the man I was hoping to see."

Basile's heart sank as he saw Waleed approaching. The self-appointed 'leader' of the camp supporters, the man always seemed to think he knew best, despite not having any experience at a dig as far as Basile could tell. Still, manners cost nothing, so he smiled, covering his distaste.

"Waleed. Everything going well, I trust?"

"I'm afraid not, my friend." Waleed shook his head, frowning slightly. "It is the workers. I hear that you have allowed them to take a break when they have barely done any work."

"That's not quite accurate," Basile began, but Waleed spoke over him.

"You need to be much firmer with them," Waleed said. "More like your colleague, the American. I fear that the workers are taking advantage of your good nature. You need to treat them like the simpletons they are. Tell them what to do and accept no excuses. Otherwise you'll be paying them to sit around sunning themselves and I'm sure the Ministry would take a dim view of such a waste of funds."

"Thank you for your input." Basile bristled at the implied threat. "I'm sure that Samuel would be on top of things were he here, but right now he isn't, so we do things my way. A kind word has always worked wonders to keep me working at my very best and I like to treat people as I expect to be treated."

"Of course, of course, my friend." Waleed clapped Basile on the back. "I only wish to help. I do not mean any--how you say?--offense. In fact, I was just about to go and assist with the packing of the scrolls and relics ready for shipping. Shall we meet at the stacks later? I have a few more ideas I would like to discuss with you that I think will make the dig truly successful."

"Thank you. Yes." Basile's brow furrowed as he watched Waleed walk away. If he was only going to help pack the artifacts now, how could he have known about the short break he'd just given the men? Basile shrugged a little Gallic shrug. In a camp like this, where everyone was on top of everyone else, it shouldn't come as any surprise that news traveled fast.

SEVEN

Josh and Nafty crowded round Samuel as he played them the footage he'd shot inside the cave system. When the recording finished, the three men looked at each other, Samuel smiling smugly at the stunned expressions on his colleagues' faces.

"And this is where the door appeared?" Nafty went over to the wall that had been transformed by the ritual, running his hands over the smooth surface that gave no hint of the secret it concealed.

"That's right," Samuel confirmed. "I filmed the doors to demonstrate that there was definitely something worth investigating here, but I sealed them up again without going through. I promised Basile that I wouldn't touch anything if there proved to be a hidden chamber until he could be here with me. I think he's feeling nostalgic for the days when he and I were the first to go into a new site back before he was promoted."

"He wouldn't mind that much, surely?" suggested Nafty. "Wouldn't it make more sense to look at what's inside so that we have actual evidence to take back to the Ministry? A couple of pretty doors aren't really proof of anything. With funding so difficult to get hold of right now, you'll need something pretty compelling to convince them to expand the excavation area to this cave, especially since you've already run over budget with the extended dig. I'm sure that Basile would rather you were able to continue working on the existing site than lose it all because of some silly promise."

"Maybe," Samuel conceded, "but there's still further investigation that needs to be carried out on the doors before I can be sure of what's going on here. There's a lot that doesn't add up. I mean, I'm pretty certain that it wasn't really a pair of ancient goddesses who opened the doors for me, so there's clearly something else going on with the ritual I performed. This cave has technology that's like nothing I've ever seen before. I need to date the doors to confirm that they really are what they appear to be and I've left the necessary equipment back at the dig site."

"Of course you have," snorted Josh. "It would have been far too easy to bring everything you need with you."

"I thought I had," Samuel confessed. "I guess I must have misplaced it back in my tent."

"What, like the time you misplaced that piece of mosaic in your dirty laundry?" Josh raised an eyebrow. "You do realize that you are supposed to look after Ministry equipment and not treat your tent like a dumping ground?"

"I know where everything is," Samuel protested. "Just because it looks chaotic doesn't mean that it's not organized."

"Uh-huh. Which is why you remembered to bring everything you needed for this investigation. Oh wait..."

"Instead of being snarky, why don't you take us to the dig site so I can fetch my equipment?" Samuel suggested. "The helicopter can get us back without any more drama, can't it?"

"Should be able to," Josh replied. "Unless there are any more invisible caves lurking about for me to fly into. When do you want to leave?"

"How does now sound?"

The two men turned to leave, but Nafty put out a hand to stop them. "We shouldn't go yet," he said.

"Why not?" asked Samuel, while Josh huffed impatiently, shaking his head at the interruption. "We've got everything we can for now. The sooner we go, the sooner we can get back and investigate more."

"There's still a chamber none of us have seen," Nafty pointed out. "You've confirmed that there aren't any armed men in there. They would have shot at you when they saw the door open, so it's perfectly safe to enter. I think we should go in and see what's really there. What if it's empty? Do you really want to waste time and even more resources on an empty tomb?"

"It won't be empty," Samuel assured him. "Besides, the technology alone makes this place worth investigating. Whatever happens, we won't be wasting our time."

"But that's the point!" Nafty whined. "Do you really think the ancients would have put such measures in place to protect nothing? There will be untold treasure hiding behind those doors. It would be so much better if we took a little..."

"And there it is. Your true colors at last." Samuel shook his head in disgust. "This has everything to do with you wanting to line your own pockets, hasn't it?"

"Of course not! How dare you!" Nafty narrowed his eyes, stepping forward to stand toe to toe with the taller American. "Just because I want to have something for my troubles doesn't mean that I don't care about the excavation. I nearly died getting here. I deserve a little reward."

"You greedy, shortsighted-" began Samuel, but Josh interrupted him.

"It's fine," he said. "Let's leave Nafty here while you and I go back to camp. I'm sure he'll be able to figure out how to conjure up the doors in the week or so it'll take for us to come back here from the Ministry with permission to investigate. In the meantime, he can loot the secret chamber to his heart's content."

"Good idea," Samuel smirked. "I hope you're good at water divining, Nafty. A man can go for weeks without food, but water? Out here in the desert, you'd be lucky to last a day, although since it's cooler in the cave, you might be able to push that to three, so you'd only miss our return by a few days. Initially, the lack of water will just make you a little bit irritable and foul tempered."

"No change there then," broke in Josh.

"Right," Samuel agreed. "As the thirst kicks in, your body will start to retain whatever moisture it can. This means that your kidneys will send less water to the bladder, so when you take a wiz and your urine's black, you know you're in trouble and really need to drink something. But since you won't have any water to hand, your temperature will go up because you'll stop sweating and your heart will beat faster to try and cope with the fact that your blood has thickened.

"But that's just the start. Eventually, your blood will become so concentrated that your skin will shrivel because there isn't enough blood pumping through your body to hydrate it. Your blood pressure drops and you'll suddenly find yourself on the floor because you've fainted. I hope you don't knock your head against the stone. Concussion can be a real bitch."

Josh sniggered as Samuel continued.

"Since your blood pressure is so low, your body will stop sending blood to the organs it considers less important, like your kidneys and gut. Since your kidneys will stop functioning, waste products will quickly build up in your blood stream. You'll be literally dying for a drink. Then you can take your pick. Go out to the desert and overheat your vital organs so you die of liver failure or stay cool in the cave and let kidney failure take you. It's entirely up to you, so pick your poison."

Nafty's usual olive complexion was now firmly green.

"All right, all right, I give in!" The man threw up his hands in surrender, racing back to the helicopter before him.

"The poor man's probably feeling very thirsty all of a sudden," laughed Josh. "Do you think you might have gone a little overboard?"

"Nah." Samuel shrugged, a self-satisfied look on his face. "I was never really serious about leaving him here. If need be, I would have just knocked him out and carried him back to the helicopter myself. I didn't go to all the trouble of saving his life just to let him throw it away."

He grinned. "Still, it was fun winding him up like that. Did you see his face?"

Josh laughed as the two men made their way to the helicopter.

EIGHT

Josh carefully eased the helicopter down to land on the temporary helipad laid out near the dig site. The sun had long since set, so he had to rely on the small colored lights marking out the space to guide him, but he still managed to make a perfect landing that was a world apart from their near crash at the cave.

Despite the lateness of the hour, the site was a hive of activity, powerful floodlights illuminating the dig with a bright, white, artificial light that was almost painful to look at. The archaeologists who were working on unearthing the site wore lights on their helmets so that they could see what they were doing, while workers carried flashlights that were almost redundant in the glare from above.

"Good old Basile," chuckled Samuel as he disembarked. "Always puts safety first!"

Nafty climbed out and stood next to him, gazing around the site.

"I bet that they don't find anything here that's half as impressive as what we've just left behind," he muttered bitterly to himself, as he turned and started to unload equipment from the helicopter.

"All right, gentlemen. This is where I'll leave you," Josh

announced from the pilot's seat, checking dials and flicking switches to prepare the helicopter for immediate takeoff.

"Are you not going to get some rest first?" Samuel asked.

Josh shook his head. "I'm heading back to Cairo for a refuel in case the Ministry decides to send me straight out again. You never know with those bureaucrats. Rest doesn't seem to factor into their plans. Apparently I can fly for days without a break and it's perfectly fine."

"Why don't you stay here?" Samuel offered. "I'm sure we can find you a spare bed somewhere in camp. It's been a long day for all of us and I'd feel better knowing that you had some shut eye."

"I'm all right." Josh reassured him. "I'd much rather go for another hour or two and collapse into my own soft bed than lie awake all night itching from sand or worrying that a poisonous insect is going to take a chunk out of me."

"Fair enough," laughed Samuel, helping Nafty take out the last of their gear. He saluted the pilot, then slid shut the helicopter door. Samuel and Nafty headed over to their camp, bags slung over their shoulders, as Josh took off into the night sky.

Seeing their approach, a number of porters rushed forward to take their bags. Samuel handed over most of the equipment, making sure that he kept tight hold of the holorecorder and his notes. He wasn't going to let them out of his sight until he'd had a chance to submit his report to the Ministry.

As he juggled his things to make sure that he didn't give the porters anything important, Samuel failed to notice Nafty slipping away into the camp.

"Samuel, my friend! Good to have you back with us."

Samuel plastered on a fake smile, as Waleed strode towards him, arms spread out to give him a welcoming hug. His hands full of equipment, Samuel awkwardly leaned towards Waleed, as he squeezed him tightly, patting him on the back.

"We were all so worried about you," Waleed told him. "Your poor colleague Basile was beside himself. I had to reassure him that you were fine, wherever you were." A cunning look flashed over his face too quick for Samuel to notice. "Where were you again?"

"Oh, just out in the desert," replied Samuel lightly, vaguely gesturing out towards the sand dunes with his head. "I figured that with such an impressive haul here, there might be something else worth exploring nearby, but we got lost and only just found our way back."

"Then we are doubly blessed!" cried Waleed. "First for you finding your way and second for you coming back safe to us. I do not know what we would do without you to lead the excavation."

"Samuel!"

"Basile!" Samuel's smile was genuine this time as he turned to greet his friend.

"Did you enjoy your vacation while you left us to slave away in your name?" asked Basile.

"Any chance to have a break from you," Samuel quipped. Waleed stepped closer to the two men so he could hear their discussion, but Samuel shooed him away. "Sorry, Waleed. Could you give us some time alone? Basile and I have some things we need to talk about."

"Of course." Waleed pressed his hands together, bowing his head a little, before turning and going back to the camp.

Samuel waited until he was out of hearing before turning to Basile and leading him away from the porters so no one else could eavesdrop.

"So?" asked Basile excitedly. "Did you have any luck?"

"And then some," grinned Samuel. "You wait until you see the footage I got."

"The map was right then," beamed Basile. "I had a good feeling about it."

"Yeah, the map told us a lot." Samuel sighed, the loss of the map still smarting. "I wish I had had more time to study it. I could have learned so much from it."

"What do you mean?" Basile's ears pricked up. "Why can't you study it anymore? What have you done with it?"

"We had a bit of drama on the way to the site," Samuel explained. "Josh lost control of the helicopter and the map was lost in the confusion."

"Lost?" Basile screeched before he could stop himself. "Lost?" he hissed, lowering his voice to a whisper so no one else could hear. "How could you be so careless? That map was priceless!"

"I know, but we found something better," Samuel soothed.

"What could be better than that map?" Basile demanded. "You told me you'd never seen anything like it before, that you could spend years studying it and still never unlock all of its secrets."

"A cave," announced Samuel smugly. If he was expecting Basile to be impressed, he was sadly disappointed.

"A cave?" echoed the Frenchman. "We've been in countless caves! What's another one to add to the list? What was inside that makes you so happy? Please tell me that it's at least the tomb of an unknown Pharoah or it contains evidence of Atlantis. Perhaps you found the Holy Grail? Please, Samuel. Enlighten me. What makes this cave so special?"

"I have no idea what's inside," Samuel confessed. "I didn't go in."

"Gah!" Basile threw up his hands in disgust. "Your whole trip was a waste of time and resources when I could have used you back here. If you'd stayed at camp instead of going on a wild duck chase, we'd still have the map."

"Wild goose chase," Samuel corrected. "And I didn't go in because I wanted you to be with me when I explored it for the first time. This isn't just any ordinary cave. It's protected by seriously advanced technology. You'd never find it if you didn't know it was there. The ancients should never have been able to develop anything like the camouflage technology on the site. This is a unique discovery."

"What do you mean?" Basile frowned.

"Here. Look at this." Samuel pulled out the holorecorder. "You can see how it looks like there's nothing there, when suddenly…"

"*Zut alors!*" gasped Basile when the cave suddenly materialized.

"We were lucky we didn't crash the helicopter," Samuel said. "The first time we saw the cave was when we nearly crashed into the rock above the entrance. Josh was bringing us in to land, and it suddenly appeared out of nowhere. It's only thanks to his flying skills we were able to avoid it, but in the confusion, we lost the map."

"I see," nodded Basile.

"Watch this part." Samuel played the footage of the door. "That wasn't there when I first went into the cave. I had to perform a little ritual to make it appear. I didn't film that part in case the recording fell into the wrong hands. Given the technology that's protecting the cave, I'd put money on it containing something hugely important. I don't want anyone else knowing how to unlock the doors until the Ministry has claimed it."

"You could be right," Basile agreed. "Come on. Let's go back to my tent so we can review your tape in greater detail before we contact the Ministry. An engineer's perspective might help identify what mechanisms are at play so you can determine whether it really is ancient technology or a terrible modern joke."

NINE

After the helicopter had touched down at the dig site, Waleed made straight for Samuel and hurried out to make the most of the opportunity to attempt to pump information out of the American about why he'd been away from the camp for so long. When Basile interrupted them, at first, Waleed thought this would improve his chances of learning more. After all, he'd spent weeks cultivating his image as a harmless porter in the hope that he'd be able to more easily eavesdrop on important conversations.

It was obvious that this was the moment he'd been waiting for.

The archaeologist had dismissed him, barely looking at the porter when he told him to leave. Still, Waleed knew to keep up appearances, pressing his hands together and bowing his head a little to hide his disappointment, before turning and going back to the camp. He couldn't help but notice the irony that only that day he'd been advising Basile on being more like the American and the second he returned, Samuel was treating him as just another lackey.

Make the most of it, my American friend, Waleed thought to himself. *Your time will come soon enough.*

As he met a group of workers heading to a different part of the camp, Waleed used them as cover to duck away and sneak back to where Samuel and Basile were talking. Hiding behind some crates, he could just about make out their conversation.

"This isn't just any ordinary cave," Samuel was telling his friend. "It's protected by advanced technology. The ancients should never have been able to build anything like it. This is a unique discovery."

Waleed knew the cautious American well enough by now to know that he didn't get excited for no reason. If Samuel thought this cave was special, then it was definitely worth finding out more.

Risking peeping out from behind the crate, Waleed watched as Samuel switched on the holorecorder. Although he was too far away to see the details of what was playing, the look of astonishment on Basile's face was unmistakable.

"Well, well, well." Waleed muttered. "Looks like all my hard work has finally paid off."

Deciding that he'd seen enough and not wanting to risk discovery, Waleed crept away from the two men, his crouched posture lengthening into a cocky strut when he thought he'd gone far enough to avoid suspicion.

You're going to have to get used to having a shadow, Samuel, thought Waleed. After what he'd just seen, he was going to stick close by the man's side. A new expedition was going to need crew and Waleed intended to be first in line to volunteer.

His mind wandering off into fantasies of breaking into the cave and pocketing enough treasure to make him wealthy for the rest of his life, Waleed almost didn't notice the man hiding in the shadows of one of the equipment tents. He'd reached a part of the camp that stored tools that were no longer in regular use, so whoever it was, they were clearly hoping to avoid the rest of the team.

Privacy is a privilege you cannot afford, my friend, Waleed grinned to himself as he snuck into the tent. It always amused him how tent walls gave the illusion of privacy, fooling people into thinking they could talk without fear of being overheard when, of course, canvas offered no real soundproofing. Waleed had learned many a useful tidbit from hanging around tents.

Making himself comfortable, he heard the sound of radio equipment tuning in to the right frequency.

Stranger and stranger.

The site had its own radio equipment for crew to use when the satellite phones failed. Why, then, was this man using his own?

"Hallo? Hallo? Can you hear me? Over."

Waleed was sure he recognized the voice. Cautiously, he lifted up the bottom of the tent wall to confirm his suspicions.

Waleed dropped the canvas as soon as he saw who was on the other side. Nafty, the third member of Samuel's team, was trying to contact someone and one thing was for certain: it wasn't the Ministry.

The radio whined, as Nafty adjusted the dials to tune into the right frequency.

"Hallo? Mr. Nam-Gi? Are you there?"

"Yes. What is it?" A bored voice finally replied.

"This is Agent 4962, sir, Nafty, speaking to you from the Ministry dig site you sent me to observe."

"Whatever it is, this better be important," snapped Mr. Nam-Gi. "Or is this another one of your flights of fancy? You have been warned about wasting my time."

"No, no, sir." Nafty was quick to reassure his superior. "I promise you that this is of utmost importance. I believe that I have found what the Bruard have been looking for."

Waleed's eyes widened in shock. The Bruard? Nafty had always seemed a little shifty, but he'd never have guessed that he was a spy for the dynasty that had ambitions of world domination. This conversation could prove to be priceless to the right buyer.

Waleed edged closer, not wanting to miss any detail, until he was practically sitting back to back with the traitor.

"Oh really?" Mr. Nam-Gi seemed less than impressed. "And what exactly might that be?"

"A hidden cave," Nafty replied.

"I take it this cave is filled with valuable relics?"

Nafty paused. "I'm not sure about that," he finally admitted.

"Then why are you wasting my time?" raged Mr. Nam-Gi.

"Because this isn't any ordinary cave." Nafty spoke quickly, needing to tell Mr. Nam-Gi everything before he cut communications. "It was hidden by a cloaking device that was far too sophisticated for an ancient civilization to have built. Its very existence suggests that there is something special about this location. There is no other explanation unless..."

"Unless this is the site we have been looking for," Mr. Nam-Gi concluded. "What else?"

"The cloaking device was so effective that we had no idea there was a cave there until our pilot almost flew into it. Once we were on the ground, we determined that it hid the cave from all angles like a bubble until you got right next to it, which begs the question of how the ancients knew that people might be able to approach from the air. Inside, there was a mysterious doorway that could only be opened with a strange ritual."

"And what was past this doorway?"

"I have no idea. I did my best to persuade McCarthy to go further in, but the American pigdog insisted on returning for Ministry support first."

"I see." There was a pause. "Then it was at least worth hearing from you, Nafty. I'm sending out another agent to relieve you of your duties. Until they arrive, stay where you are and maintain observation. You'll receive your due payment when they reach you."

"Yes, sir."

Having heard enough, Waleed slipped away. Nafty was an agent of the Bruard? Being discovered eavesdropping by him was not a chance worth taking.

As he left the tent, Waleed stumbled over one of the ropes securing it down. Muffling a curse, he abandoned his usual caution and ran to get away before Nafty could investigate the noise.

"This is not worth it. Not any more," Waleed muttered to

himself. "With the bounty on my head, the last thing I need is to stick around and wait for the Bruard to storm in. It's time to put my escape plan into practice."

Hurrying into the tent he shared with three other workers, he was relieved to see that none of them were there. Having to conceal a body before he left would have been most inconvenient.

Pulling out his backpack from under the bed, he rummaged around for the secret pocket he'd had sewn into the inner lining. Finally locating his gun, he smiled as he caressed the barrel, admiring the way the light reflected from the metal.

"Hello, old friend."

Waleed checked that it was still fully loaded before tucking it into his pants. All that was left to do now was help himself to some of the precious artifacts from the camp before heading to Cairo. It was time to start afresh somewhere new.

TEN

Samuel strode confidently through the clutter strewn around his tent, seeming not to notice the clothes, documents and equipment strewn about the floor. As the chief of the expedition, his tent was larger than most, with space for a number of tables so that he could work in peace and quiet without needing to clear away one artifact before moving on to another, as well as room to store his most precious equipment and notes.

Basile followed him, immediately tripping over a device resembling a motorcycle engine, sporting curved colored tubes on the side.

"Shouldn't that be somewhere safe?" he remarked.

"That thing?" shrugged Samuel. "I don't really know why I brought it, to be honest. It analyses dirt samples, but I haven't needed to use it on this dig. Just put it over there."

He waved vaguely in the direction of a jumble of clothes and notebooks.

"Do you really have to live like this?" asked Basile, ignoring Samuel's instructions. "How can you find anything in this mess?"

"I know where everything is if I need it," Samuel shrugged. "And

since it's my stuff, that's all that matters. Anyway, this camp is temporary and I can count on two hands the number of days I've spent here
since the dig started. I've got more important things to do with my
time than stress about housework."

"You should be setting an example," advised Basile. "Leaders
should look and live like leaders."

"I really don't think that the state of my tent has anything to do
with how I run this expedition," laughed Samuel. "Who cares? I
mean, really, who cares?"

"The Ministry might if they came by," Basile pointed out. "You
know that they like to carry out surprise inspections every now and
then. You'll want to present yourself properly for them to take you
seriously."

"You let me worry about the Ministry while you keep your focus
on taking care of the workers' safety," Samuel told him. "Now are we
going to spend all night debating the merits of dusting or do you want
to take a closer look at the footage of the cave? I know which I think is
more exciting."

He swept his hand across a table, pushing all the documents and
detritus to one side so that he could set the holorecorder down. Basile
tutted and shook his head, but pulled over a stool and sat down so
that Samuel could play the video again.

Adjusting the settings on the device, Samuel sat back as the
holorecorder projected a 3D recreation of the cave. The two men
watched, Basile's brow furrowed in deep concentration, as the video
showed the unexpected emergence of the cave and the sudden difference between the blank wall and the double doors.

"That is absolutely fascinating," breathed Basile, after he'd
viewed the film for the third time. "And you say that those carvings
are of an Egyptian and a Roman goddess?"

"That's right," Samuel confirmed. "That's Seshat, while her
companion is Moneta. It's an interesting combination and not one I
ever recall seeing anywhere else. Seshat has authority over

accounting and astrology while Moneta is a lesser known goddess who is associated with memory. Moneta is also syncretized with the Greek mother of the muses, Mnemosyne, so there's a slight crossover with Greek culture as well."

"I wonder what the significance is of the two of them being placed side by side like that?" mused Basile. "I've seen enough in my time to know that ancient carvings like this were never created randomly. There's always a reason for the choice of images."

"Obviously, any theory at the moment will be pure conjecture," Samuel replied. "However, my initial observations would suggest that the chamber was built either at the beginning of the Roman conquest of Egypt or not long after they'd taken control of the area. As I'm sure you know, the Romans were very respectful when it came to local religions. Their attitude was that if you had a goddess with similar attributes to one of their goddesses, then clearly they were the same person under a different name. Probably one of the most famous examples is that of the temple of Sulis Minerva in Bath, England. There you have the Celtic goddess Sulis conflated with the Roman goddess Minerva to create a deity that spoke to both peoples."

"So Seshat and Moneta are the same goddess here?" asked Basile. "But I thought they had different powers?"

"Exactly," Samuel snapped his fingers and pointed at Basile. "Which is one of the reasons why I think we're seeing something truly unique. I don't think this image is meant to suggest that they are the same goddess so much as whatever is contained within comes under both their auspices. I believe that the fact that the goddesses of memory and accounting are posed together like this is a clue to the purpose of the chamber. I know that it might sound a bit out there, but I think there might be some kind of mechanism inside that records dreams."

"*Mon dieu!*" exclaimed Basile. "You cannot be serious? How could an ancient civilization be capable of recording dreams?"

"I have no idea, but I can't wait to find out," beamed Samuel.

"I don't understand how you were able to restrain yourself from going inside," said Basile. "If it were me, I wouldn't be able to hold myself back. I'd be in those caves right now, drooling over all the artifacts and thinking about how my name was going to go down in history for the discovery."

"I told you. I promised you that I wouldn't go in without you and I keep my word."

Basile fixed Samuel with a look.

"All right, all right," Samuel chuckled. "That is part of the reason, but not all of it. I still haven't ruled out the possibility that this is an elaborate, modern fraud. The map might be ancient but that doesn't mean the contents of the cave are. I'd like to carbon date the doors before proceeding and I didn't have the right equipment with me to do it. Plus, of course, I didn't want to risk triggering any traps that might still be in operation. With you by my side, I can send you in first to fall into any pits."

He nudged his friend, grinning, but Basile didn't see the joke.

"Do you really think there'll be traps there?" Basile frowned.

"I *always* expect traps on these types of digs," Samuel informed him. "You just never know. Whether we're dealing with an ancient or modern technology, they've gone to a lot of trouble to keep the cave hidden all this time. I don't think they're going to rely solely on camouflage to protect their secrets, do you?"

"You're probably right," Basile agreed. "That cloaking field is the part I can't get my head around. I can't imagine how the Romans could have created something like that. It goes against everything we know about them. My gut tells me that it's modern, but then why go to all the trouble of carving those goddesses and making them look as though they're centuries old? Surely that would make people want to explore further? If they wanted people to stay away, why not just put up some good old fashioned keep out signs or booby trap the doors? *Abandon hope all ye who enter here!*"

"It's a real mystery, isn't it?" Samuel smiled at his friend and

Basile grinned back, the pair of them enjoying the buzz of knowing that they were at the start of another new adventure together.

"Of course," Samuel continued, "it could just be a former smuggler's den. It may be that they installed all the cloaking devices and one of them had a penchant for ancient art so decided to decorate the doors to throw would-be thieves off the scent. Or the doors are ancient, but whatever they were protecting has long since gone. We'll know more once I've had a chance to carry out some preliminary carbon dating."

Basile stuck his bottom lip out, pondering. At last, he nodded slowly. "Whatever the case, we ought to tell the Ministry about this. If it's smugglers who are responsible for the cave, the Ministry will want to alert the appropriate authorities and if it's the Romans, it's best if we get them started on putting a team together in case this turns out to be a solid lead. We'll want to hit the ground running on this one."

"Agreed," said Samuel. "I'll contact them first thing in the morning. Now how about a drink to celebrate? I've got a bottle of whisky somewhere that's barely been touched."

"Thanks, but no thanks." Basile shook his head, gesturing at the messy tent. "Any alcohol that's been stored in these conditions will only taste like old shirts."

"Hey!" protested Samuel.

Basile stood up. "It's been a long day, so I'm going to get some sleep." As he reached the entrance to the tent, he turned back to his friend. "I'm glad to see you back safely. I was worried about you."

"You know me," Samuel replied. "I'm the original Comeback Kid!"

"Sleep well," smiled Basile, leaving Samuel alone.

Crossing over to where his bed was buried under a pile of blankets and old clothes, Samuel pulled out a small, sturdy, oak chest from underneath the pallet. Taking a small key out of his pocket, he unlocked the chest, opening it to reveal his most important notes and documents. Pushing the papers to one side to make room, he placed the holorecorder in the chest, locking it up again to keep it safe until morning.

Just as he was about to slide the chest back into its hiding place, he felt the pressure of a gun barrel pressed against back of his head.

Click.

ELEVEN

"Turn around and stand up. Slowly. Keep your hands where I can see them and don't do anything stupid."

Samuel carefully put his hands in the air, gradually turning until he was standing facing his unknown assailant.

"Waleed," he sneered when he saw who was pointing the gun at him. "I should have guessed. There always was something suspicious about you managing to be around whenever something important was about to happen. I don't know what we've been paying you for all this time, but it hasn't been for your work."

"What can I say, my friend?" Waleed shrugged. "I have a nose for business and an eye for what's valuable. Something tells me that you are going to help me be a very rich man."

"You're kidding yourself if you think I'm going to do anything for you," Samuel scoffed. "You'd have been better off shooting me in my sleep."

"I still might," Waleed warned, waving the gun menacingly.

Samuel shook his head slowly. "You don't have the balls."

"You really don't want to push me, my friend," Waleed

cautioned. "This gun has taken twelve lives so far. Do you really want to be unlucky number thirteen?"

Samuel shrugged. "Why don't you just cut the crap and tell me what you want?"

"That's more like it," grinned Waleed. "I've come to tender my resignation and I'd like to get my severance pay. Ten thousand dollars should do it."

"Are you kidding?" Samuel raised an eyebrow. "Talk about over-valuing your worth. Never going to happen."

"Oh, I'm worth a lot more than that, I can assure you," said Waleed. "Let's just call this little bonus the cherry on the cake."

"You can call it what you like. Doesn't mean that I can pull ten thousand out of my ass," Samuel countered. "We're out in the middle of the desert. It's not like I can go down to the bank and make a withdrawal. There's no need for cash out here anyway."

"Don't treat me like a fool," snapped Waleed. "You and I both know that the Ministry gives you a sizeable lump sum for unexpected expenses, not to mention all the cash 'bonuses' that you will have been treating yourself to at every dig. You can't tell me that you don't skim off a little from the top of every project you've worked on. I think I'm being more than reasonable. I could just take everything you've got. Instead, all you have to do is give me my ten thousand and I'll let you keep your life."

"You win." Keeping his hands in the air, Samuel gestured with his head to a large chest in a corner of the tent. "You're right. I do have the money. It's all in there."

"Then go! I don't have any time to waste." Waleed motioned with the gun, indicating to Samuel to go to the chest, following close behind. As Samuel turned his back on the gunman, he sent up a silent prayer of thanks to whatever god or goddess might be watching over him that Waleed had no idea that the real treasure lay under his bed.

When he reached the chest, Samuel dropped to his knees, pulling out a large bundle of keys from his pocket.

"Now let me see. Which one is it?" he began, slowly working through the keys one by one. "I'm so absent minded these days. I think that one's for the Jeep. That's for the document box. That's for the main equipment trunk."

"Don't jerk me around," hissed Waleed, casting an anxious glance over his shoulder to see if anyone was coming. "Get the key, get the money and get on with it!"

"I think this is the right one," Samuel announced, holding up a key and shaking the bunch at Waleed. "Does that look like it's the key to a chest to you?"

"If it's not the right one, I'll shoot you in the leg, so you'd better hope it is," warned Waleed, jerking his head in the direction of the chest. "Now get a move on and open up that lock. I've got places to be and I'm sick of waiting for you."

Samuel turned and fitted the key in the padlock securing the chest. After rattling it about for a few moments, he eventually turned it, releasing the lock.

"There you go," he announced, stepping back. "Everything you want is in there."

Waleed rushed forward, shoving Samuel out of the way to start rummaging through the chest in search of riches.

"Wait–what foolishness is this?" Waleed sat back on his haunches, holding up a handful of clean sheets in bemusement.

"That's my laundry chest, sucker!"

Samuel hit Waleed over the head with a large textbook, the heaviest thing he'd been able to grab easily. As the man stumbled forward, Samuel threw himself at his back, grappling for the gun. Falling to the floor, Samuel lay on top of Waleed, pinning him in place and making it impossible for him to move. Grabbing the arm holding the gun, Samuel twisted it up behind Waleed's back, forcing him to drop the weapon. Picking up the gun, Samuel opened it to unload it, only to discover that it was already empty. Snorting, he tossed it to a corner of the tent so it was out of reach.

Pushing Waleed's arm even further up until it wouldn't move any further, Samuel dug his knee into the small of Waleed's back, making him cry out in pain. Putting his other hand on the back of Waleed's head, Samuel felt a twinge of smug satisfaction as he ground Waleed's face into the dirt.

"Did you honestly just fall for the old laundry basket trick?" chuckled Samuel, as he put all his weight onto his captive until he groaned again. "And did you really think you could rob me with an empty gun? Jeez, Waleed. I knew you weren't the brightest, but I gave you a little more credit than that. Guess I overestimated you."

"Forgive me, master," begged Waleed, trying and failing to push himself up. "I meant no harm in trying to borrow money from you. I merely needed a little financing. I would have repaid you in time. I respect you too much to cheat you."

"Uh-huh," Samuel sneered. "Next time you want to try and scare someone into giving you their money, try putting a silencer on the gun. There was no way you were going to shoot me with that and get out of here alive. A little pistol like this doesn't carry anywhere near enough bullets to shoot your way out if the crap hit the fan and the second the workers heard a gunshot, they'd have come running to help. You really didn't think this plan through, did you?"

He adjusted his position, keeping Waleed firmly in place.

"Basile!" Samuel yelled. "Basile! Get your backside in here!"

"Please, let me go," pleaded Waleed. "I'll leave and never return. We can forget this ever happened. You owe me. We were friends!"

"We were never friends," Samuel told him as Basile pushed open the tent flaps.

"*Sacre bleu!*" he exclaimed when he saw Samuel sitting on top of Waleed. "What's going on here?"

"Waleed here thought that he would treat himself to a little farewell bonus by holding me up at gunpoint," Samuel explained. "His weapon's over there if you want to grab it. Don't worry–it's not loaded."

Basile crossed over to where the gun was lying on the floor, picking it up and holding it with two fingers at arm's length as if it would bite him. "I hate these things," he said. "What do you want me to do with it?"

"Leave it on the table," Samuel told him, Basile gratefully putting it down as soon as he could. "I'm more concerned about what we do with Waleed. Do we have anywhere we can keep him locked up until we can contact the Ministry?"

"This is an archaeological dig, not a prison site," Basile reminded him. "We don't generally erect jails when we set up camp. We could tie him up though–we've got plenty of rope–and I'm sure I can find a place to keep him secure in one of the lesser used tents until you decide what to do with him."

"Excellent," nodded Samuel. "Let's do that and call the Ministry for advice. The sooner Waleed's off my site, the better."

"Wait!" cried Waleed as Basile turned to rummage around the tent for some rope. "I have information you need to hear. Let me go and I'll tell you what I know."

"You were just threatening to kill me and you think I'll let you go?" Samuel barked, incredulous.

Waleed looked around wildly, before training his eyes on Samuel. "The reason I was so desperate to get away is that you have a Bruard spy in the camp and where there's one Bruard agent, others aren't far behind. I don't want to be anywhere near those sadists when they take over the site."

"Bruard?" scoffed Samuel. "I have to give it to you, Waleed. You've got some imagination. I thought you said you had something useful to tell me."

"I'm being serious!" Waleed urged. "I heard him talking on a radio he'd smuggled in, calling for reinforcements. I need to get out of here before the Bruard arrive and if you were sensible, you'd leave too."

"Yeah, yeah." Samuel took his knees off Waleed's arms, roughly pulling them back so that he could tie them together. "Have you got that rope yet, Basile?"

"Here you go." Basile hurried forward to hand over some cord he'd found. "But don't you think we should investigate his story further? It wouldn't be the first time the Bruard infiltrated a dig to siphon off resources and treasures to further their own cause. Shouldn't we tell the Ministry immediately, just in case?"

"I don't see why," shrugged Samuel. "Waleed here would say anything to save his own skin, wouldn't you, Waleed?" He twisted Waleed's arms behind his back, roughly wrapping the rope around his wrists and tying it so tightly that the cord bit into flesh.

"I'm telling the truth," Waleed protested. "Please, you have to believe me. We're all in danger."

"Says the man who threatened me with a gun," Samuel pointed out. "Come on. The only place you're going is the most uncomfortable tent we can find to keep you in until the authorities can collect you."

"No! Please, no! I'll scream and then you'll have the whole camp wondering why you're not taking me seriously!"

"Do it and I'll give you something to *really* scream about," Samuel warned. "I've picked up a few tricks over the years and you'd be surprised at how easy it is to break a man's wrist in one quick movement."

TWELVE

Shafira sighed and sat back in her seat, swiveling her chair as she gazed at the stack of work she still had to do, her eyes glazing over. The hum of a vacuum cleaner buzzed in the background as the janitors made their way round the cubicles on her floor.

Sighing again, as she summoned more reserves of stamina, she leaned forward and clicked on the button to play the recording of yet another dig site update. Jotting down notes as she watched the video for the final time, as soon as it was finished, she clicked on her mouse to switch the screen to her word processor.

Placing her hands on the keyboard to start writing up her notes, she took them away again without typing, slumping back.

Why are you wasting your life here, Saffy? she asked herself. All her colleagues had long since gone home, making this yet another day when she'd been the first one to arrive and the last to leave. Despite all her effort, it didn't seem to make any difference to her workload and although her supervisor had promised she'd be rewarded for her diligence, she couldn't remember the last time she'd had a raise.

Was the few extra pounds she'd make in overtime really worth it?

Would the world end if she went home, curled up with a DVD and tried to kid herself that she had a life?

"Screw it," she muttered, picking up her mouse to shut down her computer.

Knock, knock!

Taking a deep breath to stifle the curse that threatened to escape, Shafira plastered on her best smile in case it was Director Haisam, but relaxed when she saw it was only Aziza, one of the mail room women.

"Hey, Aziza," she said. ""How are you?"

"Not bad, not bad," Aziza replied. "Hosein, my eldest, has just started working in the mail room with me, so I've been showing him around. He's an ambitious boy and a hard worker. I don't think he'll be there long before they give him a position more suited to his ability."

"I'll keep my eyes open for him then," Shafira told her. "I'll be able to say that I knew him when!"

"Anyway, I know that you're really busy, so I hate to disturb you, especially when it's so late," Aziza went on, "but I thought you might like to see this. It just came in from the field. It's marked urgent and since I know that it's from a region that you deal with, I thought I'd leave it on your desk before I went home so you'd see it first thing in the morning. I wasn't expecting to see you still here."

"Oh, I wouldn't dream of leaving for a while yet," Shafira lied. "Not when I've got so much to get through. Pass it over and I'll have a look now."

Aziza gave her the package and left Shafira alone again.

"The things I do to keep up appearances," she muttered to herself, turning back round to her desk. Cutting open the securely sealed envelope, Shafira shook out a USB stick and a letter. Inserting the stick into her computer, there was only one file on the USB stick. She clicked on it and a video started playing.

Shafira groaned when she realized that she recognized the footage. It was a film that she'd already reviewed–twice. Once for her job and once for her super-secret assignment from the Director. Someone must have mislabeled it as urgent.

"Home to a DVD it is," she decided, reaching forward to switch it off, when a voice started commentating.

"This is Chief Archaeologist Samuel McCarthy speaking from a site in the vicinity of the existing dig in southern Egypt," it began. "This recording should be considered highly classified due to the potential ramifications of its contents."

Hello. Shafira sat up straight, leaning forward to see what information had been missing from the other recording.

"I have already submitted a basic report of the dig site," Samuel continued, "but this extra footage concerns a location a short helicopter ride away from the dig, co-ordinates of which remain a closely guarded secret until I receive further instruction.

"I first learned of the existence of a nearby cave containing fabled treasure when I unearthed a map from the dig site. Hidden among numerous other documents on a shelf in what appeared to be a storage area, at first the map seemed to be nothing out of the ordinary. However, translations of the text indicated that the map was much more than a simple diagram. It discussed a secret cave hidden from view, as well as a number of rituals that were supposed to confer spiritual enlightenment and forbidden knowledge to the practitioner.

"It would not be the first time such a map was discovered only for its treasure to be long since gone when the site was investigated. Nevertheless, I observed protocol and kept the details on a need to know basis, taking a small team to investigate the surrounding area. At first, we found nothing, but then we fell upon a camouflaged cave–literally."

Shafira gasped as she watched the recording of the cave materializing out of nowhere, Samuel beaming, having captured the miraculous nature of the camouflage, before moving on to the sudden appearance of the carved doors leading to a hidden inner sanctum.

"I've enclosed the appropriate documentation requesting an expansion of our dig site privileges as well as extra security to protect us when we return to the cave. Although all signs suggest that this is an ancient site, possibly the greatest find of our time, there is also the possibility that this cave is a smuggler's den, in which case we will need extra firepower as well as the authority to take any offenders we encounter into custody."

When the video was over, Shafira opened up the intranet and tapped in her passcode to access Samuel's personnel file. Highly rated by the Ministry, although some of his methodology was considered highly unorthodox, there was little doubt that he got results. If he believed that a site was worth further investigation, the chances were high that it was concealing something important.

Pulling the USB stick out of her computer, Shafira rolled her chair round to the other side of her cubicle. Placing her thumb on the biometric cabinet in the corner of her room, she placed the USB stick safely inside, locking it up securely.

Next, she pulled out a requisition form, quickly filling it out to authorize the security Samuel needed, pending approval from her superior. Stamping it with her official mark, she put the form and Samuel's letter in an envelope then got up to personally take it to the mail room before going home.

Hurrying down the corridor, as she turned a corner, she ran headlong into someone coming in the opposite direction.

"Oof!"

A chill ran through Shafira as she looked up to see who she'd run into. "Director Haisam!" she gasped. "I am so sorry for my clumsiness. Are you all right?"

"Yes, yes, I'm fine." He waved away her attempts to check him over. "But I'm curious as to where you're going in such a hurry at this time of night. Is there a big party somewhere you need to get to? Can I get an invite?"

"Nothing like that." Shafira laughed nervously. "I just wanted to get this to the mail room before they closed for the evening. It's rather important."

"Is it now?" Director Haisam frowned. "I'm sure I told you that anything important that crosses your desk should go through me?"

"You did." Shafira blushed. "But this seemed urgent, so I used my initiative to expedite the matter and approach the President. I didn't think you'd mind when it was something that seemed to need his input."

"I'll be the judge of that," Director Haisam reminded her. "What's happened?"

"I've received a recording from Samuel McCarthy out in the field," Shafira told him. "He thinks he's uncovered a new area of interest close to the site he's currently working on and has requested extra support. Based on my analysis of the situation, I think that his request is warranted."

"I see." Director Haisam's brow furrowed. "I think you should hand the recording over to me for review, and let me deal with any resource allocations. It is highly probable that this concerns the matter that we discussed previously. This is exactly the sort of thing I was talking about and I'm most disappointed that you didn't think to come to me before anyone else."

"Shouldn't we bring this to the President's attention?" Shafira asked.

"The President is already aware," replied Director Haisam loftily. "He has asked me to handle all aspects of the situation, which is why you should give me everything you have and let me deal with it."

"But, sir..." Shafira struggled to keep her tone respectful. "This discovery could hold great cultural significance. Protocol would dictate that I go through the proper channels to ensure that it's afforded the appropriate protection right from the start. The Bruard would love to strip it bare and use what they find to force concessions from us. Look at the impact the Elgin marbles have had on Greek/British relations. If the Bruard steal whatever is in this site from Egypt, this could be far, far worse according to McCarthy's preliminary theories."

"Exactly," Director Haisam told her. "It is precisely because this is such an important site that we have to do what the President wishes and keep this hush hush. Let me see the letter McCarthy sent."

Reluctantly, Shafira gave him the envelope she was carrying. Ripping it open, Director Haisam quickly scanned the contents.

"Hmmm. Where is the recording he mentions? I think it best if I look after it."

"You don't need to worry about that, sir. It's perfectly safe," Shafira reassured him.

"I didn't ask if it was safe," hissed Director Haisam. "I asked where it was."

Shafira gulped, as the Director stepped closer to her.

"Do I need to mention your insubordination in your next career review?" he threatened. "I do not expect to have to face the third degree when I make a simple access request. Do not make me ask you again to give me the recording."

"N... no, sir. It's locked in the safe in my office."

"Then don't just stand there, girl," Director Haisam barked. "Take me to it!"

Shafira hurried back to her cubicle, the Director hot on her heels.

"Come on, Shafira. Get a move on!"

Shafira frowned, struggling to understand the Director's sudden shift in attitude. He'd always been such a pleasure to deal with in all the other cases she'd worked on. What was so different about this one?

THIRTEEN

"It's just in here." Shafira leaned over the biometric cabinet, pressing her thumb to the mechanism to open it. "You don't have to worry about anyone taking it. It's completely secure. I'm the only person who can open this door."

"No system is completely secure," sneered Director Haisam. "It's that kind of slapdash attitude that allows mistakes to happen. You should always be vigilant. Always."

"Yes, sir," replied Shafira, groaning inwardly as he retrieved the USB stick and turned to the Director. "I hope you don't mind my asking, but what is it about this particular recording that's so special? As McCarthy himself says, it may just be a smuggler's den. There may not be anything ancient there at all."

Director Haisam huffed. "I suppose you deserve an explanation after all your hard work. However, I shouldn't need to have to stress to you that what I am about to say to you needs to remain strictly confidential. I am trusting you, Shafira. Don't let me down."

"I won't, sir." Shafira gave the Director the USB stick as he leaned into her, keeping his voice low, despite the absence of staff in the office.

"The President has received intelligence that the Bruard have turned their attention away from the Chinese border, having failed to make major inroads in the area. Instead, we have received reports that they are active in the area you have responsibility for. Given the number of significant dig sites in the area, this news should come as no surprise. The Bruard are notorious for stealing ancient artifacts and trading them on the black market to fund their campaigns. Since this particular site is reputed to be especially rich in treasure, we have to be particularly alert.

"McCarthy is right to request extra security, although not for the reasons you might think. I doubt there are any smugglers there. If the cave is in active use, it'll be the Bruard using it as a base for their activities in the area. I wouldn't be at all surprised if they used it to keep hostages and torture victims knowing that they would be unlikely to be disturbed in such a remote area."

"Torture?" Shafira gasped.

"Oh yes." Director Haisam nodded gravely. "We do our best to keep reports of the worst Bruard behavior out of the media. We don't want to give the Bruard any kind of free publicity, but I'm sure you don't need me to tell you that they are utterly brutal, willing to do whatever's necessary to get what they want. This means that if McCarthy has discovered an important site, details of the investigation will be on a strictly need to know basis. You are not the only one in your department who has been working on this project for me, but I have intentionally isolated you all from each other for your own protection. The less you know about the big picture, the safer you all are."

"Thank you, sir." Shafira couldn't help but wonder who else might be helping the Director. If they were able to pool their findings, surely they could find what the Director needed faster? She was just an admin clerk. The Bruard wouldn't care about her, would they?

"What about the requisition forms?" Shafira asked. "Would you still like me to send them out?"

"Hold fire for now, Shafira," Director Haisam instructed her. "I'll review it personally and draft a report to the President. He can decide what measures are most appropriate."

"Will do, sir." Shafira nodded.

"I have to say that I'm very impressed by your dedication to your work," Director Haisam told her. "Your kind of work ethic will take you far. However, I suggest that you turn in for now, act naturally when you come in tomorrow as if there's nothing of concern going on."

"But there isn't, is there, sir?" asked Shafira. "Nothing of concern happening, that is. Surely I'd only need to put on an act if I had information that could spark off a riot if it got into the wrong hands or a spy had infiltrated the department."

She laughed, but the Director remained po-faced until her laugh faded away.

"You don't really think there's a spy in the department, do you?"

"I always expect spies when it comes to the Bruard," sniffed Director Haisam. "Hope for the best and prepare for the worst, Shafira. It's the only policy that makes sense."

"So does that mean that the Ministry will be inspecting the site after all?"

"It is entirely possible that we will be authorizing an investigation," the Director confirmed.

Shafira's heart beat a little faster. "In that case, sir, might I request that I be allowed to join the expedition? I mean, I'm already familiar with the project and you did say that I would go far within the Ministry. This would be the perfect opportunity for me to prove myself."

Director Haisam chuckled and shook his head. "Much as I applaud your enthusiasm, I'm afraid that that is completely out of the question. This kind of operation requires specialist skills and experience. It would be utterly inappropriate for a mere admin clerk to go along. It would be restricted to essential staff only on a need-to-know basis. However, don't be disappointed. You are still a vital member of the team. Your work is just as important as any archaeologist's, even if it's less glamorous. I'm reliant on you continuing to send me detailed reports so that I can assess the situation as it changes."

He checked his watch. "My goodness. Is that the time? I've been keeping you far too long. I suggest you do as I told you—go home and get a good night's sleep. There'll be plenty of work waiting for you in the morning."

"Yes, sir." Shafira nodded as Director Haisam took his leave.

Frowning, she turned to tidy her desk before heading out. Something didn't add up, but she couldn't put her finger on what exactly.

If only she was further up the food chain. Then she'd be on the Director's need-to-know list and she could help out more, maybe even go on the expedition.

As it was, she was just 'a mere admin clerk.'

Shafira decided to take Director Haisam's advice. She'd go home, have a nice, relaxing bubble bath and watch a DVD in bed. Staying here wasn't going to make any real difference to the amount of work she'd have to do in the morning and her encounter with the Director had left her feeling a little unsettled.

Picking up her purse, she looked round her cubicle to make sure that she hadn't left anything behind before finally logging off for the night.

FOURTEEN

Director Haisam returned to his office, where his secretary was still sitting at her desk outside his door, busy typing up dictation from a tape he'd recorded earlier.

Pulling on a light coat, he collected his briefcase.

"Make sure all those documents are on my desk by morning, Feme," he instructed. "They're highly time sensitive, not to mention confidential."

"Of course, Director Haisam," she replied, as he left, unaware of the dark look she threw at his back without missing a keystroke.

"Goodnight, Director Haisam," called the security guard manning the door as the Director strode past, nodding an acknowledgment.

Walking out of the Ministry building, the Director turned left, heading in the opposite direction to the official parking lot. As he strode along the sidewalk, a car with dark tinted windows pulled up alongside him. Director Haisam got into the back of the car, the vehicle moving away almost before he'd had a chance to shut the door.

"Ugh. Thank goodness I'm free of that dreadful place," tutted the

Director, pulling off his gloves and dousing his hands with liberal amounts of sanitizer before squirting some inside the gloves to disinfect them.

"Was today just as awful as the past two days?" asked Gord, as he drove his master, Pin, away.

"You cannot imagine." Pin rolled his eyes. "Today was the worst yet. A woman dared to question my orders. A woman! Such insolence would be unthinkable were the Bruard in charge. There is such decadence everywhere I look. Women working in the Ministry, women overstepping their authority, overestimating themselves everywhere. It is unbearable, quite unbearable!"

"Don't worry, sir," Gord soothed. "We will be able to correct all of that once the Bruard takes its rightful position at the head of the new world order. We will restore everything to the way it should be and you will be justly rewarded for everything you've done to rid the world of corruption."

"I tell you something, Gord," snarled Pin. "When we overthrow the Ministry, that woman will be the first to face punishment. Shafira will learn that you should obey my word without question. Women cannot think logically. Her idea of 'initiative' will only cause trouble."

Gord listened patiently as his boss ranted, letting out all his pent up frustration from the day. It wasn't the first time he'd heard this tirade and it was unlikely to be the last.

"Has there been any progress on the special project?" Gord eventually asked when Pin paused long enough for him to speak.

"Potentially," Pin told him. "A Samuel McCarthy has apparently uncovered a cave network that was hidden by a sophisticated cloaking tech yet bears all the features of an ancient chamber. There are no signs of any recent smuggling activity and, of course, we know it is not a Bruard outpost either."

"Very odd, sir," remarked Gord.

"Indeed," Pin nodded.

"Have they recovered any valuables from the site?"

"Pah!" Pin sniffed. "The idiot that reported it decided for reasons best known to himself that he wasn't going to actually look inside the vault, so nobody knows what it contains. I don't know. Maybe he was afraid of catching some ancient virus or some other equally foolish nonsense. I hoped for better from a professional archaeologist, but what do you expect from an American? I'll need to authorize an official expedition to investigate further if we want to know what's there."

"Maybe you should just leave it alone for now," Gord shrugged. "Come up with an excuse to make this McCarthy move on and come back when the opportunity presents itself. If you don't know what's inside, the Bruard won't want to expend precious resources only to find that the chamber is empty, looted by thieves centuries ago. You know what the consequences are for those who waste Bruard money."

"I do," agreed Pin, "but there's something about this site that tells me it's worth pursuing. I want nothing more than to see the Bruard take over the world and I genuinely believe that there is something here that will enable them to do so. The technology at this site is incredible, while the ancient door markings are like nothing I've ever seen. This is too big to ignore. I can't risk leaving it for the Ministry to grab the artifacts before the Bruard can get there. It's a gamble, but my instincts tell me that we should take this further. And my instincts are never wrong."

"Very well," Gord nodded. "In that case, there is another issue we need to discuss."

"Yes?"

"The Director's children. How do you want me to handle them?"

"For goodness' sake, Gord. We're not monsters," retorted Pin. "I'll make arrangements for them to visit family indefinitely. Besides, Haisam will be making his last appearance at home tonight. It won't be long before they'll be mourning their dear, departed father."

"Does that mean that you need me to dispose of Haisam?" confirmed Gord.

"I don't know why you kept him around this long anyway," said

Pin. "Why waste good food on a dead man? We've already mined him for any valuable information. He's got nothing more to offer."

"He's good company," chuckled Gord. "His face when I describe what I'm going to do to his wife is hilarious!"

Pin shook his head, sneering in disgust. "Crude, Gord, even for you. I'm afraid the fun and games are over. Haisam is surplus to requirements. Eliminate him and then return to collect me when I call for you. I'll arrange for the children to leave and then we can move on to the next phase in the plan."

"Yes, sir."

Pin pressed the button to close the window between the passenger and driver sections, spending the rest of the journey lost in thought as Gord drove to Haisam's home. Pulling up outside the modest house, the henchmen came round to open the door for Pin before getting back into the car once he'd seen his master go inside, tires screeching as he gunned the engine, eager to have one final night of fun with the real Director.

FIFTEEN

Samuel checked over the ropes securing Waleed to the chair Basile had dragged into the middle of one of the lesser used storage tents.

"I'm beginning to wish that I'd ordered the prison cell tent when I took inventory," he joked. "Still, this will do for the moment. Don't worry, Waleed. I'll make sure that you're reasonably well looked after until I can find someone to take you to Cairo to turn you over to the authorities. You won't be our highest priority, but we'll throw food in your general direction on occasion."

"Mmm-mmm-mmm!" Waleed fought to speak against the gag tied around his mouth.

"Don't try to claim that you need the toilet again," Samuel warned, as he loosened the gag to see what he had to say.

"Please," begged Waleed. "I beseech you. Let me go before it's too late! You have to believe me. I had good reason to run away."

"What–the Bruard?" Samuel laughed. "You'll have to come up with something better than that if you want us to believe you." He reached out to put the gag back in place, but Waleed jerked his head away, determined to be heard.

"I'm being honest," he urged.

"For the first time in your life," muttered Basile.

"I *did* see a spy," Waleed insisted. "He was speaking to someone higher up reporting on what he'd seen. Some kind of secret cave, he said."

Samuel and Basile exchanged nervous glances. "Go on," Samuel said, folding his arms in an attempt to hide his concern.

Heartened by having permission to speak, Waleed repeated the conversation he'd overheard. "He talked about a cloaking device, something that was way beyond ancient capabilities, and strange rituals required to enter the inner cave system. There was also something about a doorway but he didn't know what was behind it."

"And who was the spy?" Samuel asked.

"I don't know," Waleed admitted. "He was sitting in shadows and I couldn't get close enough to see. He must be someone with access to your reports though. He knew too much to be a mere worker."

"Basile, a word?"

Samuel took Basile to the other end of the tent, out of Waleed's hearing. "What do you think?" he whispered.

"Much as I hate to say it, I think he's telling the truth," Basile replied. "Very few people know about the cave and for him to have all that detail means that he must have got it from somewhere. It's plausible that he overheard a spy talking about it, although it's also possible that he rifled through your reports while he was waiting for you in your tent and then made up this spy as a cover story."

"I agree," nodded Samuel. "It goes against every fiber in my being to say it, but Waleed could be right. There might be a spy in our midst. We'll have to warn Nafty to be on high alert. Clearly someone is paying close attention to our movements. They must have seen the report I sent back to head office. I tried to keep it confidential, but it's always possible that someone hacked into the system and downloaded the files or even went into my tent before Waleed and copied my document.

"I'll tell Nafty to keep anything related to the cave under lock and key. If we do have a traitor on the site, we'll need to make sure that he doesn't learn any more than he already knows. I can't impress upon you enough the importance of tighter security now. I'm putting you in charge of Waleed. Go outside and keep watch for anyone acting suspicious while I question him further. If we do have a spy in the camp, I don't want us to be overheard."

"*Oui, biensur.*"

Basile ducked outside to stand guard while Samuel walked back to Waleed, who looked up at him with hope in his eyes.

"You can see that I'm telling the truth, can't you, my friend?" he said. "That information was worth a reward, yes? I know I can't expect any money from you now and it was foolish of me to try and steal, but if you let me go, I promise I will leave straight away and never return. We can consider ourselves even..."

"Sorry, Waleed." Samuel shook his head. "After what you've done, you're stuck where you are for the time being. I'm going to place a guard on you while I get some of the workers to build a makeshift cage for you. We have the facilities to put together some-thing secure enough to hold you and I'm not cruel enough to keep you tied up like this indefinitely. I'll make sure you're as comfortable as possible while you wait for justice."

"But... but.... You can't!" protested Waleed. "I'm too delicate to be behind bars! I have a letter from my doctor. It's bad for my mental health!"

Samuel chuckled. "There's nothing delicate about you, desert rat. You should have thought of that before you pulled out a gun and tried to steal from me."

"If you lock me up in this heat I could catch the plague! Malaria! Dengue fever! Ebola!" Waleed babbled wildly. "I have medication in my bag to protect me from infection. If I don't take it, I could die!"

"I think you'll survive just fine," Samuel told him. "Slimeballs like you always do."

"But the Bruard! If they find me trussed up like a turkey, they'll gut me. Please, you can't keep me here. You are condemning me to death by your actions. When you find my body, it will be on your conscience. Can you live with that, McCarthy?"

"I'll cope," Samuel shrugged. "But, I'll tell you what. I promise you that if I find evidence, *real* evidence and not just your say-so, that the Bruard is involved with the dig, I will release you." He stepped closer to the restrained man, squatting so that he could look him straight in the face. "But if you ever point a gun at me again, loaded or not, all bets are off. I'll stake you out in the desert for the Bruard to do whatever they like to you and I won't lose any sleep over it."

"Thank you, my friend. Thank you." Waleed's relief was palpable. "I know that a man as noble and honorable as you will keep your word when you find the evidence you seek. Can I beg a favor from you?"

"Another one?" Samuel huffed. "Do you want anything else while I'm at it? Lobster Thermidor on a silver platter or the moon on a stick?"

"No, no. Don't worry. I don't need anything expensive." Samuel's sarcasm appeared to have completely bypassed Waleed. "If the Bruard are coming, I need to be out of here before they arrive. Please, my friend. Promise me that the instant that you find proof that I'm telling the truth–and I know you will–you will come back and release me so I can get to safety."

"Why should I do that? If I find out the Bruard are active in the area, you're going to be the last thing on my mind."

"You have no idea what they're like," warned Waleed. "Those men are brutes. I'm deathly allergic to blood. They're likely to come in guns blazing to wipe out the camp. They don't like leaving any survivors as witness to their wicked deeds. I wouldn't survive a serious firefight."

"You had no problem pointing a gun at me," Samuel observed.

"An *unloaded* gun," Waleed corrected. "I would never have seriously hurt you."

"And those twelve men that gun has killed?"

"A mere fabrication designed to add a little spice to my story."

Samuel narrowed his eyes, considering everything Waleed had told him. One thing was for sure. Whatever else he might be lying about, it was clear that he was genuinely terrified of the Bruard, a fear that went beyond anything he might have read about in the media. What was his history with the organization?

"All right. I'll see what I can do. That's the best I can offer," Samuel told him before going out to confer with Basile.

"Have you seen anyone spying on us?" he asked.

"No one as far as I can tell," Basile replied. "Nobody cares about what goes on in this part of the camp. What do you make of his story? The man's a weasel. He'll say anything to save his skin. I wouldn't trust a word he tells you."

"That he is," Samuel agreed, "but I think he's telling the truth, at least as far as he's capable. How else could he have found out about the cave? That's the one thing that doesn't add up. It's a weird thing for him to invent as an excuse for his behavior."

"Someone as slippery as him will have his resources," Basile pointed out. "But whatever's going on, one thing's for sure: the sooner we get him out of the camp, the better."

"Agreed," nodded Samuel. "Until then, we need to find a guard we can trust. Anyone could be in league with the spy." He thought for a moment. "What about Nafty? He isn't essential to the dig, so right now, he's just waiting around for instruction from the Ministry and he seemed loyal when he was out at the cave. He might like the chance to do something useful. Can you wait here while I go and fill him in?"

"*Oui, oui.*" Basile nodded.

"I'll warn him to be careful with his things as well," Samuel said. "Maybe Nafty can help us figure out who the spy is. He might have seen someone lurking about his tent."

He headed out to fetch Nafty to help out with guard duties, leaving Basile to watch over Waleed, wondering just how true his story really was.

SIXTEEN

Shafira sat by the window in her favorite café, idly stirring her coffee. Slowly, she flipped through the latest copy of *Egyptology Studies*, imagining that she was the archaeologist featured in one of the articles. There'd be pictures of her posing in front of a recently discovered tomb, a big smile on her face as she held up an ancient vase.

Anything had to be better than being stuck in an office cubicle.

She sat up a little straighter when she saw the next headline.

McCarthy Discovery Reveals More About Ramses II.

McCarthy! That was the name of the archaeologist in charge of the dig that had made Director Haisam behave so peculiarly. Intrigued, she read on.

A mile north of the pyramids of Giza, renowned Egyptology and archaeology specialist Samuel McCarthy has uncovered a temple that provides further evidence of the connection between King Ramses II and his status as a supposed sun god.

Built in honor of the pharaoh, the temple features a wooden carving of Ramses II placed in perfect alignment for the sun to hit it twice a year, once on his birthday, October 22, and also on the date of his coronation, February 22, potentially as part of a religious ritual.

Carbon dating suggests that the temple was completed in 1281 BC, some six years before his more famous temple that was previously unearthed in Aswan, meaning that the Pharaoh's construction projects were even more extensive than existing evidence had suggested.

Ramses II was born in 1315 BC and came to the throne as a young man in 1290 BC to become one of the more popular pharaohs. Having inherited a country that was already flourishing under his father's reign, Ramses II had been an ardent student of the theory of war, rule, and politics, enabling him to put this theory into practice to build upon his father's success and defeat the Hittites, who were a massive military power at the time.

Ramses II was obsessed with leaving a permanent legacy in honor of himself and is responsible for constructing more shrines, palaces, statues and obelisks than any other previous ruler as part of his bid for immortality. As well as numerous self-aggrandizing monuments, he also oversaw the development of Pi-Ramesses, Egypt's new capital, which would become a major city in the ancient Near East.

McCarthy told us that the discovery of this new temple is particularly exciting because of the exceptional quality of the surviving artifacts. Containing both wooden and stone carvings, the level of detail provides more information about Ramses II's rule, including a well-preserved mosaic that tells the story of a battle against the Hittites.

"There is no doubt that there are countless more secrets waiting to be discovered in this temple," said McCarthy. "As we unearth more of the site, it is likely to become one of the most significant finds in recent years, deepening our understanding of this important period in Egyptian history."

Shafira sighed for what felt like the thousandth time that day, slumping so that her chin rested on her hand as a twinge of jealousy ran through her. Imagine being the first person to discover a temple. A whole temple! McCarthy was American, yet he was doing more for her country's heritage than she ever had.

Not for the first time, Shafira wished that her father had acceded to her pleas to study archaeology instead of insisting that she take up an administrative position. Her life would be very different if she were out in the field instead of filing papers at the Ministry.

Picking up her cup, she took a sip, blanching and wincing at the taste as she swallowed a mouthful of cold coffee.

"That's what happens when you stir a cup for half an hour," laughed Omar, the waiter behind the counter, who'd been watching her. "Some things are best not savored for *too* long."

"I guess I got lost in thought," Shafira confessed, bashfully. "Could I get a refill, please?"

Omar poured out another cup, crossing over to replace her barely touched coffee. "You're one of my best tippers, so call this one on the house," he told her. "Just don't tell the boss, okay?"

Shafira laughed. "Your secret's safe with me."

Omar craned his neck, trying to make out what she'd been reading. "So what was so interesting you ignored my beautifully made coffee?"

"Oh. This?" Shafira turned the magazine over so he could see the cover.

"*Egyptology Studies*," he read. "Interesting. Are you a student, then?"

"No." Shafira shook her head. "I'm just a clerk at the Ministry of State for Antiquities. The closest I get to being on a dig is when I read the reports sent in after all the fun is over."

"It sounds like you're in the wrong career," Omar observed.

"There's more job security at the Ministry than out in the field," Shafira told him. "All the archaeologists are self-employed freelancers with no guarantee that their contract will be renewed at the end of a dig. At least I have a permanent position and know how much money I'll take home at the end of the month. My older brother, Yusuf, followed his heart and ended up partying a little too hard to be able to keep any job for too long. He's still bouncing from one dead end job to another. I don't want to disappoint my parents the way that he did."

"Don't you think they'd be proud of you if they saw your photo in a magazine like that?" Omar nodded at the picture of McCarthy.

"They'd probably tell me that it's no place for a woman," Shafira replied. "And wonder why I'd been mad enough to leave a position with such potential." She put on a thick accent, imitating her father. *"You could have your own secretary one day, Shafira, if you work hard enough."*

"But do you want your own secretary?" Omar asked. "Sometimes when we live our life for others, we forget to live it for ourselves. Do you want to look back when you're older and ask yourself what if? Maybe you should live a little, do what makes you happy for a change instead of ending up resenting the decisions you made for the sake of your parents. Think about it."

Omar turned and headed back to take up his position behind the counter as Shafira picked up her coffee, drinking it before it grew cold this time. Throwing a generous tip on the table, she swept the magazine into her bag, ready to go home.

SHAFIRA DAWDLED DOWN THE SIDEWALK, taking her time as she thought about what Omar had said. He had a point. She was doing what her parents expected and how happy was it making her? Whatever you could say about her brother, at least he enjoyed himself. At the same time, she knew how badly Yusuf had hurt them. It was her duty as their daughter to show that they'd brought up at least one of their children properly.

Reaching the intersection with the turn off to her house, she paused. Turn left and she'd be home in five minutes. Turn right and she'd stroll through Al-Azhar Park and wouldn't be back for at least another half hour. She'd bought her house precisely because it was so close to the park, yet she'd spent so much time at work, she'd rarely come here.

Deciding that Omar was right and she needed to do what made

her happy, in a tiny gesture of defiance, Shafira headed right to detour through the park. It was a beautiful evening. A little fresh air was just what she needed to clear her head after a hard day's work.

A balmy breeze blew across her face, a pleasant, warm caress that confirmed that she'd made the right choice in cutting through the park. She could feel all the tension from work draining away with every step. There was a path up ahead that she could take that would lead out to the back of her road, eventually bringing her home. Shafira resolved to come this way more often after work and not be in such a hurry to get to her destination that she forgot to enjoy the journey. There was something wonderfully soothing about being out here.

THUD!

A loud noise came from behind the bushes she was walking past, sending the birds that had been snoozing in the trees flying into the air in panic. Frowning, Shafira left the path and headed in the direction of the sound.

As she pushed through the undergrowth, she heard more strange thumps and thuds. Trying to stay as silent as possible, she crept towards the sound, a sickening feeling of dread building in the pit of her stomach.

Concealed in the bush, she cautiously pried apart the branches to peep through. She clapped a hand over her mouth to stifle a scream as she saw a large man in the center of a small, secluded clearing, a mirthless grin on his face as he punched and kicked some poor soul who was lying limp on the ground.

For a moment she stood frozen in fear, unsure of what to do for the best. Run or hide? A man that brutal wouldn't hesitate to eliminate any witnesses.

The thug gave his victim a final kick, causing him to roll towards her hiding place. Shafira bit down on her hand to hold back her cries as the bloody, bruised face of Director Haisam stared lifelessly up at her.

SEVENTEEN

Shafira gazed helplessly at the face of the man she'd been talking to just a few short hours ago.

Closing her eyes, she willed her body to break free of the terror that was trapping her inside herself. *"Move, Saffy,"* she thought *"Move your frigging feet or you're next."*

Slowly, slowly, she began to retreat, edging backwards inch by painful inch, but, seeing the brute marching towards her, she stopped.

"Dammit!"

What to do? What to do? He was twice her size. She had no chance of fighting him off. Shafira didn't kid herself that the self-defense class she'd taken at the community center would do anything against a ruthless giant.

She reached out for her purse, her fingers fumbling as she searched for the zip. Slowly, slowly, ever so slowly, she pulled it down, the sound of the teeth unlocking sounding impossibly loud.

After what seemed like an eternity, she'd opened the bag enough to slip her hand inside, keeping her attention firmly fixed on the killer as she rooted around for the ancient can of pepper spray her mother had given her 'just in case.' It had been in her purse for so long, Shafira had no idea if it would still work, but it was the only chance she had to gain some kind of an advantage in a fist fight.

Adrenaline coursing through her body, her hand shook as she lifted up the can, finger on the button ready to spray it in the man's face. If it could only buy her a few minutes' head start, she might be able make it back to her street, even her house, before he caught up with her.

Shafira bit her lip, holding her breath as the man came closer and closer, tensing herself to leap out at him.

He whistled tunelessly as he scooped up a bag that had been lying on the floor near the body. Was he going to use it to suffocate her?

Shafira put her other arm in front of her eyes to shield them as she readied herself to fire the spray…

…when, instead of reaching out into the bushes for her, the man bent over the body, a streetlight reflecting from his sweaty forehead for a second, dragging his victim back into the middle of the clearing as if he were light as a feather.

"Well, Haisam, it's been fun knowing you, but all good things must come to an end," he muttered to the body of the director. "Although I must say that I am a little disappointed. I'd have thought that you'd put up a little more of a fight, if only for your lovely wife and delightful children. I know that Mr. Nam-Gi promised you that we'd take care of them, but my idea of care is a little different to his. I hate leaving loose ends, so you have my word that I'll make sure that everything is neat and tidy before we move on to our next assignment."

Shafira watched in horror as the man crammed her boss' body into the bag, not showing any sign of respect while he treated it like a piece of trash. Her stomach lurched as she heard the snap of a limb.

"All right, Haisam. Let's get this over with." The corpse finally concealed in the bag, the director's murderer lifted up the body, easily tossing it over his shoulder as if it were full of wastepaper

instead of the remains of a human being. Whistling the same uniden-
tifiable tune, he turned and strode off in the opposite direction to
Shafira's hiding place.

When he was out of sight, she turned and threw up everything
she'd eaten that day, her stomach still retching long after it
was empty.

"Pull yourself together, Saffy," she moaned, her legs feeling like
jelly as the adrenaline wore off. "It's not too late to help his family."

Hauling herself to her feet, Shafira headed back to the entrance
to the park. She fought every instinct to run screaming for help,
instead doing her best to walk along nonchalantly, as if she hadn't just
witnessed a murder. She had no idea where the killer had taken the
body and there was still a chance that he might see her and realize
that he had another loose end to take care of.

"Oh God, oh God, oh God, oh God," she chanted over and over
under her breath, her mind churning as she attempted to process
what she'd just seen and wondered what to do for the best. This was
a sick nightmare there was no waking from.

As she approached the park entrance, relief flooded through her
body as she saw a police officer walking past.

"Thank goodness. Officer! Officer!" Shafira ran towards the
policeman, shouting and waving to get his attention.

"Yes?" The policeman turned to her, his bored gaze taking in her
disheveled appearance, sneering at the state of her clothes.

"You have to come quickly. There's been a murder!" Shafira
gasped. "Back there. A man was beaten to death."

The policeman's demeanor changed in an instant, going from
disinterest to high alert. "What exactly happened?"

"In the bushes, just up that path. I saw a man kicking and
punching my boss. He killed him."

Shafira burst into tears, the trauma of what she'd been through
finally catching up with her.

The policeman, pulled out his walkie-talkie. "Back up requested
at the west entrance to the Al-Azhar Park. Possible homicide

reported, repeat, possible homicide reported." He turned to Shafira, placing a hand on her shoulder reassuringly. "Don't worry. We'll get to the bottom of this."

Shafira sniffed and nodded.

"Do you have any ID?" the officer requested. "We'll need to take a formal statement from you."

"Of course." Shafira rummaged in her bag, taking out a business card to give to the policeman. "I work at the Ministry with the man who was killed. But don't you think you should go after the murderer? He could still be in the park. He was heading in that direction."

"Stay here," ordered the policeman. "More officers will be here momentarily and they'll need to talk to you."

He hurried off in the direction Shafira had indicated, leaving her on her own. Standing in the illuminating beam of a streetlight, Shafira shivered, despite the heat. She'd never felt so exposed. There was only one policeman and he'd left her here. There was no knowing when his backup would arrive and what would happen if the killer came back this way after hearing her shout? He might guess that Shafira was the one who'd called the cops on him.

Shafira shook her head, turning to hurry home. Much as she wanted to do her civic duty, it was too risky. She'd given the policeman her details. They could contact her after they had the killer behind bars.

Once she was safe in her house, Shafira headed to the kitchen, putting on the kettle. Going to the cupboard, she pulled out a box of chamomile tea to try and help her get to sleep.

"Screw it," she muttered, putting the tea back and going to where she kept her secret stash of alcohol saved for special occasions. Grabbing a bottle of whisky that had barely been touched, she headed off to bed to drink herself into oblivion.

EIGHTEEN

Waleed frowned, his tongue protruding from a corner of his mouth as he wriggled around like a fish out of water, desperately trying to free himself from his bonds. Let the American sit here and wait for the Bruard to come and slaughter them all if he wanted. Waleed had every intention of being on the other side of Egypt when that happened.

"A-ha!" he crowed as, with a final tug, he felt the ropes around his wrists loosen and start to slip away. However, his celebration was short lived, as someone started to open the tent flap. Grabbing at the rope before it tumbled to the ground, Waleed did his best to wrap it back around his wrists in a vague simulacrum of the knots that had held him. It was unlikely to fool anyone who looked closely, but he prayed to Allah that whoever his guard was, they wouldn't bother checking.

Waleed suppressed a gasp when he saw who was coming to watch over him.

"Well, well, well," said a familiar voice. "Why am I unsurprised to find you here?"

"Nafty, my brother," greeted Waleed, trying to keep his tone light. "You couldn't do me a favor and let me out of here, could you? I have somewhere important I need to be."

"I don't think so," tutted Nafty. "You and I need to have a little talk about how you came to be in this... predicament. I hear that you have uncovered a spy in our midst, a spy for the Bruard, no less. The irony is delicious, don't you think? After all, you've always been the first to volunteer for extra duties. Don't think I haven't noticed you take any opportunity to stand around listening to those more important than you discuss the issues facing the dig. Are you sure that the spy isn't, in fact, you?"

"What can I say?" shrugged Waleed. "I relish the chance to learn from those wiser than I. It does not make me a spy."

"No," conceded Nafty. "But the fact that you've been observed snooping around where you do not belong would certainly suggest such a thing. Nevertheless, let us assume that I am willing to give you the benefit of the doubt. Why would a man like you, a man so desperate to be of assistance whenever he can, suddenly turn on those he has been so intent on helping? What could possibly have happened that would make you turn your back on your colleagues and hurl accusations of Bruard involvement?"

"There is no grand mystery," Waleed told him. "I simply grew bored of being on a dig site when I was never given the chance to prove my worth. I could have helped recover artifacts, served as McCarthy's right hand man, yet no matter how hard I tried, I was relegated to a mere skivvy, a slave to the Americans. Any man would tire of such treatment given enough time. I thought I could earn good money here. I was wrong. I am not so foolish as to not recognize the right moment to cut my losses and leave."

"And yet that moment coincides with the discovery of a double agent," pointed out Nafty. "Wonderfully convenient, is it not?"

"Allah moves in mysterious ways," Waleed proclaimed.

"Not so mysterious when men are involved," Nafty pointed out. "We are, at our heart, much simpler creatures. Although I have to say, Waleed, that I am surprised by the path you chose to take. Why try to rob the American? Surely there would be more money to be made confronting the spy and blackmailing him?"

"I would never dream of going against the Bruard," Waleed assured him. "I always intended to steal from the American before I left. After all, that's what his people have done to us, coming to our country, stealing our ancient treasures with no regard for our heritage. A few thousand dollars is nothing to a man like him and no less than we deserve."

"So why tell him about the spy?" Nafty asked. "If you have so little regard for the American's wellbeing, why not keep quiet and let him suffer when the Bruard arrive–assuming that they are, in fact, coming at all."

"I just want to get out of here," pleaded Waleed. "If telling him a story about a spy on the camp wins me my freedom, then I will tell him about ten spies, a hundred, even! Please, my friend. Can you not turn your back and let me leave? If it would help, I'd be more than happy to make it look as though I overpowered you, much as it would pain me to hurt you."

Nafty gazed at him, mulling over his options. "You're just an idiot who thought he could steal and run," he announced at last. "I owe you nothing. You will stay here and face the consequences of your actions." He patted his jacket, suggesting that Waleed wasn't the only one who'd brought a gun to camp. "Behave yourself and this evening will go by just fine. But trust me. I will lose no sleep if you decide to test me. I suggest you try to get some rest. You'll be out of here soon enough."

"Very well," Waleed said, hanging his head in resignation. "I'll give you no trouble."

"Good." Nafty turned and left the tent to take up his position outside the entrance.

As soon as he was gone, Waleed dropped the ropes, padding silently across the tent and pressing his ear at the tent flap. The sound of a cough told him that Nafty was indeed standing guard right outside, so he couldn't simply walk out.

Waleed moved round the tent, tugging at the canvas where it met the ground, but it was too securely fastened for him to be able to squeeze out without risking attracting attention. Nafty might have been bluffing when he implied that he had a weapon on him, but he didn't strike Waleed as someone who would hesitate before taking a shot. There was a certain steel to him that the American lacked. Where McCarthy was all talk, Nafty was a man of fewer words and more action.

Resigning himself to a long, uncomfortable night, Waleed returned to his chair. Picking up the rope, he did his best to redo the knots with his mouth. He couldn't think of a plausible story that would explain to Samuel or Basile how he'd managed to get loose and he wasn't going to give Nafty any excuse to hurt him. It would be terribly convenient for the American if Waleed were to suffer an 'accident.'

NINETEEN

Samuel walked into his tent, a towel wrapped around his waist, having just showered. Picking up the shirt that was lying over the back of a chair, he sniffed at it, tossing it towards the ever-growing pile of dirty laundry on top of one of the side tables before rummaging around in the pile of clothes by his bed to find something clean enough to wear.

There was a fumbling at his tent flap just as Samuel finished buttoning up his pants. Looking over, he smiled when he saw Basile walk in.

"Good timing!" he remarked. "A moment earlier and you would have seen me in my tighty-whities."

"Don't make jokes at me, not today," growled Basile. "I'm never in a good humor when I'm woken up to do your job."

"What have I done now?" asked Samuel. "Or rather, what *haven't* I done?"

"The radio tech has been trying to contact you for the past hour," Basile raged. "Why haven't you responded?"

"I didn't hear anything," shrugged Samuel.

Basile crossed over to where the radio sat on a small table.

Gingerly removing some underwear from it and tossing them to one side with a grimace, he flicked the switch turn the set on.

"Of course you're not going to hear it if you've turned it off," he snapped.

"I shut it off every night," Samuel explained. "The crackling disturbs me, so I shut it off so I can get some sleep. There didn't seem to be much point in switching it on while I had a shower. It's not as though I can hear anything with water in my ears." He grinned to take the edge off his words.

Basile shook his head, his mood lightening a little. "No one but you can get away with this kind of behavior," he told him. "You're lucky it wasn't an emergency."

"If it were, my good friend Basile would have come to find me," Samuel pointed out. Basile groaned and shook his head, but the two of them both knew it was true. "Do you know what the Ministry wanted?"

"They've reviewed your reports on the cave and not only have they granted approval to extend the excavation, they're sending one of their own to observe the exploration."

"Yay." Samuel put his thumbs up halfheartedly.

"What's wrong?" Basile asked. "The Ministry is going to fund further investigation. Surely that's a good thing?"

"Not when it comes with strings attached," Samuel told him. "In my experience, when they send someone to 'observe' what they really mean is interfere."

"Does it happen often, then?"

"I've had observers attached to a few of my digs over the years," Samuel replied. "It happens more often than you'd think, although it's always for reasons outside the scope of the dig."

"You mean-?"

"Yes." Samuel nodded grimly. "If the Ministry is that keen to supervise what we're doing first-hand, then either they saw something in the recordings I missed or they share our concerns about smugglers or Bruard agents."

"I fear you're right," Basile agreed. "But what can we do? It's the Ministry. They're paying for this dig after all. What they say goes. Speaking of which, their official should arrive within the next day or two, so perhaps you should take this opportunity to clean up your tent. We don't want the Ministry to take one look at this mess and immediately rescind their funding."

"It'll never happen," Samuel reassured him. "I'm too good at what I do. But if it will make you happy, I'll tidy a little, just for you."

"Really? Promise?" Basile looked dubious.

"Have I ever broken a promise to you?"

"Well, there was that time when..."

Samuel held up a hand to interrupt him. "All right, all right. No need to go into details. I take your point. I really will clear up a bit. Changing the subject, has anyone had a chance to check on Waleed?"

"According to Nafty, he was a model prisoner all night. He's asked for some breakfast to be taken to him."

"Then why don't you take some food to our guest?" suggested Samuel. "Maybe he'll tell you something he wouldn't say to Nafty or me. After all, you are the good cop to my bad."

"Like what?"

"I've been thinking more about the story he told us," said Samuel. "After a night tied to a chair, maybe he'll have changed his mind about whether the Bruard are coming. Or maybe he'll have remembered some more details about the alleged spy that will help us identify him. Either way, I wouldn't mind getting your opinion on the veracity of his claims. I trust your judgment."

"All right," nodded Basile. "I'll sound him out."

"Just don't discuss what he says with anyone other than me or Nafty, okay?" Samuel instructed. "We don't want to start a panic. I still haven't ruled out the possibility he's lying to us."

"*Bien sur,*" Basile agreed. "What will you be doing while I'm exchanging pleasantries with Waleed? Are you sure you wouldn't rather interrogate him yourself?"

Samuel shook his head. "I want to review the scrolls that were found with the map. It's possible that they may have a clue I missed about what could be waiting for us in the cave. I want to be as prepared as possible before the Ministry official arrives and starts asking a million questions."

"Good idea." Basile headed out to put together some food for Waleed, while Samuel flicked the switch to get the coffee maker started. The way this expedition was shaping up, he was going to need a lot of caffeine to get through the next few weeks.

TWENTY

By the time Shafira pushed through the rotating door to enter the Ministry building, she was a nervous wreck. It didn't help that her head was pounding with the mother of all headaches. Using whisky as a sleep aid had not been the best idea she'd ever had and had done nothing to chase away Haisam's death playing in an endless loop in her mind. She'd practically run to work, seeing Haisam's murderer lurking in every shadow. Even now, in the safety of the Ministry, she was gazing around, looking to see if the killer had somehow followed her here and was waiting for a chance to leap out at her.

She'd feel better if the police had spoken to her last night, perhaps offered some form of protection, but since the officer she'd spoken to had run into the park in search of Haisam's killer, she hadn't heard a thing, not even to ask her to make a statement. Surely they should treat a murder more seriously than they seemed to be? There should have been a cordon placed around the park immediately, a crime scene investigation team brought in to go over the area with a fine-toothed comb, but when Shafira had gazed in the direction of the park as she went through the intersection, she couldn't make out any sign of police activity. The park looked like it did on any other ordinary day.

Pressing the button for the elevator, Faroukh came to stand by her as she waited for it to descend.

"Good morning, Shafira," he beamed. "And how are you this beautiful morning?"

"Oh, er, fine, fine." Shafira barely glanced at Faroukh as she gazed up at the numbers above the elevator counting down the floors until it would arrive, her foot nervously tapping away the seconds.

"I do hope that you aren't still burning the candle at both ends," he advised. "I keep telling you, this place does not reward hard work. You are better to do what everyone else does. Clock in at 9, do what you can for the next few hours, then head home the minute the clock strikes five."

"That sounds lovely," Shafira murmured, barely aware of what Faroukh was saying.

"You're not listening to a word I say, are you?"

"What?" Shafira blinked, attempting to push away the image of Haisam's dead eyes.

"It's all right," he reassured her jovially. "I'd probably tune out if I were you. The youth of today think they know it all. Until you get old and discover that you know nothing!"

He laughed at his own joke, nudging Shafira with his elbow, but she didn't join in.

"Hey, are you all right, Shafira?" Faroukh asked, frowning. "Now that I can see you, you're looking a little pale. Are you feeling okay?"

Shafira said nothing. How did you tell a colleague that their boss had been brutally murdered? Was it even her place to say anything before the news was made public? Would she get into trouble with the police if she discussed the Director's death with anyone before she spoke to them?

She was saved from having to reply by the ding of the elevator announcing its arrival.

"After you." Faroukh bowed, stepping back so she could go in first. "You know, if you're not feeling well, it's not too late for you to go home. I'm sure I could cover for you."

"That's very kind of you, but there's no need," Shafira assured him, as the elevator sped up to their floor. As the doors opened again, the first thing Shafira noticed was the uniformed police officer standing outside her cubicle chatting to one of the secretaries. The woman laughed coquettishly at something the policeman said, but when she saw Shafira walking towards them, her mood shifted in an instant as she glared at her colleague.

"That's the woman you're looking for," the secretary said coldly, turning away as Shafira came to stand next to the officer.

"Are you Shafira Khouri?" asked the policeman, checking in his notebook that he had the right name.

"I am." Shafira's heart leapt to her throat as the policeman tutted and read over his notes, seeming to take an eternity to remind himself of the details of the case he was investigating.

"Is there somewhere private we can talk?" he asked at last.

"Meeting room three is free, Officer Ali," suggested the secretary helpfully. "Just through that door there."

"Thank you, Rasheeda," smiled the officer. "And thank you for the coffee too–just what I needed!"

"You're welcome." Rasheeda blushed, fiddling with her hair as she wiggled her fingers in a goodbye wave before returning to her desk to gossip with the other secretaries.

"What's going on, Officer?" asked Shafira. "Have you found Director Haisam's body?"

"I think it best if we discuss this in the meeting room," replied the policeman curtly, indicating to Shafira that she should lead the way.

Once inside the meeting room, the policeman gestured to Shafira to take a seat as he closed the door behind them. She sat down, clasping her hands together to stop them shaking.

"Have you found Director Haisam's body?" Shafira repeated as the officer flicked through his notebook to find a blank page.

"Before I update you on our investigation, I'd like you to go over once again what happened last night," Officer Ali told her.

"I was walking home after work," Shafira began. "Usually I'd go straight to my house, but it was so lovely I decided to take a detour through the park. As I walked past some bushes, I heard a thud that was so loud that it scared the birds from the trees. I went to see what had made the noise and I saw a man kicking and punching someone. At first I thought it was a mugging, but it soon became clear that something more serious was going on. When the attacker was finished, they shoved the body in my direction, which is when I saw that it was Director Haisam. Luckily, I was hidden by the bushes or I might have been killed too.

"As I watched, the murderer wrapped the Director's body in a bag and then left, so I went to get help. I saw a policeman by the entrance to the park, so I gave him my card, told him what had happened and went home." She hung her head in embarrassment. "I should have waited for the officer to return, but I was afraid. I didn't know whether the killer had seen me or if he'd come back, so I decided to wait for the officer in the security of my own home, only nobody came to check on me."

"Were you drinking last night?" asked the officer abruptly.

"Was I-? No!" Shafira blushed. Could the policeman still smell whisky on her breath? What did it matter if she'd had a drink or two after what she'd witnessed? She was stone cold sober when she saw Haisam die.

"It's just that we have a rather peculiar situation here," the officer explained. "It's this alleged death that puzzles me the most."

"Alleged?" Shafira frowned. "Officer, I can assure you that Director Haisam was dead. Nobody could have survived what he went through. I saw it with my own eyes. Somebody killed him, and you need to find the murderer before they strike again."

"We found blood in the park in the area you directed us to," the policeman confirmed. "Given the seriousness of your allegations, we wanted to test it immediately, so we came to the Ministry to try and obtain a DNA sample to confirm the identity of the victim. I'm sure you can imagine our embarrassment when we found the Director in his office working late. He was most surprised to learn that he was supposed to have been murdered a few hours previously."

"But... but I don't understand," stammered Shafira. "How did he look? Was he bruised?"

"He was fine," replied the officer. "Not a scratch on him. He was more than happy to supply us a sample for us to compare against the blood. We are waiting for the lab results to confirm, but even without them, I think it safe to say that you were mistaken about the victim– assuming there was even a victim in the first place."

"But there was!" protested Shafira. "You said yourself you found blood at the area."

"There are plenty of explanations for why there was blood there," the officer told her. He carried on talking, but Shafira wasn't listening. She was distracted by the sight of the Director walking past the meeting room window. She watched as he stopped to talk to staff, shaking hands and exchanging pleasantries as he made his way through the department.

The detective was right. Director Haisam was in perfect health.

"I'm sorry, Officer Ali," murmured Shafira. "I guess I must have been mistaken after all. I'm sorry for having wasted your time."

"Perjury is a serious offence," the policeman warned. "I'm afraid I have to inform you that your case will be referred to my superiors who may decide to charge you. I must request that you remain in Cairo until we have concluded our investigations. Should it transpire that there was a victim after all, we will still need to identify who they were, since you were clearly mistaken about it being the Director and you will be required to give evidence. Make sure that we have your updated contact details at all time."

"Yes, of course." Shafira stood as the man got up to go, her mind whirling. She wasn't perjuring herself. She knew what she'd seen. There had to be a rational explanation for what had happened last night, but whatever it was, the police weren't interested in uncovering it.

She escorted the officer to the elevator. As the doors closed behind him, she turned and watched the Director as he smiled and joked with Rasheeda and the other secretaries. There wasn't a scratch on him.

It made absolutely no sense. Something was very wrong here. Shafira was determined to find out what it was.

TWENTY-ONE

Basile ducked into the tent that served as Waleed's jail cell, a bowl of porridge in his hand.

"Thanks for keeping an eye on him," he said to the porter who was currently sitting with the prisoner. "I'll take over from here. I'd like to have a word with him in private."

"I'm not sure that that's a good idea," countered the porter. "He's a tricky character who almost persuaded one of the guards to set him free. You should have some back up with you, just in case."

"I'm sure I can deal with *un petit salaud* like him," Basile reassured the porter. "Besides, Waleed and I have things to discuss. Private things."

"Are you sure?" The porter looked dubious.

"I'm sure," Basile insisted. "We're wasting enough resources on him as it is. Go and do the job we're paying you to do."

"If you say so." The porter shrugged and walked out, leaving Basile alone with Waleed.

"Hope you're hungry," Basile said to Waleed, dragging over another chair to sit opposite him as he spooned out some porridge, shoving it into Waleed's mouth without caring if any fell down his clothes.

"Thank you," mumbled Waleed, through his food. "Nobody brought me any dinner last night so I'm starving."

"You're lucky to get anything at all," Basile told him. "After the stunt you pulled, we should be staking you out in the middle of the desert for the fire ants."

Waleed sucked air through his teeth. "You're a harsh man," he said. "Have you been spending too much time in the company of Samuel McCarthy?"

"Samuel's not harsh," protested Basile. "He takes a dim view of thieves, that's all. And I can't blame him."

Waleed barked a laugh. "I get it. You don't want to risk your standing in the camp. But it's all right. You're among friends now. You can tell me the truth. Samuel won't learn about anything you say from me."

"Hold your tongue." Basile roughly shoveled another spoonful of porridge into Waleed's mouth. The man grinned as he chewed, which only angered Basile more.

"See–I can see Samuel's influence finally coming out in you," Waleed chuckled. "I told you that you should take lessons from the American. I'm glad to see you finally listening to me."

"Don't think I can't see what you're doing," warned Basile. "You're trying to get under my skin. I know your sort. All you want to do is cause trouble. No doubt that's why you're claiming that the Bruard have infiltrated the camp. It's just another one of your little mind games. For all we know, it's you who is the Bruard agent. You've been cagey and suspicious from the moment you first came here. You were leaving to meet up with your masters and you're annoyed that we've thwarted your plans."

"I'm no Bruard." For a moment, Waleed lost his swagger, as he practically spat out his words.

Basile was taken aback by Waleed's intensity, but he tried not to let it show. "The Ministry will be here in day or so. If you don't give them the answers they want, you'll be turned over to be questioned by the government's expert interrogators and make no mistake—they *will* make you talk."

"The Ministry is coming?" mused Waleed. "An interesting development. Are you not curious as to why the Ministry is sending one of their own to visit the camp after all this time? They wouldn't be coming just for little old me. What else is going on, I wonder?"

"It's no great mystery," Basile told him. "Either their experts saw something in McCarthy's recording he missed or they're as concerned as we are by the possibility of the Bruard using the cave."

"That's one explanation," conceded Waleed, smirking.

"What?" snapped Basile. "What are you trying to say?"

"It's just that I've had encounters with the Bruard before," Waleed confessed. "It is not something I'm proud of, but I once ran a con that went awry, incurring the wrath of the Bruard. I did a lot of research on them in preparation for the scam. I learned how to spot their cells so I could manipulate them better. The Bruard is involved here, of that there is no doubt, but I do not believe that it is how you think it is, my friend."

"Is that right?" Basile attempted to act nonchalant.

"How is this, my friend?" Waleed offered. "I'll be more than happy to stay at the camp and assist you in the fight against the Bruard, but in order for me to be effective, I'll need to be free of my bindings. You help me and I'll help you. I can't uncover the spy if I'm trapped in here, can I?"

"I don't think so," sniffed Basile. "I can't imagine Samuel would like it if he knew that you were running around camp unsupervised. It's going to take him a while to forgive you for putting a gun to his head, even if it was all a bluff."

"What can I say? I was desperate," Waleed told him. "But with your support, I think we can find the truth." He thought for a moment. "How is this for a compromise: what about if you let me investigate the camp without us telling Samuel for three days? That will give me plenty of time to compile a full report on the Bruard agent and what is really going on behind the scenes at camp. If I haven't found anything after three days then I will willingly hand myself over to the authorities. You can't say fairer than that, my friend."

"I don't know..."

Waleed pressed on. "I'm swift and quiet, so no one will see me moving around and I promise that I'll be back here in my prison before Samuel comes to check on me. He'll never know I've been gone. Give me a chance to prove myself to you, one way or another."

"I'm still not sure if we shouldn't tell Samuel," said Basile.

"You know what will happen if we do," replied Waleed. "He'll tell you that you're wrong about me, that I'm dangerous, that I should be restrained until I can be handed over to the authorities, blah, blah, blah. If that happens, you'll never know who the spy is until it's too late. Samuel is an intelligent man, but sometimes he can be blinkered by his own brilliance. You have much better people skills than he. You always have. It's why everyone loves you on the camp while Samuel would be eating his meals on his own if you weren't here. He is your friend. I understand your loyalty to him. But this is not betraying him. This is helping him. Together we will keep him safe. When you unmask the spy, you'll be a hero. Your name will be on the front page of all the papers, with the details of how you persuaded your quiet little apprentice help you to prove your suspicions. I will just be a small footnote to your brilliance. Don't you want to be the hero of the story instead of Samuel for a change?"

"It would be nice," Basile conceded. He paused for a long moment. "All right. You have a deal. I will give you your freedom for the next three days as long as nobody sees you and you return here for questioning whenever Samuel wants to talk to you. If you do not uncover evidence of the Bruard's involvement during that time, you will let me hand you over to the authorities myself."

"It is a deal, my friend," cried Waleed joyously as Basile went round to untie his hands. "Now here's my plan..."

TWENTY-TWO

Samuel walked through the dig site, paying careful attention to everything around him as he inspected the progress. Thanks to the generosity of the Ministry, he'd been able to hire a large crew, so they'd managed to unearth a great deal of the palace they'd discovered, but there was still a long way to go before they could consider the site fully excavated. It was a large site, one of the biggest digs Samuel had worked on so far, and with the discovery of the cave adding to his workload, there was still a lot left to do.

"Mr. McCarthy!" beamed one of the workers as Samuel went past. "It's good to see you here."

"Good to see you too, Suleiman. Keep it up! You're doing great." Samuel made a point of knowing all the workers' names, even if he'd only met them briefly. It was one of the many little ways in which he won the respect of all his team. Well, almost all. There were always exceptions like Waleed.

"Oh, Suleiman, do you know whether the scrolls we recovered from the library last week are still in storage tent B?"

"Yes, Mr. McCarthy," nodded Suleiman. "Categorized and ordered just the way you requested."

"Excellent."

Samuel headed off to the section of the camp set aside for the safe storage of documentation. After centuries sealed underground, they required strict climate control to preserve them before they were safely transported to the city for further study.

Making his way to storage tent B, Samuel entered the outer part of the tent. Unlike accommodation tents, extra layers had been constructed around the artifact storage tents designed to keep out dust, moisture, bacteria, and anything else that might degrade the documents.

Liberally covering his hands with the antibacterial soap stored by the entrance, Samuel scrubbed up, making sure that his hands were perfectly clean before going into the inner sanctum of the tent. Holding his hands in the air so that he didn't sully them when he pushed the door open, Samuel turned to push open the entrance with his back. He could hear the sounds of someone shuffling around inside the tent, presumably another archaeologist.

Samuel opened his mouth to call out a warning that the doors were about to open when he heard the familiar crackling sound of a radio tuning in. Remembering what Waleed had claimed about the spy, Samuel bit back his cry, leaning his head against the door to listen in. Samuel strained his ears, but he couldn't make out any of the words beyond a vague muttering. Leaning closer to try and hear better, the door suddenly gave way beneath him and he fell into the storage tent, landing painfully on his backside.

Ignoring the agony in his lower back, Samuel pulled himself to his feet as he heard the sound of a case snapping shut. Footsteps ran away as Samuel gave chase in the direction of the noise.

"A-ha!" he crowed as the figure turned and ran down a stack of crates that Samuel knew ended in a dead end. "I've got you now!"

Turning the corner to see who he was chasing, Samuel was just in time to catch sight of a foot disappearing underneath the canvas as the spy scrambled out to freedom.

Stifling a curse, Samuel threw himself after him, forcing himself underneath the canvas to race after the traitor, fighting his way through the extra layers to get outside. The imposter was fast. In the heat of the midday sun, Samuel quickly found himself flagging as he ploughed through the sand in a vain attempt to catch up, each footstep becoming heavier and heavier.

Eventually, he was forced to give up, panting and clutching at the stitch in his side to watch helplessly as a solitary figure fled through the dunes to freedom, running over the sand as easily as if it were asphalt.

"Not fair," growled Samuel. "Why does the Bruard give out sandskimmer tech shoes while the Ministry barely issues even basic boots?"

The spy disappeared from view, safe in the knowledge that it would be too dangerous for Samuel to go after him. There was nothing Samuel could do but head back into the storage tent and check that the artifacts were all secure, in case the spy had sabotaged them.

Reentering Storage Tent B, Samuel reached the section where the map had been stored. He found a number of the scrolls were out of their cases, unrolled and laid out on white paper. Had the spy been photographing them for his own nefarious purpose? Samuel had a horrible feeling that Waleed may well be right on the money. And if that was the case, the entire camp could be in terrible danger.

TWENTY-THREE

"Hey, Faroukh." Shafira smiled as she walked up to her colleague who was helping himself to coffee from the machine. "How's your day going?"

"All the better for seeing you," came the smarmy reply. "I must say that it is very pleasant seeing you out here, socializing with the rest of us mere mortals instead of beavering away at your desk. What brought about such a welcome change in attitude?"

"Let's just say that I've been thinking about what you said and you're right," Shafira told him. "I've been spending hours trying to clear my backlog and it never makes any difference. Reports come in faster than I can process them. I might as well relax a little. You get paid the same either way, right?"

"Exactly!" beamed Faroukh, as Malik, another clerk, came to join them in the kitchen. "Malik, look who's emerged from her cubicle to join us."

"Hi Shafira." Malik poured himself a coffee. "To what do we owe the honor of your company?"

"I guess I got tired of staring at the same gray walls day in, day out," Shafira replied.

"There must be something in the air," observed Faroukh. "The Director has been friendlier recently as well. He's spending an awful lot of time in our department and I can't say that I'm completely happy about knowing that he's breathing down my neck, watching my every move."

Shafira bit her lip, trying to hide her excitement at hearing the Director's name mentioned. "You noticed that too, huh?" she asked casually. "I thought it was just me who thought he was acting strangely."

"I don't know that I'd describe him as acting strange," said Malik. "I thought he was just being nice, figured he'd been on one of those modern management courses where they teach you that if you want to inspire your staff you need to be their best friend. It's a sad day for the world when someone being friendly is considered odd behavior."

"Even so, you don't think he's been a bit different recently?" Shafira pressed.

"I suppose he's been a little pushier than normal," Malik conceded. "He does seem to be a lot more interested in my work than he used to be."

"Now that *is* weird," joked Faroukh. "Who'd find the boring reports you produce interesting?"

"Very funny." Malik shook his head. "Oh, and then there was that time when he shook my hand and then I saw him washing it immediately afterwards as if it were covered in dung. It was really offensive. Does he think he's going to catch something from me?"

"There was that flu bug going around," Shafira reminded him, topping up her coffee. "Maybe he's worried about that. Anyway, much as I've enjoyed our little chat, I really do need to get back to work. I don't want to get too sloppy!"

She raised her mug in salute to her colleagues and headed back to her cubicle. Her heart started beating faster when she saw Director Haisam walking down the corridor towards her.

"Ah, Shafira." He raised a hand in greeting. "Just the woman I was hoping to see. Do you have a moment? I'd like to speak with you in my office."

"Of course," Shafira agreed. "I'll just put this on my desk." She went into her cubicle and placed her mug on a coaster, trying to control the shaking of her hands. How could the Director still be walking around without a scratch on him? It just didn't make sense. She knew what she'd seen. The Director had been beaten to a pulp in front of her eyes.

Haisam led the way through the warren of corridors that criss-crossed the Ministry until they reached his office, Shafira close on his heels. She watched his movements closely, looking for any clue that would explain his sudden health, perhaps a hint that he was covering his pain, but he seemed to be the same Director she'd worked with ever since she started at the Ministry, even if he was a little more familiar with the staff.

As he unlocked the door to his office, Director Haisam stepped to one side, gesturing to Shafira to lead the way. "Take a seat," he instructed, closing the door behind them before going to take his place behind the desk.

"I want to share a funny story I heard recently." The Director steepled his fingers together, gently swiveling his chair from side to side. "Apparently I'm supposed to be dead! According to this story, I was beaten to a pulp in a nearby park then shoved in a bag, my body taken to be dumped who knows where! Can you believe it?"

"No." Shafira frowned, doing her best to appear ignorant. "What a peculiar rumor. Who would say such a terrible thing?"

"I was rather hoping that you'd tell me," Haisam replied. "A friend of mine in the police force told me that while he couldn't give me the name of who made such a ridiculous claim, he did strongly suggest that it was one of my employees, someone with whom I've been working closely. Do you have any idea who that might be?"

Shafira stuck out her bottom lip as she pretended to ponder the question. "I can't think of anyone," she finally replied.

"Is that right?" Haisam leaned back in his chair, clasping his hands across his belly as he twiddled his thumbs. "Because I have my suspicions."

"You do?"

"I have been observing my staff very closely recently," the Director told her. "I'm sure that you can appreciate that when you have tasked a number of people with working on different aspects of a highly confidential project, it's important to be certain that they are all observing the correct protocols. We cannot afford any leaks, not when there are enemies of the state everywhere. As such, I've become very familiar with my team's work patterns, habits and behavior. Almost everyone seems to acting as normal, which would make pinpointing the alleged witness difficult apart from one thing."

"Which is?"

"There is one individual who's suddenly become very jumpy and nervous. Could you explain why that might be?"

"Not without knowing who we're talking about." Shafira's scalp prickled, her stomach clenching as she fought hard to remain calm and not run screaming from the room. She wanted nothing more but to trust the Director, but there was something threatening about his manner that set her on edge.

"All right." Haisam sat up and leaned forward. "Let's try a different approach. Is everything all right, Shafira?"

Yusuf had always taught Shafira that the best lie was one that contained as much truth as possible. Remembering his advice, she paused then shook her head. "No."

"I thought as much." The Director smiled. Shafira was sure that he meant it to be reassuring but there was something predatory about the look. "Would you like to tell me why you went to the police with such an absurd story?"

"What? You think I-?" Shafira laughed and shook her head. "I'm sorry if I gave the impression that I was the one responsible for going to the police. It wasn't me! I've been having a few personal problems and I'm afraid that last night I let them get the better of me. I took a little something to help me sleep and I'm suffering the after effects this morning. Next time I'll stick to chamomile tea." She smiled again, winking at the Director to hint at the fact that she trusted him not to tell anyone that she'd been drinking.

"I see." The Director gazed at her thoughtfully. "I'm sorry to hear that you have been having some difficulties. You can always talk to me if you need some support, even with non-work issues."

"Thank you, Director."

"Perhaps it would help if you were to get away from things for a few days?" the Director suggested. "I will shortly be visiting a dig site to inspect progress. Maybe you would like to accompany me as my assistant?"

Any other time and Shafira would have jumped at the opportunity. This trip could be the stepping stone to a promotion, the chance to do the kind of work that really excited her. But how could she go away with someone she'd seen die before her very eyes?

Director Haisam was doing a very good impression of being the benevolent, kindly boss he'd always been, but until she had an explanation for what had happened last night, she couldn't trust him. Even assuming that it was nothing but an elaborate hoax, what kind of sick individual would pretend that he'd been beaten?

"I'd love to, Director," she replied, "but with all the extra work you've requested as well as my usual duties, I simply have too much to get through to be able to take any time away. Perhaps next time?"

"Hmm." The Director gazed at her impassively. "That's what I like about you, Shafira. Your dedication to your work. Anyone else would jump at the opportunity to have a break from the office." He shifted some papers around on his desk, picking up one and pretending to examine it. "I shall be heading out this afternoon on the expedition. I would appreciate it if you could carry out your tasks in my office until I leave."

"Why?" Shafira asked. "I mean, everything's in my cubicle. It would be very difficult to work here."

"I'm sure we can find a way to accommodate your needs," smiled the Director. "Since you have declined my offer to come with me, I'd like to get your perspective on everything you know about the dig so that I can be fully briefed on what I should be looking out for when I arrive on site. After all, you review inspections on a daily basis and your attention to detail is second to none. Your input would be invaluable."

Shafira knew when to pick her battles. "I'll go and collect my things," she told him. "I'll be right back."

"I shall come with you," the Director announced. "I'm sure you would appreciate an extra pair of hands to carry all the essential documents."

"Thank you. That's very kind." Shafira smiled, but inside she was panicking. It seemed that the Director wasn't going to let her out of his sight, taking away any chance for her to tell someone what was going on. Maybe she'd sound like she'd escaped from the asylum, but knowing that someone else knew about the weird things that were happening would give her a small feeling of security.

The pair marched to Shafira's cubicle in silence. Normally, the Director would make small talk, but he was lost in thought and Shafira was too caught up with worrying about how to get away from him to keep up the pretense that everything was fine.

At last, they reached her desk. Shafira grabbed a bundle of files at random, passing them to the Director.

"There you go," she told him. "If you could carry those, it would be a huge help."

"Of course."

Shafira picked up her bag, rummaging around in it as if to check that she had everything she needed. Instead, she palmed her pepper spray, surreptitiously tucking it into her blazer pocket as she zipped the bag closed and picked up a few more files.

"I think that's everything," she smiled.

"Excellent."

Shafira strode alongside her boss as they made their way back to his office.

"Now, Shafira," he began, as he closed the door behind them, shutting out the outside world. "Why don't you tell me what you know about inspection protocol out in the field...?"

TWENTY-FOUR

Samuel put his tray down next to Basile's, taking a seat at the long table in the dining tent.

"Falafel! My favorite," he beamed, as he took a large bite out of his lunch, ignoring the large blob of sauce that dripped out and down his shirt.

"Samuel!" scolded Basile, but his friend merely grinned and scooped up the sauce with his finger to lick it clean.

Looking around to see if anyone was within earshot, Samuel pretended to focus on his wrap as he spoke.

"Has Waleed said anything interesting yet?" he asked. "Or is he still repeating the same old tired story?"

"Nothing new." Basile shook his head. "Just that he was trying to steal a few things to line his pockets before he left and the Bruard story was an attempt to win some sympathy."

"Really?" Samuel put his food down on his plate, clasping his hands in front of his mouth with his elbows resting on the table to try and disguise what he was saying in case anyone attempted to lip read. "Because I think there could be some truth to his story."

"*Mon dieu!*" Basile gasped. "How can this be?"

"I just saw someone suspicious at the storage tent," Samuel explained. "I heard the sound of a radio, but I couldn't make out what was being said. When I tried to get closer, I fell, alerting whoever it was. They ran off into the dunes."

"And you didn't catch them? You're getting slow in your old age." Basile nudged Samuel with his elbow.

"They had sand skimmers on," Samuel protested. "How can I compete in these tatty old shoes? If it wasn't for that, I would have easily chased them down."

"I hope he finds the spy soon," Basile muttered.

"What do you mean?" frowned Samuel.

"What?" Basile did a double take. "I hope *we* find the spy soon. Funnily enough, a camp follower also mentioned that he saw someone acting suspicious around the storage area, but I didn't think anything of it. You know what some of the workers are like. Too superstitious for their own good."

"Basile!" Samuel scolded. "Why didn't you tell me? That could have been a major clue."

"Sorry, Samuel," Basile said. "It all seems so unbelievable. Bruard spies, ancient mysteries... Whatever happened to the days of digging up relics and going home without all this fuss and drama?"

"Times have changed," Samuel shrugged.

"Did you see if anything was taken?" Basile asked.

"Not that I could determine." Samuel shook his head. "However, I did find a load of scrolls laid out on the table. Judging by the white paper that had been placed underneath them, I think that the spy may have been taking photos or filming them, but I'm not quite sure why."

The two friends fell into puzzled silence, Basile finishing the final few bites of his meal.

"So what's our next step?" he asked, throwing his fork down on the plate when he was done.

"I guess we just be extra vigilant for the moment," Samuel replied. "Until the Ministry arrives, we can only work with what we have. We're not exactly equipped to defend ourselves from a Bruard plot."

"Tell me about it." Basile nodded, thinking about Waleed and wondering whether he'd uncovered any more information about the spy's identity since they'd last spoke. "I'm glad that I have the right man on the case." He caught himself and pointed to Samuel. "And by the right man, I mean *you*! You're the right man for the case."

"You Frenchmen are weird." Samuel shook his head and took another bite of falafel.

"All right. I need to go and check the western shaft," Basile told him. "Bruard or no, we're still here to do a job and I need my paycheck."

He got up and headed out of the dining tent, leaving Samuel to finish his lunch alone.

TWENTY-FIVE

Shafira closed the file that she was working on and opened the next, surreptitiously glancing at the Director out of the corner of her eye. She'd been working in his office all day and hadn't seen anything suspicious, but she'd still have felt a lot more comfortable back in her cubicle.

Haisam checked his watch.

"Almost three. My ride should be here at any moment. I suppose I ought to go down to meet him. My pilot hates it when he takes off late." He started to gather together some documents, putting them in his briefcase to study during his flight.

"I'll be heading back to my cubicle, then, if that's all right?" Shafira asked.

"Of course, of course. Thank you for your help this afternoon." Haisam barely looked at her as he waved her away.

Shafira left his office, nodding an acknowledgment to his secretary as she left, but once she was out of sight, she paused. The police might not believe her story and put it down to a drunken fantasy, but if she got evidence that something strange was going on, they'd have to investigate.

One of the mail room staff walked towards her, whistling as he pushed a cart filled with letters and packages. His face looked strangely familiar.

Acting on an impulse, Shafira stepped in front of him. "It's Hosein, isn't it?" she asked. "Aziza's son?"

"Yes, miss." The youth seemed barely old enough to be hired, but his resemblance to his mother was unmistakable.

"Please, call me Shafira." She smiled warmly at the boy, who could barely bring himself to look her in the eye. "I know that we're not supposed to send mail room staff on personal errands, but I was wondering whether you could do me a favor?"

"I don't know." Hosein shuffled about uncomfortably. "Mom would kill me if I lost this job."

"It's nothing that will get you into trouble. I promise," Shafira reassured him. "It's just that I need to get these documents back to my cubicle and I've realized that I'm late for a meeting on the other side of the building. It would look very unprofessional if I showed up with armfuls of paperwork, so it would really help me out if you could take them back to my desk for me."

"I guess it's not too different to delivering the mail," Hosein conceded. "Put them on my cart and I'll drop them off for you."

"Thanks, Hosein. You're a lifesaver!"

Pulling out a file at random, pretending that she'd need it for her 'meeting,' Shafira gave the rest of her paperwork to Hosein. The mailman trundled his trolley down the corridor as Shafira headed out towards the entrance to the building where the Director had gone. Punching out, she told herself that all those hours of overtime were going to come in handy when her pay was docked for leaving early.

Approaching the reception area, she heard Director Haisam say goodbye to Tarek, the security guard on duty, so she pressed herself up against the wall round the corner, counting to five to give the Director a chance to get ahead so he wouldn't see her following him.

"You're leaving early," remarked Tarek when Shafira finally emerged from her hiding place. "It's not like you to be out in the hours of daylight, let alone go home early. I was beginning to think that you were a vampire!"

"The Director forgot an important document," Shafira lied, waving the file in her hand at the guard. "I need to get it to him before he takes off."

"He's only just left," Tarek pointed through the doors. "If you hurry, you should catch him before he gets into his car."

"Thanks." Shafira rushed through the revolving door, but slowed down again as she exited the Ministry, not wanting to actually catch up with the Director if he was waiting outside. However, instead of hailing a cab as usual, she saw the Director walking away from the Ministry.

Keeping her distance, Shafira followed him as he turned onto the sidewalk leading toward downtown Cairo. As she watched, a black car with dark tinted windows pulled up alongside him. The driver got out to open the door for the Director, who got into the back of the unmarked vehicle.

"How strange," she murmured to herself. It wasn't a cab from the Ministry's preferred company.

The car pulled away. Shafira was no closer to finding out what had really happened in the park. Using private transport to drive you to the airport was hardly a crime. Impulsively, she put out her arm, hailing a cab that was approaching.

"The man in that black vehicle is my boss," she told the driver. "But he's forgotten an important document." She showed him the file in her hand. "If I don't get this to him before he gets to his meeting, I'll lose my job. Is there any chance you could follow that car?"

"No problem." The driver turned on the meter and Shafira climbed into the back as he pulled out into traffic after the black car. "I've always wanted to have someone tell me to follow that car. It's just like being in the movies!"

He prattled on about explosive car chases from his favorite films, seeming not to care that Shafira wasn't saying anything as she gazed anxiously at the black car up ahead. Who was driving? She couldn't see any detail through the dark glass, but she could have sworn that the man who had opened the door for the Director was of similar build to the man who'd attacked her boss the night before. It made no sense.

Still, it was the middle of the day and she was surrounded by people. She might have been vulnerable in the park, but she couldn't possibly be in any danger in broad daylight.

As they took the freeway ramp, it soon became clear that they were going to the airport, just as the Director said he was. However, although her driver had made good time in keeping up with Haisam's vehicle, as they approached the waiting area, traffic ground to a stop. Shafira caught a glimpse of the Director striding into the airport.

"I'm so sorry, miss," her driver apologized, as he pulled up to the terminal. "It's not usually this bad at this time of day. I hope you can still catch up with your boss."

"It's not a problem," she reassured him, throwing money through the window at him without waiting for a receipt. At least the Director wouldn't have been able to spot her chasing him.

Running into the airport lobby, at first, there was no sign of Haisam. Biting her lip and looking around nervously, she finally caught sight of him just as he disappeared through a door marked 'Private Flights Only.'

Hurrying after him, she was about to push through the door, when a large man stepped out to block her way.

"Ticket?" asked the guard.

"Oh." Shafira patted herself over before treating him to her most charming smile. "I'm so sorry. I appear to have misplaced it. If you could just let me go through, I'm sure the staff on the other side can sort something out for me."

"If you haven't got a ticket, you're not going through that door." The guard folded his arms and glared at her.

"But it's an emergency," Shafira begged. "I'm supposed to be visiting my dying grandmother. If I don't catch my flight, I may never see her again."

"If you cared that much about her, you wouldn't have lost your ticket, would you?"

Realizing she was wasting her time pleading with the guard, Shafira turned and pulled out her cell to call the police. She tapped the first digit, then changed her mind and put her phone away. If she rang them without any proof of wrongdoing, they really would charge her with perjury this time. The Director had got away, at least for now. What if he'd been corrupted by the Bruard, which is why he was so keen to get details of her more unusual cases? Had she been tricked into feeding information to the enemy by the one man she was supposed to be able to trust?

"I have to warn Samuel McCarthy!" she gasped, turning and running back towards the cab stand, praying that she'd be able to reach him on the radio before Director Haisam arrived at the dig site.

TWENTY-SIX

Pin strode through the airport, Gord by his side carrying a small suitcase.

"Director Haisam," beamed a security guard, as Gord put the case on the scanner. "Always a pleasure to have you fly with us. Going anywhere nice?"

"Just another site inspection," replied Pin, as Gord went to collect the suitcase from the other side. "Business with very little pleasure, I'm afraid."

"I'm sorry to hear that, sir. Have a good flight." The guard saluted before handing the case back to Gord.

Pin and Gord headed out to the section of the airport reserved for private planes. Their Cessna VTOL was waiting for them, a small mobile stairway pushed up against the side. As they approached, a small group of people crossed the asphalt to meet them, a motley crew dressed in the typical casual, practical garb of archaeologists. Anyone looking closer would notice that these were no ordinary researchers, however. Suspicious bulges under jackets hinted at the presence of firearms, while a woman pulled a lethal knife out of a hidden holster, inspecting the blade before securing it out of sight again.

Gord stepped back to allow Pin to board the plane first, before he and the rest of the team followed their leader. The pilot was already seated, making his final few checks in preparation for takeoff. Hearing his passengers arrived, he turned round and nodded a greeting.

"Welcome aboard, everyone," he smiled. "My name is Captain Ali. Flying conditions are excellent, so we should reach our destination with no drama." He muttered the last sentence under his breath.

Pin's smile faded a little as Gord glared at him, the rest of the team ignoring his welcome as they took their seats in silence.

"All right then." He cleared his throat nervously, as Gord closed the plane door, twisting the security handle firmly closed. "If you could all fasten your seatbelts and prepare for takeoff, we'll be in the air in next to no time."

The pilot finished his preflight checks, before radioing in to control that they were ready to leave. Taxiing out onto the landing strip, he called back to his passengers, "Keep your seatbelts securely fastened until I instruct you otherwise. You'll be able to move about the plane once we're airborne, but until we're steady, stay in place for your safety."

Pin gazed disinterestedly out of the window, watching as the airport buildings receded into the background. With a roar of engine thrust, the craft leapt vertically into the air.

"You are now free to unbuckle your seatbelts," Captain Ali announced, a minute later, as the VTOL began to build up some forward speed. Pin unclipped his seatbelt, moving forward into the cockpit to sit in the co-pilot's seat.

"I couldn't help but notice that our destination is rather out of the way," the pilot said, as he nodded respectfully by way of a greeting. "Has the Ministry discovered a new tomb? Or ancient palace? I must admit to having more than a passing interest in archaeology. You have no idea how excited I was when I was assigned this flight."

"You will be even more excited when you know what we are looking for then," Pin told him. "Would you like to hear all about it?"

"Would I?" The pilot grinned. "You just wait until I tell my wife that I flew an important Ministry official. She won't believe it! She says that it's not fair that I have all the luck when it comes to clients. She keeps warning me that all the other pilots will get jealous. I can't wait to see their faces when I tell them about your mission."

Pin stifled a yawn as the pilot babbled on. It was always so tedious dealing with civilians. They were impressed by the most pathetic of things. If 'the Director' hadn't needed a pilot to fly him to the site, Pin would have just taken control of the flight from the start.

"As you've so cleverly surmised," he said when he could finally get a word in, "we are indeed on our way out to a dig site, but this one is no ordinary excavation. Archaeologists have unearthed a cave system concealing ancient ruins."

"A cave?" The pilot frowned. "I didn't think there were any caves out in that region and I've flown over it so many times I've lost count."

"This cave has been hidden from view by a very sophisticated camouflage technology," Pin explained. "If it was not for the persistence of one Samuel McCarthy, it may have remained hidden for who knows how long?"

"Samuel McCarthy!" exclaimed the pilot. "I'm a huge fan of his. I'm not surprised that he's behind this discovery. If anyone can find hidden treasure, it's him. But wait a minute—you mentioned sophisticated technology. Surely that means that this can't be an ancient ruin?"

"You would be surprised," Pin told him. "Ancient civilizations had access to untold wisdom. We are still nowhere near to recovering all the knowledge that was held in the Royal Library of Alexandria and that was but one library and a famous one at that. We have barely scratched the surface of the hidden numinous knowledge of our ancestors. Of course, there is the possibility that there is nothing ancient about this site and it's merely a smuggler's den, in which case we will ensure that the miscreants are brought to justice. However, I have a feeling that this is no smuggler's lair. I think that we are about to unearth something that far exceeds anything our current understanding could conceive of. If I am right, then it is essential that I secure it for my superiors in the Bruard before McCarthy takes it to the Ministry."

"The Bru-"

The pilot didn't get the chance to finish his cry, as Pin expertly stabbed him in the back of the neck with a small blade he'd concealed in his hand. Taking out a handkerchief to wipe the blood from his hands, Pin sneered with distaste at the sensation of the warm fluid sullying his flesh. He would have to fully purify himself later to rid himself of the taint of the unclean. The pilot's head lolled to the side, his eyes wide with terror, as his spinal cord was severed. The rising and falling of his chest ceased.

"Gord!" Pin snapped. His henchman hurried forward to pull the pilot out of his seat, dragging him to the back of the plane where he could more easily dispose of the body, while Pin moved to the pilot's position.

Taking hold of the controls, Pin called over his shoulder. "Has the weapons drop arrived at the first stop?"

"Yes, sir," came the reply. "It's all ready and waiting. All we need to do is retrieve it."

"Excellent," nodded Pin. "With any luck, we can finish our mission while this identity is still of value. Unfortunately, you screwed up. It's only a matter of time before my cover is entirely blown, so I want to make as much use out of the Director as possible while I still can."

"What do you mean?" Gord lumbered up to take the co-pilot's seat next to his superior. "I did everything you told me to."

"Yes," sighed Pin. "I suppose it's my fault not to give you explicit instruction to ensure that there were no witnesses when you disposed of Haisam. I should have known that I couldn't trust you to use your initiative."

"It was the middle of the night," Gord protested. "No one was around. There's no way I was seen."

"And yet it would appear that Shafira Khouri knows, or at least suspects, that her beloved boss isn't who he seems. I had a visit from the police thanks to your incompetence. Fortunately for me, Haisam was on good terms with the chief, so I was able to persuade him that Ms. Khouri was mistaken, but she's not the kind of person to know when to leave well alone, which is why I've arranged a little surprise for her when she goes home this evening. I believe suffering, at least, is something you get."

Gord nodded, his face alight with satisfaction. "Yes, boss, it is."

TWENTY-SEVEN

Shafira raced to her cubicle and started rifling through the files that Hosein had placed on her desk for her. "Come on, come on, where are you?" she muttered as she frantically pawed through the paperwork in search of the file on McCarthy's dig site.

Finally finding the right file, she plopped down in her chair, as she jotted down the coordinates of the dig site on a notepad. Pressing the space key a few times to bring her computer out of sleep mode, she typed in her password and pulled up the encrypted email interface that allowed her secure wireless communication with the field. If the Director was in the air, it wouldn't be long before he reached the site and McCarthy and his men could all be in danger. She had to get word through before he touched down.

As the program opened, an error message flashed up on the screen.

"*Outgoing communications unavailable at this time. Please check your internet connection and try again.*"

"Are you kidding me?" she cursed, as grumbles and complaints started to rise from surrounding cubicles.

"Who switched off the internet?" she heard Malik cry. "When are they going to sort out the computers in this place?"

"Afternoon off for everyone!" whooped Faroukh, as Shafira went back to the hard copy file. Scanning through the documents, she searched in vain for a telephone number, but all she could find was the general helpline for the Ministry, which would only put her through to someone else in the building. With the internet down, they wouldn't be any more successful in contacting the site.

Shafira tapped a finger against her computer keyboard as she considered her options. Although it was possible that there would be more contact details held in the staff records, Shafira would need to go through someone in HR to obtain them and there was no one there she could trust. What if they'd been subverted to help whoever the Director was working for?

There was no other choice. She was going to have to go old school and see if she could find something useful hiding in the paperwork.

Going to her filing cabinet, she searched for the file that contained the personnel details for the project. Making her way down the list, most of the names were unfamiliar, but Shafira was flooded with hope when she saw a name she recognized. "Josh Bradley!" she gasped. Of course he'd be the preferred helicopter pilot for this project. He was the best in the business!

Gathering up the McCarthy files, Shafira prayed that Josh was home and not still on site.

———

LIVING within walking distance of the Ministry had its benefits, but today, Shafira cursed every step it took to get home, and hence to her car. As she walked past the sign for the park, she couldn't help but shudder as she remembered what she'd witnessed there. She was going to get justice, no matter what it took.

The memory of almost being splattered with Haisam's blood

made her guts twist, and she picked up the pace. Although the killer would be long gone by now, she couldn't shake the feeling of a foul presence, a lengthening shadow of evil over that place.

As she stepped between two cars to cross the road towards where her trusty Nissan was parked, she caught a glimpse of movement behind her in the rearview mirror of the vehicle she was standing behind. Hurrying across the road, she heard footsteps coming up behind her.

Not caring whether she looked stupid, Shafira broke into a run, racing towards her car, and thanking the heavens that she was wearing flat shoes. The footsteps behind her picked up the pace as whoever it was ran after her, confirming that she was being pursued and it wasn't an innocent pedestrian. Fear gave her wings and she ran faster than she ever had in her life, seeing the familiar blue of her Nissan up ahead. Running so fast that she almost ran into the door, Shafira reached into her bag, yanking out her keys and rifling through them to find the one for her car.

Hands shaking, she stabbed at the button that would unlock the doors when a hand landed on her shoulder.

She screamed, as her pursuer yanked her away from the car, causing her to fall to the ground. Seeing the glint of a knife coming towards her, Shafira yanked the pepper spray from her pocket, and sprayed a cloud of pain into the face of her assailant. As he clawed at his eyes, Shafira aimed a powerful kick at his groin. He uttered a guttural growl of agony, as he crumpled to the ground.

Scrambling to her car, Shafira pulled the door open and threw herself into the driver's seat. Slamming down the button to lock the doors, she gunned the engine, tires screaming in protest as she put her foot down.

There was a loud bang. Her rear windshield shattered. Shafira screamed, ducking down instinctively.

Reaching into her bag, the other hand trying to keep the steering wheel under control, Shafira took out her cell and scrolled through her contacts to find Josh's number, babbling incoherent prayers, while trying not to crash.

"Pick up, Josh, please pick up," she whimpered, as his phone rang and rang and rang.

TWENTY-EIGHT

Flying was one of life's very few true pleasures, and a little smile played on Pin's lips as he switched off the autopilot in readiness to land. One day, when his masters had gained their rightful position ruling the world, he would retire and spend his days flying to remote destinations. Until that day, he would savor moments like these, brief glimpses of pure joy as he experienced the freedom of movement high above the earth.

Behind him came the familiar clicking of weapons as his team checked that their guns were loaded, and ready to fire when he gave the command. Now that the pilot had been disposed of, their archaeologist disguises had been replaced by military uniforms, Gord straightening his beret to ensure that his insignia was facing the correct direction as he came to join his boss in the cockpit.

Pin hovered over the makeshift landing strip. "Keep your mouth shut when we get there," he instructed. "Tell everyone to follow my lead until I've had a chance to gauge the situation. At the moment, as far as the archaeologists are concerned, the soldiers are simply accompanying the Director in case of smugglers at the cave. We don't want to blow our cover unless we don't have any choice. I'd rather not have to cover up another dig site massacre. It's so inconvenient."

"Yes, sir," nodded Gord, returning to his seat to inform the rest of the team of Pin's instructions.

The engines strained as Pin expertly brought the VTOL in to land, touching down with barely a bump. Two men rushed to open the door, dropping a makeshift ladder so they could exit the VTOL. Climbing down, they stood to attention on either side of the ladder, saluting smartly as Pin climbed out of the plane.

As he took in his first sight of the excavation, he noticed a man coming towards them. Tall, with light brown hair, the kind of man who women would find attractive for some inexplicable reason, Pin suppressed a sneer of disgust as he observed that the man's shirt was hanging out of his pants, a smear of sauce staining the front of his shirt. Some people had no self-respect.

"I'm Samuel McCarthy," said the man, reaching out a hand to introduce himself. "Are you the director I've been told to expect?"

"I am." Pin gritted his teeth as he took McCarthy's hand before reaching into his jacket pocket for his credentials. "Director Haisam. It is an honor to meet you."

"The pleasure's all mine," replied Samuel, barely glancing at the Director's ID, his attention caught by the group of soldiers disembarking.

"Ah." Pin followed Samuel's gaze. "Yes, I have brought some support with me. Your recording had some of my superiors concerned about the possibility of smugglers in the area. I've been granted a small platoon of solders, just as a precaution. I'm sure this will be just another boring assignment for them, but it's better to be safe than sorry, don't you think?"

"Sure," agreed the American. "Something strange is going on here, that's for sure."

"Why don't you go over your research so far as we walk back to the dig site," Pin suggested. "I've read the reports, but there's nothing like hearing your first-hand account."

"Of course," Samuel nodded. "It started when we uncovered a map among some scrolls in what appeared to be a storage area in the palace we've been excavating. At first, it seemed to be just a map of a pretty featureless area of desert until I started translating the inscriptions, which suggested that there was cave in the vicinity, a cave that held treasures too important and precious to be stored in the palace. They had been taken to a secure location to be safe from the unworthy."

"Interesting," mused Pin. "One would think that the palace treasure room would be the safest place for whatever these artifacts are."

"Exactly," said Samuel. "Which is why I wanted to see if I could find the cave. I haven't been able to determine what the nature of whatever it is we'll find there, which has made me doubly curious. The scrolls are written in riddles and ciphers, plus they're in a rather archaic form of Sanskrit. It's taking me a while to decipher them.

"I took a helicopter out to search the area and after a few false leads, we uncovered the cave. In fact, we almost flew the helicopter into the rocks because it was so well camouflaged. I've never seen such effective technology, which is confusing. If this technology is ancient, it calls into question everything we think we know about ancient civilization. On the other hand, it could just be that modern smugglers or even the Bruard found the cave, stripped it of whatever was inside and have repurposed it for their own uses, setting up some kind of holo-tech in addition to the existing security measures."

"I think it highly unlikely the Bruard are involved," Pin sniffed. "There have been no reports of Bruard activity in the region and I can't imagine that they would requisition a cave in the middle of nowhere if it wasn't going to benefit them militarily. There aren't any important targets within the vicinity. I think it far more likely that we're dealing with smugglers here, assuming any relics have already been looted. What did you see inside the cave?"

"At first, nothing," Samuel replied. "It took a while for me to figure out that a ritual needed to be performed that revealed a set of double doors. Superstitious ancients would have thought that their gods were opening the doors, although the reality is that it's simply a clever mechanism that relies on a combination of sound and weight distribution to trigger the opening.

"The double doors were intricately carved with two goddesses, one Egyptian, one Roman. The symbolism on the doors alone contain a wealth of information as to what might be contained within the inner sanctum."

"And what did you find in there?"

"I didn't explore any further," Samuel told him. "I wanted to wait for approval to send a team in. It was too potentially dangerous. There could have been lethal traps, and there were only three of us in the initial investigative team. Given the level of sophistication used to conceal the cave and the entrance, I wouldn't assume that that was the only defense built into the cave system. And, of course, we can't rule out the possibility of armed men inside. I must admit that I'm relieved to see soldiers with you. They'll be able to secure the area so that my archaeologists can work safely."

"And these two goddesses," Pin continued. "What do you suppose they might mean?"

"Like many Egyptian and Roman deities, they both have multiple associations with complex meanings," Samuel replied. "However, my preliminary theory is that the cave system contain something associated with dream recordings. Given the sophistication of what we've uncovered so far, this really could be the most exciting discovery anyone's ever seen."

"Fascinating," murmured Pin. "How soon can we get to the caves and start work?"

"Now that you're here, we just need to finalize a few details and we're good to go," smiled Samuel. "Let's get back to the camp and I can introduce you to some of my key team members."

As they approached the camp, Samuel spotted Basile. "Basile! Over here!" he beckoned.

Basile came over to join Samuel and the Director, his eyes narrowing as he assessed the newcomer.

"Basile, this is Director Haisam," Samuel introduced. "He's here from the Ministry to oversee the cave investigation."

"Is he?" Basile looked the Director up and down. "Let's see some ID. We've had a few problems recently with thieves. I need to be certain of who I'm dealing with."

"Are you kidding me?" hissed Samuel, pulling Basile to one side. "Do you see the soldiers he's brought with him? Do you really think that a con artist is going to pay for a frigging *Cessna*, fill it with soldiers and come all the way out here just in case they happen to bump into an important archaeological investigation?"

"A lot of strange things have been happening ever since you came back from that cave," Basile pointed out. "How can you be sure that this man is who he says he is? I'm not telling him anything until I'm satisfied that he's really from the Ministry."

Samuel sighed and shook his head. "I'm so sorry, Director Haisam," he said, turning back to the Ministry official. "My colleague is a cautious man who takes site safety very seriously. Would you mind showing him your proof of identity?"

"Not at all." Pin's voice was cold, despite his politeness, as he took out his wallet to show Basile his Ministry ID. "I also have a copy of the letter you sent with your recording, just to show that we weren't randomly wandering the desert in the hope of 'bumping into an important archaeological investigation.'"

Basile took the documents the Director offered him, inspecting them carefully to satisfy himself that they were genuine.

At last, he handed them back. "Sorry about that," he told the Director. "I'm sure you can appreciate that we're all a little jumpy around here ever since we discovered the caves and thought they might be associated with the Bruard."

Pin laughed. "I think your men have overactive imaginations. We may find some smugglers, but my team can deal with them. You have nothing to worry about. Now, why don't we go to your Mr. McCarthy's quarters to discuss things further? I don't know about you, but I'm getting more than a little uncomfortable in this sun."

"Of course, of course."

Pin gestured to Gord to keep their men by the plane before following Samuel and Basile into the camp. The sooner they told him everything they knew about the cave, the sooner the real work could begin.

TWENTY-NINE

Shafira anxiously looked around, trying to see if she was being followed by mysterious black cars as she drove through central Cairo. Every building seemed to hide a sniper, every alley contained a car waiting to ram her off the road. She'd almost had a heart attack when a vehicle cut her off as she was driving down the freeway. Every blast of a horn sent her heart racing.

By the time she pulled up outside the entrance to Josh's house, she was a nervous wreck. She sat in the car gripping the steering wheel so hard her knuckles turned white as she tried to gather up the courage to get out and run the few meters to his door.

After a few deep breaths, she opened the car door and scurried to the house, knowing that it couldn't protect her from a bullet. Banging on the door, her head remained on a swivel as she scanned the street for pursuers. When Josh opened the front door, she practically fell into his arms.

"Woah!" He helped her stand up. "Where's the fire?"

"Josh! Thank goodness you're all right." Shafira practically cried with relief. "Can we talk?"

"Of course." Josh stepped aside to let Shafira in, shaking his head in bemusement as she hurried through to the living room.

Normally, Shafira loved coming to Josh's home. An old family friend, it had been a source of endless fascination whenever she visited him with her parents.

The walls of every room were filled with photographs taken on countless flights around the world, shelves groaning under the weight of souvenirs and mementoes. Shafira always enjoyed hearing the stories behind each item. It seemed that it wouldn't matter how many times she came, she would never learn all the details of Josh's adventures.

The pilot was a gifted storyteller and listening to him tell her about his escapades was almost as good as being there with him. He'd worked for a commercial airline in Texas before moving on to the Ministry, and some of the tales he'd told her about the passengers he'd encountered would have her in gales of laughter.

There would be no laughter today. It was Shafira's turn to tell a story.

"Do you want some sweet tea?" Josh offered. "You look like you could do with something to calm you down."

"No, no, I don't need any tea. This is too important."

"You sounded stressed on the phone, but you hung up before I could ask what was going on. What's up?"

"I couldn't tell you anything because I didn't know if my cell was being tapped, so I all I could do was confirm you were home and hang up before they could get a fix on my location."

Josh raised an eyebrow at Shafira's reply, but didn't say anything, waiting for her to go on.

"Plus I didn't want to say your name or mention your address in case they followed me," she explained.

"They?" Josh shook his head. "Are you on something, Shafira? You're acting really weird."

"Believe me, I'm stone cold sober," Shafira reassured him. "But you'd be acting weird if someone tried to shoot you."

"Shoot you?" Josh grimaced. "What on earth are you talking about? What the hell is going on, Shafira?"

"I wish I knew. It's all so messed up."

"Start from the beginning," Josh advised. "Whatever you've got yourself involved in, I'm sure we can work it out together."

"I think I saw someone murdered."

"You *think*? How can you not be sure if you saw someone die or not? The more you talk, the less I understand."

Shafira sighed. "This is what happened. I swear I'm not making it up or imagining things. I was walking home and I decided to take a detour through the park. I heard a strange noise, so I went to investigate, when I saw a man punching and kicking someone else to death. It was dark, but I was able to catch a glimpse of his face as the body rolled towards me. It was my boss, Director Haisam."

"Director Haisam?" Josh frowned. "Why haven't I seen anything in the papers about this? The media would have been all over the murder of a prominent Ministry official."

"Because he was at work the next day without a scratch on him," Shafira explained.

Josh raised an eyebrow.

"I know, I know, it sounds crazy. I still don't understand it myself. That's why I followed him when he left the Ministry today. He's supposed to be going to the dig site where your friend Samuel McCarthy is working, but instead of using Ministry transportation, he got into a car with a strange man who took him to the airport. That's where I lost him. Then, when I went home after work, someone attacked me. I managed to get into my car, but they shot at me as I drove away. You can see my shattered back windshield if you don't believe me. Someone tried to kill me, Josh, just as they killed that poor man in the park, whoever he was."

"But why?" Josh paced up and down as he tried to make sense of Shafira's story. "Why would someone try to kill you?"

"I can only assume that they know that I witnessed the murder and they're trying to shut me up, permanently," Shafira replied. "If I was wrong and the Director was fine, then why would they send an assassin after me if they weren't trying to cover something up? I can't help but think that it's got something to do with Samuel's dig and what he found there. I tried to send him a message, but I haven't been able to contact him, which worries me. The only other thing I can think to do is warn him in person, which is why I'm here, talking to the only pilot I know."

She smiled hopefully at Josh, who shook his head.

"I don't know, Shafira. This all sounds way above my paygrade. You need to call the police about this."

"Don't you think that was the first thing I tried?" she cried. "But I think that the Director or his imposter has connections on the force. They threatened to charge me with perjury unless I dropped it. I don't think they'll take me seriously unless I can get better proof that something terrible has happened."

"Alright," Josh decided. "Then we go to the Ministry."

"And speak to who? Director Haisam?" Shafira glared at Josh. "Come on, Josh. You've got more intelligence than that. I don't have the authority to go over his head and whatever's happening, it's obvious that the Director's at the heart of it. Please, Josh. Can't we take your helicopter and go to the dig site? It could save lives. Nobody at the Ministry is going to pay any attention to me. I know that I sound like a mad woman, but you've known me all my life. You're my Uncle Josh, the man Yusuf could call when he got into trouble and didn't want our parents to know. You've always helped my brother out of a tight spot. Can't you do the same for me, just this once?"

"I don't know." Josh ran a hand through his hair, undecided. "I still think it would be best to go to the Ministry. If you told them what you've just told me, I'm sure we can persuade them to help us."

"But what if the Director is involved in something big?" countered Shafira. "What if he's involved with the Bruard? Assuming we can persuade someone at the Ministry to believe us and we don't just go straight to another traitor, they'll start an investigation and it'll let the Director know that we're on to him. Whatever it is he's planning, don't you think it's better to warn your friend first?"

"I guess so," Josh conceded. "But this seems too big for us to handle on our own."

I know," Shafira agreed. "I feel overwhelmed by it all, but after that assassin attacked me, I knew I needed help and you were the only person I knew I could trust. I know that between us we'll find the proof we need to get the authorities involved. They can take it from there. Please, Josh? You'd do it if Yusuf asked."

"I don't know that I would," Josh grumbled. "But all right. I'll help you. I just need to make a call first."

For the first time since she'd witnessed the murder, Shafira could finally relax a little as Josh dialed his boss.

"Hey, Daniel," he greeted. "I know that I'm supposed to be ferrying around that team in Alexandria, but I'm going to have to take some last minute leave... I know, I know, it's really short notice and I'm sorry for the inconvenience, but when did I last take a vacation? ... I don't know how long. But I promise I'll be back as soon as I can. You know me. I wouldn't ask if it wasn't important... Thanks, Daniel. I really appreciate it."

Josh hung up and turned to Shafira. "Looks like you got yourself a pilot. I guess that you'll finally get up close and personal with one of those excavations you've always been so curious about."

"Thanks, Josh." Shafira threw herself at the Josh, giving him a big hug. "I owe you big time."

"Yes, you do," Josh smiled.

"How soon can we leave?" Shafira asked.

"Just as soon as we get to my helicopter." Josh grabbed his keys. "Come on. I'll drive us to the heliport. If someone is after you, they'll be watching out for your car. Hopefully we can buy a bit more time by switching vehicles."

Shafira hurried after him, grateful that she wasn't on her own anymore.

THIRTY

Samuel ducked inside his tent, holding open the flap for the Director and Basile to follow.

Basile looked around, nodding his approval at Samuel behind the Director's back at the sight of a tidier tent. The table had been cleared so they had room to work, and the tent looked organized--as long as one didn't look too closely.

Haisam gazed disdainfully around the tent.

"They say a messy workspace is a sign of a creative mind," joked Samuel, noticing the Director's reaction. "You should have been here a week or so ago. I was *really* creative then. I've tidied up a bit in honor of your visit."

"I keep telling him to sort the place out," Basile told the director. "You're lucky–he's actually made an effort for you."

"Then it is a good job I wasn't here a week ago, isn't it?" sneered Haisam. "Now why doesn't one of you fetch a map so we can determine exactly where we're going? I don't really want to spend any longer here than absolutely necessary. I have important business to take care of back at the Ministry and every minute we're here costs the Ministry money."

"Of course." Samuel pulled out his geoscanner, placing it in the middle of the table and hitting the button that projected a 3D image of the area. "This is where we are now." He pointed at one section of the map. Then, with a swipe of his hand, the parched sandy-brown terrain scrolled. "And this is where the cave is."

Director Haisam squinted and stroked his chin thoughtfully. Then he turned to Samuel. "We leave now in my VTOL."

"Uhh, okay," Samuel said uncertainly.

"Now remind me again. Who was with you when you found the cave?" asked Haisam.

"Josh, the pilot, of course, and Nafty, another one of my team."

"And what did this Nafty think of the cave? Did he agree with your decision to wait for backup?"

"No. He wanted to see what was inside," Samuel admitted. "I was the one who insisted on coming back first."

"In that case, I think we should invite Nafty to join us," Haisam decided. "It seems only fair, no?"

"It would be useful to have someone else there who has an idea of what to expect," Samuel agreed. "And I'm sure Nafty would jump at the chance to investigate further. Basile, could you go and tell Nafty to join us? I think he's on guard duty with Waleed."

"*Bien sur,*" Basile nodded, as he headed out to tell Nafty the good news. Samuel and Director Haisam halted.

"Waleed was a member of our crew who decided that he would be better off trying to rob me instead of earning an honest wage," Samuel explained to the Director. "He could have sabotaged the entire excavation if we hadn't managed to stop him. We've got him restrained in one of the storage tents until we can transport him back to Cairo to face the authorities. Maybe you could take him back on your plane with you? I'm sure the Ministry takes a dim view of anyone who tries to steal from one of your digs."

"These matters are none of my concern," the Director replied curtly. "Site security is your remit."

"Fair enough," Samuel shrugged. "So what *are* your responsibilities at the Ministry? Do you frequently come out to visit dig sites?"

"Mr. McCarthy, the nature of my work at the Ministry does not concern you," snapped Haisam. "It is irrelevant to your research and you are answerable to me, not the other way round. It would be better if you were to confine your thoughts to the nature of your latest discovery instead of wasting energy on small talk and petty thieves. For example, have you come up with any theories as to how ancient engineers could have constructed the doors concealed in the cave?"

"I have a few," Samuel replied, while turning over the Director's seemingly self-contradictory response in his mind. "Obviously, Basile is the true expert when it comes to engineering, but when you sit back and look critically at the construction, although the door mechanism is highly sophisticated, it's based on sound engineering principles that those who built it would have understood given other structures we've analyzed. Of course, we still don't know a great deal about a lot of ancient construction. We haven't solved the mystery of how they built Stonehenge, for example, and attempts to recreate the transportation of the stones using the techniques that we do know about have failed to even come close to success.

"It is possible that this is an example of the ancients knowing far more than we give them credit for. Scholars have been arguing for a long time that we underestimate their ability and this could be the proof they need. It might simply be that this is the first time such an impressive construction has survived but it would have been by no means the only example at the time. Alternatively, the doors might be ancient, but the cloaking mechanism itself could be a later addition when smugglers decided that they could use such an isolated hiding place."

"I see."

An awkward silence descended as Samuel ran out of things to say to the taciturn Director. He'd never been so relieved to see Basile as when he returned to the tent.

"Is Nafty excited about coming?" Samuel asked.

"He probably would be if I could find him," Basile replied. "As far as I can make out, the last time anyone saw him he was loading supplies in the main relics' tent, but it's been a few hours before anyone can confirm they spoke to him."

Samuel tapped his fingers in the table as he thought about where Nafty could be. The man he'd disturbed in the storage tent was of a similar build. Now that he thought about it, it was entirely possible that Nafty was the person he'd chased into the dunes.

He kept his thoughts to himself, however, as the Director sighed with impatience, checking his watch.

"I'm sorry, Director Haisam," Samuel apologized. "It would appear that Nafty is busy elsewhere on the site. Would you like us to look further for him before we leave? He's bound to be around somewhere."

"It is of no consequence." The Director waved him away. "We'll just have to cope without this Nafty's insights."

"Would you like me to come along instead?" offered Basile. "I understand civil and structural engineering better than anyone in the camp. I may be able to help you determine the provenance of the various technologies at the cave."

"Even if we manage to find Nafty, I think Basile should accompany us regardless," Samuel told the Director, in a last-ditch effort. "His input would be invaluable. If there are any traps waiting for us, Basile is most likely to spot them before we trigger anything deadly."

The Director thought for a moment, then nodded. "Very well. Basile may come along."

Haisam strode out of the tent, leaving Samuel to gather together a few things.

"Here's my radio equipment and Bluetooth," he told Basile, showing him the communication devices before placing them in his backpack. "If you need it, the comm code is 47582-b."

"Why would I need the code?" frowned Basile. "I'm going to be with you."

"We might get separated," Samuel explained. "I want to make

sure that we can keep in touch with each other. Director Haisam might be from the Ministry, but he's not exactly the most touchy-feely person I've ever met and there's something about him that doesn't feel right. I'd feel more secure knowing that you've got my back rather than trusting to some stranger."

"*Oui, oui,*" nodded Basile. "That makes sense. Give me the matching commset."

Basile jotted down the code, storing it safely in his jacket pocket before picking up the other commset.

"I've got a long range radio as well," Samuel told him. "The code's the same. Now are you ready to go and see what's buried in that cave?"

"Ready as I'll ever be," grinned Basile.

THIRTY-ONE

As the desert slipped by below the VTOL, Samuel turned to his right, cupped his hands up to Basile's ear, and said, "So what do you think about our man from the Ministry?"

"Pah!" Basile shook his head. Both men swiveled their heads so Basile could now talk directly into Samuel's ear without being overheard by the Director in the row in front of them, over the drone of the engines. "He reminds me of all the reasons why I never want to work in an office. I'd rather have sand in my pants than deal with people like him. I've had results-based managers before and they're always obsessed with micro-managing me instead of recognizing that I know more about engineering than they could ever hope to comprehend. You wait; I bet he'll try to tell us how we should explore the cave instead of leaving it to the experts."

"He's not exactly the friendliest of people, is he?" Samuel agreed. "Do you think maybe he's stressed about what we might find when we go through the doors? Perhaps he's never had to face smugglers in real life and doesn't want to get caught up in a gunfight."

"Isn't that the whole point of bringing so many armed men?" Basile pointed out. "They take the bullets so we don't have to. Maybe the good Director doesn't like leaving the comfort of his air conditioned office, but that's no excuse for rudeness. We should be working as a team. For all he knows, we could be about to open the doors to priceless artifacts. Surely that's something to get excited about?"

"Unless it's already been stolen," Samuel pointed out. "Speaking of thieves, did you get a chance to speak to Waleed before we left?"

"I did," Basile confirmed. "He's sticking to his story. If it's not true, he's a darned good liar. Still, that's not our problem. I've left a couple of my assistants in charge of him, so he'll be fed and cared for until we can send him back with the Director when we return from this expedition."

"Don't you think it's strange that the Director didn't want to know more about him?" Samuel remarked. "I mean, I told him that Waleed could have sabotaged the entire expedition and he didn't seem to care."

"Maybe he thinks that it wasn't worth bothering about?" Basile suggested. "After all, we have him under lock and key. How much harm can one man do on his own?"

"I suppose." Samuel frowned, then shrugged. "Oh well. It's not down to me to question how the Director does his job. I'm going to get some rest while we wait for the sun to lower a little more. Not long now and we'll have the answer to what really is hiding in that cave." He turned to look outside, and then back to Basile. "We're coming in a little lower now."

"You told them *not* to land right at the cave, right?" Basile said.

"Yes, I was most emphatic. Two hundred yards south, minimum. Don't want a repeat of my first near crash landing there."

The featureless terrain came up to meet them, and the machine was soon on the ground, its extra wide tires keeping it comfortably "afloat" on the sea of sand. Samuel leaned over Director Haisam's shoulder, to check the GPS coordinates on the aircraft's display. "There it is. The cave." Samuel beamed, spreading his arms wide to indicate their final destination, as the doors slid open and the suffocating, hot desert air filled the cabin.

"Are you sure?" Director Haisam frowned. "It doesn't look any different to the rest of the desert."

"Oh, I'm very sure," Samuel assured him.

"If you're right, that cloaking device is incredible," breathed Basile. "It just looks like another dune. If it were anyone other than you, I'd think you were nuts. How on earth did you figure out this was the right location?"

"That's why they pay me the big bucks," Samuel grinned. "If I didn't have years of experience and training, there's no way I could have deciphered the map that led me here, but trust me. This is where we need to be. Come on. See for yourself."

The Director and Basile looked at each other, then decamped from the VTOL and strode forward. They hadn't gone far before they disappeared. Even the usually unflappable soldiers couldn't help but be impressed.

Basile reappeared, beckoning to Samuel and the rest of the team. "You guys need to see this."

Samuel hurried after his friend, enjoying the reactions to his discovery as the soldiers followed close behind.

"Isn't it amazing?" he said to Basile, but the engineer shook his head, frowning. "Look. Over there."

"Uh-oh." Samuel's heart sank. He saw a number of desert striders, trucks that had been specially adapted to traveling across the sand dunes by the additional of four powerful hydraulic legs.

"I guess it's a smuggler's den after all," Basile sighed. "Sorry, Samuel. I know how much you were looking forward to unearthing the find of the century. We'll just have to step back and let the soldiers do their job."

"There's still a chance that there's something ancient in that cave," Samuel replied. "The question is whether we can get to it."

"Don't worry," said Director Haisam. "This is why we brought an armed guard. Whoever it is that thinks they can take advantage of an important Egyptian monument for their own nefarious purposes, we'll soon teach them a lesson they'll never forget. Gord! Take a couple of men with you and check out the vehicles."

"Yes, sir." Gord snapped to attention, gesturing to a couple of soldiers to come with him as they went to inspect the desert striders. The rest stood by as they examined the vehicles from all angles. Once they were satisfied that the desert striders weren't booby trapped, they started opening up the storage units and taking out some crates that had been placed inside.

"Don't open those," Samuel called out, hurrying over to intervene, closely followed by Basile and Director Haisam. "They might contain artifacts. They'll need special handling to make sure the contents aren't damaged. That's assuming that whoever dug them up hasn't already irreparably harmed them. There's no guarantee that they have any training in how to handle ancient relics."

"The engines are cool," Gord told Samuel. "Whoever drove here, they've been here for awhile."

"They must still be inside the cave," Samuel replied. "I suggest you put some men on guard while Basile and I look through the crates to see what's been retrieved from the cave. Basile, you've learned enough through being on digs with me to help me take a preliminary look at what we've got. If it turns out to be smuggler's goods, we let the guards deal with them."

Samuel pulled a pack of latex gloves from his pocket, peeling off a pair for Basile before putting on some himself. "Start with the crates you find in that strider. I'll look through these ones."

"*Oui*," Basile nodded, as Samuel took out his Swiss army knife and used it to pry open the nearest crate.

"Well, well, well," murmured Samuel as he saw what was inside. "The plot thickens."

Carefully, he picked up a scroll that was at the top of the crate, whistling as he unrolled it to read what it says. "Director, you might want to come look at this."

"What is it?" The Director's face was inscrutable as he leaned over to see what Samuel had found.

"I'll need to test the parchment to be certain, but unless this is an exceptional forgery, this scroll is of ancient origin. It would appear that whoever drove these striders here came to the cave with the explicit purpose of looting. We got here just in time. Egypt could have lost something truly valuable."

Carefully placing the scroll back in the crate to keep it safe for transportation, Samuel's concentration was broken by an ear splitting scream.

"Basile?" Samuel raced over to his friend's side. "Are you all right?"

"*Vous ne m'avez pas dit que nous aurions affaire à des corps. C'est trop. Je ne peux pas faire face à ça. Ramenez-moi à la fouille en ce moment. Je veux juste sortir d'ici.*"

The Frenchman spoke too fast for Samuel to be able to follow what he was saying, but when he saw what was inside the large crate he'd just opened, Samuel paled, his blood turning to ice in his veins.

"Nafty!"

His former colleague was lying in a long, coffin-like crate, laid out with his arms crossed against his chest as if he were a mummy.

"Do you know this man?" The Director came to stand next to Samuel, gazing down at the body with a disdainful look.

"Yes," Samuel confirmed. "This is Nafty, the man I told you about. He was with me when I first discovered the cave. He must have come here to try and loot the cave ahead of us, although I didn't tell him how to open the doors. The fact that whoever he was working with has started removing relics raises all sorts of questions. Unless these have come from another nearby site. So many unanswered questions..."

"None of which are worth considering," the Director told him. "Whatever unfortunate end your colleague has suffered is none of our concern. His demise means there's one less problem for us to deal with. Still, it is clear that he wasn't working alone. Gord–assign a small detail to secure the cave entrance should we need to make a quick exit. Then take the rest of the men and come with us into the cave."

Gord shouted instructions to his men as Samuel closed the crate over Nafty's body.

"Rest in peace," he murmured. "I might not have known you well, and maybe you were a Bruard traitor, but nobody deserves to die alone in the desert."

"This is a bad sign." Basile shuddered. "I think we should leave. Whatever is in that cave, it's not worth dying for."

"We'll be all right," Samuel reassured him. "We have a brutish-looking security force on our side.

"You two!" Gord barked. "Stop wasting time and get your butts into the cave. Your friend isn't going anywhere now."

Basile and Samuel exchanged a look, as they took out headlamps and put them on. They then took out their Maglites, switching them on as they walked into the cave, staying on high alert for Nafty's killer.

THIRTY-TWO

Gord took point, leading the expedition into the dark mouth of the cave, the cooler air enveloping the men. Samuel followed close behind him, with soldiers alternating between the Director and Basile to make sure that the unarmed men would be protected in the event of an ambush.

Samuel's heart was pounding so hard that he was sure that the others could hear it. Seeing Nafty's body had really brought the danger home.

"Is that it?" Gord came to a halt in front of a blank wall. "We came all this way for *this*? There's nothing here."

"That's the beauty of this place." In a rare show of emotion, the Director smiled, running his hand over the smooth, blank surface of the wall in front of them. "There's plenty here for those with eyes to see. McCarthy, open the door."

"Sure, but have you seen those footprints?" He indicated at the ground in front of the wall. "I don't think those are from when Josh, Nafty and I were here. They look recent. Either someone is in the cave with the door shut or they're nearby hiding in some unnoticed nook. Either way, we should proceed with caution."

Gord stepped towards Samuel, looming over him.

Although the American didn't like to show he felt intimidated, he got the hint. "I suggest that you get your men to set up a defensive perimeter, just in case," Samuel said.

Gord nodded, snapping his fingers to direct the soldiers as Samuel set out the bowl and offering he'd brought for the ritual. When everyone was in place, he closed his eyes, taking a moment to center himself. Although he knew that the doors weren't really going to be opened by Roman and Egyptian goddesses, Samuel always liked to show appropriate respect when he worked on a site. It felt like the right thing to do.

"*Magna matres, aperi ostium mihi.*" Samuel lifted up the bowl, repeating the gestures he'd made the first time he'd performed the ritual.

"*Ego sum non mortuus est.*" Carefully, he placed the bowl in the groove carved into the middle of the floor.

"*Testor ego tueri arcana.*"

Samuel sat back, waiting for the click that would signal the triggering of the door mechanism. When it came, the bowl started to move, its smooth progress giving the illusion that it was moving of its own accord.

Just as before, when the bowl reached the stone it disappeared. The whole cave started to shake with a threatening rumble. Small stone chips clattered to the floor.

"Earthquake!" cried Gord. "Everybody out!"

"Wait!" Samuel barked, waving his arms around to get the others' attention before they evacuated. "It's fine. Look!"

Jaws dropped as the cave settled down and double doors materialized behind Samuel. Seshat smiled benignly on one side, while Moneta looked over them on the other.

As they watched, the doors silently swung open a crack, the goddesses stepping aside to grant access to the inner chamber.

"Remarkable," breathed the Director. "I've never seen anything like this. How could something this incredible possibly have remained hidden for centuries?"

"This entire site has been built for deception," Samuel pointed out. "Given how well it's been concealed, it's likely its existence was a closely kept secret right from the moment of construction. It was not unknown for slaves to be executed after building secret chambers to ensure that nobody spoke of their existence.

"However, there's so much about it that intrigues me. Here. Look at the condition of the door. There is a veneer of dust covering it, which would suggest years of disuse. Yet, the joints are still in pristine condition. It is possible that someone has been maintaining it all this time. It's a conundrum."

"I didn't think the Romans put doors on tombs," Basile remarked.

"Although it might be unusual, it's not unheard of," Samuel corrected. "For example, an ancient temple was unearthed in Pompeii that was still under construction when Vesuvius blew and buried the city under layers of ash. There was a marble door there that was carved to resemble typical wooden Roman doors and it's possible that there were plans to add statues such as these at a later date. It needs more study, but so far, there is plenty of evidence to suggest that this could be of Roman provenance."

"It's just a door," huffed Director Haisam. "Do we really need to waste all this time debating it when there are more exciting things waiting for us in the inner sanctum?"

"I understand that it might seem like we're wasting time, but archaeology is a slow and delicate process," Samuel explained. "The more information we can have before we enter the cave system, the better prepared we'll be for whatever lies within. Remember, when the door closes, all this carving disappears and it becomes a blank wall again. Unlike the camouflage that hides the cave entrance until you get close, the wall takes that technology a step further. It is only when you perform the ritual that the true nature of the doors is revealed. Otherwise, they're invisible."

"Very impressive." The Director shook his head in disbelief.

"But Samuel, surely you can't seriously be considering the notion that these are genuinely ancient doors?" burst in Basile. "This kind of camouflage technology wasn't around during Roman times. There's just no way that this can be an ancient tomb."

"Normally I'd agree with you," Samuel told him. "I'd doubt it myself if it wasn't for one thing: the map. We know that the document was Roman. I tested it myself. The composition and grain of the parchment were undeniably Roman. And it was the map that gave me the directions to find this place and had the details of the ritual required to open the door. How do you explain that if this door isn't ancient?"

"I can't," Basile conceded. "So I guess we have to go further in to solve the mystery. Did your map tell you whether the opening ritual works from the other side of the door? I'd hate for us to be trapped inside and starve to death."

"You don't need to worry about that, gentlemen," The Director reassured them. "That's why we'll have men outside. They can always blow the wall to let us out if we need."

Samuel glared at him. "You can't be serious? These doors have stood here for centuries. You're a Director of the Ministry. You can't be thinking about destroying something so valuable unless it's an absolute last resort."

"Of course not." The Director waved away Samuel's protests. "It was just a little Ministry joke. Your precious doors are perfectly safe."

Samuel clenched his jaw, biting back the retort he would have made if Haisam wasn't his superior.

"You!" The Director pointed at one of the soldiers. "Open the doors properly so we can see what's inside. It's time we discovered what's really going on here."

"Sir." The soldier saluted and jumped forward to push on the doors. He managed to get them halfway open before they stuck on something. Sticking his head through the gap, he was the first to see what the doors had been hiding.

A second later came the shout: "Hostiles!"

THUNK!

The man slowly fell back, an arrow protruding from his chest.

"What do we do?" cried Samuel as he and Basile threw themselves to the ground. The Director ignored them, gesturing to the soldiers to get them into position.

"You and you, provide cover," he ordered. "You and you, push forward. Whoever is inside, we need to flush them out into the open. Now, attack!"

Director Haisam pulled a gun out from a hidden holster, ignoring Samuel and Basile as the two men army-crawled along the ground to take shelter behind a boulder.

"What the hell is going on?" whispered Basile, as he and Samuel watched the Director rush out of the cave to fetch reinforcements, acting for all the world as if he'd had specialist military training. "I thought he was a Ministry official, not a soldier."

"I have no idea," Samuel replied. "If we survive this, he's going to have some explaining to do."

THIRTY-THREE

The large cavern was dimly lit by the quivering flicker of torches. Shots echoed, bullets pinging from the walls, as Haisam's henchmen and the soldiers attempted to take out the hidden assailants concealed inside the cave. Samuel risked peering out over the top of the boulder he and Basile were using for shelter.

"What can you see?" hissed Basile, tugging at Samuel's shirt to get him back under cover as a bullet ricocheted inches away from his foot.

"Looks like there's a huge room behind the doors," Samuel told him. "There appear to be rows of sarcophagi lining the walls, which will help us date the chamber–assuming we survive this."

One of the soldiers fell to the ground next to them, clutching at the arrow in his shoulder. Samuel reached out and dragged him to the safety of the boulder.

"I have to help them," Samuel said, as the soldier groaned in agony. "They're being slaughtered."

"You can't," Basile gasped. "Those men are professional soldiers. If they can't defeat whoever's inside, we don't stand a chance. We need to stay out of the way and let the professionals do their job."

"Aargh!" Another soldier fell to the ground, a victim of the deadly archers, leaving just two soldiers to defend the archaeologist and engineer.

"Sorry, Basile. It's just not in me to sit back and not do something to help."

Keeping a careful watch out to gauge timing, Samuel dashed out from behind the rock and over to the doors. Sitting with his back against the door, he dug his heels into the ground, pushing with all his might to open them fully so the soldiers had more room to maneuver.

The doors fully open, the two remaining soldiers were able to run through together, taking cover behind stone pillars. A few seconds later, buzzsaw-like sounds came from their small, automatic weapons, as they sprayed tiny caliber rounds towards the archers. Samuel raced after them, hiding in a corner while the soldiers attempted to secure the area.

"This is madness," Basile muttered, shaking his head as he watched his friend taking up position in the heart of the melee. "All right, Samuel. I'm coming for you!"

Crawling out to the dead soldier still lying in the doorway, he pried the gun from his hand. Aiming in the general direction of the doors, Basile closed his eyes and pulled the large pistol's trigger.

"Hey!" Samuel yelled back at him. "Watch where you're pointing that thing! You almost took my head off! Do you want to do those archers' job for them?"

"Sorry!" Basile called back. This time, when he fired the gun, he aimed at the ceiling, hoping that the extra shots would scatter their attackers. Lying on the ground, he got his first good look at who was firing the arrows. He couldn't count how many of them there were, and it was impossible to identify who was attacking them thanks to the large gas mask-like contraptions covering their faces, which were hooked up to water sacks on their backs.

"Samuel!" He called out. "Do you see the masks?"

"Yes!" came the reply. "I recognize them. They're called Dervish pumps. They're great for supplying water when you're journeying across the desert, but they've got one fatal flaw. Which gives me an idea..."

"Samuel!" warned Basile. "Stay where you are! Don't do anything stupid!"

His warning was useless as he watched Samuel throw himself around the stone pillar he was using for shelter, edging closer to the archers who were too distracted by the firefight to notice his approach.

"*Américain stupide!*" Basile exclaimed, doing his best to provide cover for his friend as, somehow, he managed to get within reach of one of their attackers. "Stupid American! Look out behind you!"

Samuel whirled round to see a masked man rushing towards him, dagger in hand. There was nothing he could do but throw his hands up in front of his face, closing his eyes so that he wouldn't see the inevitable fatal thrust.

"Die, scum!" The Director came running into the chamber, leading the rest of the soldiers as they fired indiscriminately into the tomb. The knife-wielding attacker's back was shredded by a hail of steel, and he crumpled to the floor with a cry of agony.

Taking advantage of the sudden surprise attack, Samuel hurled himself back at the archer he had been targeting. The man dropped his bow as Samuel managed to get in a couple of jabs to the kidney with his right fist. However, once he recovered, it was quickly clear that Samuel was outclassed. Basile could only watch helplessly as the archer punched the archaeologist in the face, sending him stumbling towards the soldiers and directly into the line of fire. Undeterred, Samuel nimbly regained his footing and launched himself back at the man, grabbing him round the waist in a tackle, and pinning him against the wall. Samuel ground his forearm against his victim's throat.

Reaching round to the back at the mask, Samuel grabbed at the failsafe valve that controlled the flow of water into his mask. Giving it a firm twist, the valve broke off in his hand.

"Bleurch!" gargled the archer, grabbing at his mask to pull it off as it filled with water. Samuel ducked out of the way, pressing himself up against the wall as the man stumbled into the path of one of the soldiers.

"Take him prisoner!" Samuel called. "We can question hi... Nooooo!"

He cried out in horror as the soldier callously placed his gun against the head of the archer and pulled the trigger.

"Director Haisam!" Samuel yelled. "Call off the attack! We've won! We've won!"

The Director either didn't hear him or ignored his pleas, as he steadied himself in the middle of the room, aiming at the remaining men who were retreating into a corridor opposite the entrance that lead deeper into the cave network. Another man fell to the ground, one of Haisam's bullets hitting him square in the back.

"Enough!" shouted Samuel, waving his arms about to attract the Director's attention. "This fight is over! Let the rest go."

The Director snarled, steadying his gun for another shot, before pausing and then lowering his weapon. "Cease fire!" he called out. Immediately the soldiers stopped shooting.

Samuel stepped forward, gazing around the chamber in dismay. "In my entire archaeological career, I have never started an excavation with a shootout," he raged at the Director.

"So you're lucky that my men were here to save you," replied Haisam, coolly. "You're welcome."

"I'm welcome?" Samuel shook his head in disbelief. "Look at the damage you've done! Those sarcophagi are centuries old and you've caused irreparable harm with your trigger-happy ways. There isn't a single one that you haven't damaged."

"They shot first," Haisam shrugged. "What would you have preferred us to do? Let them slaughter us all? Ask politely if they would be so kind as to please stop killing us?" He sniffed in disgust. "Whilst I appreciate your concerns, my duty is to my men and my country first and foremost. It is clear that this is the tip of the iceberg. I do not believe that this chamber contains the most valuable relics to be found on this site. Mourn the loss of a few items if you must, but my focus is on the true treasure concealed somewhere in the catacombs."

"Until we've uncovered everything, we have no idea what the 'true treasure' is," Samuel argued. "Your men were out of control. They killed indiscriminately. We could have learned so much from questioning our attackers, but they're dead, butchered at the hands of your men."

"They are soldiers," Haisam shrugged. "It's what soldiers do."

Samuel opened his mouth to point out that Haisam was an administrator, yet had been equally violent, but something told him that now was not the time.

"Now if your delicate American sensibilities can cope with the notion of doing the job you are paid to do, I suggest that we press on with our search," said the Director. "I do not believe that we will have any more trouble from our enemies. They've seen what we will do to anyone who dares to attack us. Nevertheless, I will send a couple of men on ahead to secure the area."

He gestured to a couple of the soldiers, who started down the corridor, after the archers.

Samuel stared at the Director, debating his next move.

"Do we have a problem, McCarthy?" said Haisam, narrowing his eyes slightly.

"I don't know. Do we?" countered Samuel. "Basile and I are here to do a job as you so rightly point out, but we can't do it while your men slaughter everyone in sight. I need your word that you'll show restraint if we encounter anyone else."

"All I can say is that I will not kill anyone I do not have to," the Director promised. "But you need to remember that my soldiers are here for your safety. Unless you would like to return home with an arrow in your chest? They shot first, remember?"

"Nevertheless," Samuel said. "If we encounter anyone else, I feel it would be better if we were to attempt to capture them alive. They know this cave system better than us. It could save us a lot of time if we were to interrogate them instead of kill them."

"We will do our best." The Director turned and strode down the corridor after his soldiers. Samuel made to follow him, but Basile pulled him to one side, trying to get as far away from listening ears as possible.

"Do you believe him?" he whispered. "More importantly, do you *trust* him?"

"I'm not sure," Samuel replied, "but what choice do we have? We can't leave on our own and I want to know what's so important about this place that people are willing to die for it."

Basile sighed. "Me too," he confessed. "I just hope it was worth all this bloodshed. Come on. Let's go and see what's lurking in the catacombs."

They crossed the chamber to go into the corridor, following the archers.

"The crossfire destroyed so much of the interior of this chamber," tutted Samuel in dismay, stopping to examine a shattered carving. "I would have thought the Ministry would have cared more about protecting the site. At least the men who attacked us used arrows."

"And not a single one hit any of the artifacts," Basile observed. "All the damage was caused by the Director's men."

THIRTY-FOUR

Shafira gazed out over the complex of rectangular holes, walls, and tents that was the excavation site as Josh expertly brought the helicopter down close to the landing strip. This was it! She was finally out in the field, free from the constraints of an office. If only it were under better circumstances...

When they'd safely touched down, Josh switched off the helicopter's engines, swiveling in his seat to face Shafira as the loud whine decreased. "What's the plan, Stan?"

Shafira adjusted her uniform, making sure that her Ministry badge was clearly visible.

"Hopefully Samuel won't have left the site yet," she replied. "Since he's your friend, do you think you could come up with some excuse to get him away from the Director so that I can talk to him alone, warn him that he can't trust anyone until we've solved the mystery of what's going on here?"

"I can do that," Josh nodded. "What do we do if he's already left though?"

"Then we'll have to fly to the cave site," Shafira decided. "I brought some files with me so that if I do have to face Director Haisam, I can pretend that they were too important to wait."

"Is he likely to buy that?"

"Maybe not," Shafira sighed. "But he did initially ask me to accompany him. I can tell him that I reconsidered his offer after I did more research into the site and wanted to see it for myself. After all, it's the female prerogative to change my mind!"

"I really hope you know what you're doing," Josh warned.

"I wish. I'm making it up as I go along," Shafira admitted. "That's why I'm lucky to have a friend like you by my side. I couldn't have got here without you. Do you remember where the cave is if we have to fly out there?"

Josh winced. "Not really. I was just going where Samuel told me to. The biggest problem is that damn camo-tech hiding the cave. We could be right on top of it and not know. There weren't any obvious landmarks that would be able to give us a clue to where to go. It took us forever to find it first time around and that was with the assistance of Samuel's map. Since he lost it when we almost crashed into the cave, I wouldn't want to risk running out of fuel trying to find the site again."

Shafira tapped a finger against the dashboard as she thought. "All right. Cross your fingers that McCarthy is still on site. If we've missed him, we'll just have to search his tent to see if he's left any clue to their whereabouts."

"I guess that'll work," Josh agreed, before indicating to the men that were coming towards the helicopter. "Looks like they've sent out a welcoming party. Let's go and see if they can tell us where Samuel is."

Josh and Shafira disembarked, and headed over to meet a single, tall figure dressed in a patterned headscarf and gray tunic.

"*Marhaban*," Shafira greeted as they met, holding up the ID in her wallet so that they could see that she was from the Ministry. "I'm looking for Samuel McCarthy or Basile Rossignol. Are they here?"

"I'm sorry, ma'am," the man replied. "You've missed them. They left with one of your fellows and some soldiers a few hours ago. But surely you'd know that?"

"I was caught up on another assignment," Shafira explained, as Josh looked at her sharply. "I'm running behind, which is why I had to commandeer a helicopter. I have some important documents for the Director. It is imperative that I get them to him." She glanced away and then back again, smiling at the man as she batted her eyelids at him. "I don't suppose you could tell me where they've gone?"

"I have no idea, miss." The man shook his head. "But he might have left a note in his tent. Would you like me to show you where it is?"

"That would be very helpful. Thank you," said Shafira, as their guide turned to lead them through the camp, out to where Samuel's tent was pitched.

"Call out if you need any help," offered the worker, holding open the tent flap for Shafira and Josh. "I'm working nearby."

"I will." Shafira thanked the man again before ducking inside the tent. Her smile faded as she took in the state of Samuel's tent. "Oh my goodness. How on earth is Samuel supposed to find anything in this place?" She moved over to a table, picking up a dirty T-shirt that was covering some equipment, holding it at arm's length.

"Samuel's never been the world's tidiest person," Josh told her. "Claims that disorganization is the sign of a brilliant mind, but I think he's just lazy."

"Help me sift through this mess," Shafira replied testily. She began sifting through books and papers on the table next to her. "If Samuel's out in the middle of the deserts with those thugs, we need to let him know. They could be agents of the Bruard."

"Speaking of the Bruard, don't you think you should have warned that worker about what's going on?" Josh asked as he rifled through some paperwork.

"Like he was going to believe me," Shafira pointed out. "I'm not supposed to be here as it is. What if they demanded proof that *we're* not the frauds? They could ring my office, who'll tell them that I'm supposed to be back in Cairo. No, if the Bruard are here, then they're with Samuel looking for the cave. The camp is safe, at least for the time being."

"Fair enough," Josh agreed. "But Samuel's a likeable guy. I'm sure the team would help us out if they thought he was in trouble. We could get to the cave much faster with their help."

"Maybe," Shafira said, "but who can we trust? Whatever Haisam's mixed up in, it's big. For all we know, the camp could be rife with spies and agents left to make sure that no one interferes. Do you want to risk telling the wrong person our suspicions? The best thing to do is find out where Samuel's gone and get there as fast as we can. So keep looking for clues. We might get interrupted at any moment, especially if someone's decided to ring the Ministry to check on my story."

Josh and Shafira redoubled their efforts, the occasional sounds of a voice or a chisel against stone their only companions as they searched for a clue to where Samuel and his team had gone.

"Shafira!" Josh beckoned to her. "Over here."

He held up the device containing the geo-map Samuel had used to show the Director where they were going. "This should have a record of all the recent searches Samuel's carried out. The chances are high that he's used it to locate the cave site so they could plan out their return route." He tapped on a few buttons to bring up the map. "Dammit! It's password-protected. What do we do now?"

"Give it here." Shafira held out a hand for the device. Hitting a few buttons, she passed it back to Josh. "There you go."

Josh looked at the display and saw that Shafira had unlocked the map.

"How did you do that?" he gasped. "Have you taken up hacking in your spare time?"

"Nothing like that," Shafira laughed. "But hang around offices for long enough and you soon find that the same old passwords get used over and over. There are people who still use 'password' would you

THE ETERNAL CHAMBER: AN ARCHAEOLOGICAL THRILLER   173

believe, while there are others who think they're being clever by using a sequence of letters or numbers or even their name written backwards without realizing that just about everyone else is doing the same thing."

"So what was Samuel's?"

"1q2w3e4r," Shafira replied. "It looks random, but it's just the first few keys from the top two lines of the keyboard. Now what were the last plotted coordinates?"

Josh called up the log of previous searches. "Yes!" he crowed. "Gotcha!"

"Have you found the cave?"

"Yes," Josh beamed. "I recognize the area. I know exactly where we're going and this time I won't nearly crash into the rocks."

"Excellent. Let's get going then. I just hope that we can find a way to warn Samuel without alerting the Director to our suspicions."

Josh and Shafira grinned at each other, but their joy turned to dread as they heard someone opening up the tent and coming in.

THIRTY-FIVE

"Who are you?" demanded Shafira, as an unfamiliar man walked into the tent. Short and stocky with black hair and eyes, there was something about him that raised her hackles.

"Shouldn't I be asking you that question?" he countered. "You're the ones rifling through Samuel McCarthy's tent."

Josh and Shafira exchanged a glance as she indicated the badge attached to her lapel. "Shafira Khouri from the Ministry of State for Antiquities," she announced. "And you are?"

"Waleed at your service." Waleed sketched an elaborate bow, but Josh was unimpressed.

"Do you have a surname, Waleed at-your-service?" he asked.

"Just Waleed will do," came the evasive reply. "But I'm curious. What is a Ministry official doing here when we had no less than a Director arrive today?"

"I have an important message for Samuel and the Director," Shafira replied. "It's on a need-to-know basis, so I can't say further than that."

"Of course, of course. I understand." Waleed shrugged expansively. "I am but a humble worker, here to support Samuel in any way that I can. Still, if it is such an important message, I don't understand why you weren't here sooner. Surely you must appreciate how difficult it will be to find Samuel in the field?"

"There were some complications," Shafira told him coolly. "Which means that it is crucial that we get to McCarthy as soon as we possibly can."

"Complications like... the Bruard?" Waleed raised his eyebrows, looking from Shafira to Josh and back again to gauge their reaction.

Shafira's eyes widened, while Josh shook his head.

"You don't need to worry about me, my friends," Waleed reassured them. "You are not the only ones to suspect Bruard involvement in this excavation. I've been working undercover for Basile. We suspect that there are Bruard spies in the camp. I've been tasked with discovering their identity. Perhaps we can combine our knowledge and work together?"

"A word, Shafira?" Seeing that she was about to tell Waleed everything, Josh pulled her to one side.

"This is it!" she whispered excitedly. "This is exactly what we were looking for. I *knew* that something big was going on. It's the only way the Director could have been compromised. If this Waleed has information on the Bruard, we need to know about it."

"Don't go buying what he's selling," Josh warned. "He seems a little too upfront with his suspicions. Be careful that he's not just spreading honey to trap flies. We know nothing about him. For all you know, he could be a Bruard agent himself, left on duty here to head off anyone who suspects what's happening."

"I'm not a Bruard agent!" Waleed protested, making Josh and Shafira jump. He smiled obsequiously. "I'm sorry, but I couldn't help but overhear. I know you have no reason to trust me, but believe me, I hate the Bruard as much as you do. It's thanks to them that I was placed under supervision in the camp. It was Basile who saw through their lies and set me free. I owe him and I'd like to help him as he helped me. If you could only let me come with you, I promise that I'll prove to you that I'm on your side."

Shafira bit her lip in indecision, glancing at Josh, who frowned and shook his head.

"Look at this." Waleed pulled a piece of paper out of his pocket. "Basile trusted me with the comm signal code to his and Samuel's radio equipment. He wouldn't have done that if he hadn't wanted me to help. When we get within range, I can help you contact your friends without alerting any traitors who may be with them. What do you say? Shall we go defeat the Bruard?"

"I really don't trust this guy," Josh cautioned, but Shafira waved away his concerns.

"You can come with us," she decided. "But the first sign of any trouble and we'll throw you out of the helicopter. Don't think we won't!"

"Don't worry. I won't give you any trouble," Waleed grinned.

As Josh and Shafira left the tent, Waleed surreptitiously grabbed one of Samuel's hooded shirts, throwing it on to conceal his appearance as he followed them to the helicopter.

THIRTY-SIX

Samuel paid close attention to the ancient surroundings him as his party made their way deeper into the catacombs. He swung his Maglite around, trying to take in all the details, as exciting new discoveries greeted him with every step.

When they'd first entered the corridor that lead away from the entrance chamber, stone pillars had been placed every few feet decorated with simple carvings that only hinted at what would be found further down the passageway. Romans loved symbolism, rarely using decorations that didn't hold multiple meanings, and as they got further into the cave network, the rough pillars gave way to Roman mosaics interspersed with statues of Seshat and Moneta, benevolently watching over passersby.

"I didn't realize that Romans had such gaudy taste," Basile remarked. "I had no idea that they used such bright colors in their designs."

"It's cool, isn't it?" beamed Samuel. "This is a remarkable example of Roman art and architecture. We can thank whoever sealed the caves off from the outside world for them being so well preserved. Most people think of Roman culture as being all white and bland, but they loved color and used it on everything."

"Look at those images." Basile pointed to a detailed mosaic. "Who were those people?"

"I'd need to examine the surrounding iconography to identify them accurately," Samuel replied, going over to look at the picture. "But at first glance, judging by the clothing and how they are positioned, these are either Pharaohs or important aristocrats, indicating that whatever was stored in this place was reserved for the rich and wealthy. This figure here appears to be dreaming, while if we look over here, this one is examining the stars. Of course, back in those times, astrology was considered to be a science, so the positioning of the stars and planets in this picture will have a specific significance."

"What else can you tell us?" Overhearing Samuel and Basile's conversation, the Director held back to walk alongside them.

"Anything I say now is only a preliminary observation and may prove to be inaccurate once I've had a chance to carry out further investigation," Samuel cautioned. "But based on what I've seen so far, I believe that the design at the start of this corridor dates towards the end of the Egyptian dynasty. I can confirm that theory once I've had a chance to date the sarcophagi in the entrance chamber, assuming there's anything left after your men shot the place up." He glared at the Director, who ignored the jibe.

"However," Samuel continued, "as we've progressed further into the cave network, we're seeing Egyptian work giving way to an increasingly heavy influence from Roman styles, giving us a blend of the two cultures that would have naturally occurred after the Romans conquered the area."

"Seshat. She is Egyptian, is she not?" mused the Director, lightly waving his hand in front of the face of one of the statues.

"Yes, although I would have thought you'd know that already," frowned Samuel.

"I wonder whether she was included as a form of rebellion, a desire to go against orders from the invaders. I can't imagine anyone being willing to share their culture with those who have overthrown them."

"You'd be surprised. The Romans were very laid back when it came to the gods. They viewed local deities as having their counterpart within their pantheon, so didn't have a problem with cultures maintaining their own religions and forms of worship. They would have seen Seshat as being simply another Roman goddess known by an Egyptian name. Allowing those they conquered a certain level of autonomy was one of the reasons why they were so successful at taking over vast swathes of land."

"I see." The Director nodded and then turned to join his soldiers up ahead, leaving Samuel and Basile to examine the mosaic further.

"This is incredible, Samuel," breathed Basile. "But I have to say that I'm impressed by your restraint. Why aren't you rushing ahead? Surely this is just a fraction of what we'll find later."

Samuel's reply was lost as there was a sudden thud. The sound of a metal blade swiping through the air was closely followed by a cry of alarm.

"Because of that." Samuel pointed to the ground where a spike had suddenly burst through, narrowly missing a careless soldier.

"Phew!" Basile whistled. "I get it now. I guess it's not so bad after all having the Director in the lead to guide us past the traps."

"I'm not so sure that our Director friend is the type of guide we want," murmured Samuel out of the corner of his mouth so he wouldn't be overheard this time. "If he wasn't my superior, I'd tell him to get lost."

"I get that," nodded Basile. "Director Haisam is nothing like any other Ministry official I've ever encountered."

"Quiet back there!" Gord hissed. "Or do you want us to miss another trap?"

"Last I checked, this was an archaeological expedition that I'm still in charge of," Samuel retorted. "If I want to talk, I'll talk."

Gord strode angrily towards the archaeologist, but the Director put out an arm to stop him.

"Enough, all of you. Need I remind you that we're still in hostile territory? Save the petty arguments for when we're out of here."

Gord glared at Samuel before spitting on the ground in front of him, barely missing Samuel's feet. He then turned and marched off.

"*Tête de bite*," Basile swore. "What an a-hole."

"Don't worry about it," Samuel advised. "Every group of soldiers has that one guy with a big chip on his shoulder. He's just trying to assert what little authority he has to try and make himself feel like the big man. He probably resents being in an inferior position to an archaeologist."

"You should be honored that the gorilla views you as a rival," Basile joked.

"Yeah, lucky me." Samuel beat his chest Tarzan style before slowly carrying on down the passage, still fascinated by the Roman décor covering the walls.

"Keep up, McCarthy," barked the Director. "We still have a long way to go. There'll be plenty of time for you to come back and look at these walls in greater depth later."

"If you don't destroy them with bullets," Samuel muttered, picking up the pace until they reached a fork in the corridor. To the left, they could see a flickering light in the distance illuminating the fact that the passageway suddenly turned sharply left. To the right, an ominous dark tunnel opened up before them. It seemed to swallow every scrap of light.

"Stay here," Director Haisam ordered. "Gord, go check out the tunnels and report back."

For once, Samuel was happy to do as he was told, as the large soldier strode forward to investigate their options. After walking down both corridors a few paces and thoroughly banging on the walls and examining the floor, he returned.

"They went that way." He pointed down the darkened tunnel in the direction their attackers had fled.

"Then we go the other way," Samuel decided. "It's madness to follow people in the dark when they know the territory and we don't.

Even with all our flashlights, we're still going in blind. They'll just pick us off one by one."

"You're correct," the Director agreed. "This is why you and Basile will go down the tunnel first to see if perhaps the enemy are trying to trick us into going the wrong way."

"Me and Basile?" Samuel laughed. "I don't think so. You're the one with the trained soldiers. Send one of them to check it out."

"I'm afraid I must insist." The Director pointed a silver handgun at them, clicking the safety off.

"Are you crazy?" gasped Basile. "What are you doing?"

"I think it is time I introduced myself properly." Director Haisam reached up to his lapel and pressed a tiny button. In an instant, his disguise melted away, revealing his true identity. "My name is Pin Nam-Gi and you *will* go down that corridor before us."

THIRTY-SEVEN

"Now, get yourselves down that corridor," Pin ordered, gesturing at Samuel and Basile. "We need to wipe out the remaining archers so that we can explore the rest of this network without looking over our shoulders every step of the way. If that's the way they've gone, that's the way you're going. You're expendable, so if anyone's going to get hit by an arrow, it needs to be one of you two. Unless you'd prefer a bullet?"

"No, no, you've made your point." Samuel put up his hands in surrender and turned to go down the tunnel, Basile by his side. "But tell me, Haisam–sorry, Pin–who are you really working for? The Ministry only believes in death by paperwork. Ministry employees might wither away waiting for a permit to come through, but last I checked, they didn't use violence to get people to do what they wanted them to do."

"Do you really not have any idea?" laughed Pin.

"I have my suspicions," Samuel admitted. "I can't prove anything just yet though, so I'd rather keep my ideas to myself for now."

"Ah well. You'll just have to keep guessing for the time being," Pin shrugged. "However, I'll make you a deal. If you survive long enough for us to get to the heart of the catacombs and we retrieve what's waiting for us, I'll tell you everything."

"It sounds like you already know what's there," Samuel observed. "Why do you need us then if you already have all the answers?"

"Good question," Pin chuckled. "But then I don't pretend to have all the answers. Let's just say that I was curious about the cloaking field, just like you. Regardless of who's responsible for it, it's clear that there's something here that's of inestimable value. Whether my masters use it or sell it for a fortune is meaningless to me. It's my duty to retrieve it, so that's what I'll do."

"If it's your duty, then surely it should be you going down the tunnel, not us?" Samuel pointed out.

Pin laughed. "In this instance, I am willing to step aside and let you have that honor. Now we've delayed long enough. I am a man of my word. I *must* insist you go ahead," he said gesturing with his gun barrel.

Basile recognized the twitch in Samuel's jaw. It meant Samuel was about to lose his temper. Basile grabbed hold of his friend's arm and pulled him in the direction of the darkened corridor. "Let's just do what he says," he advised. *"Nous pouvons trouver comment échapper à ce crétin une fois que nous sommes dans le tunnel. Ne risque pas ta vie en l'attaquant ici. Ça ne vaut pas le coup."*

"English, please," said Pin, as Samuel nodded slightly at Basile to show he understood. The Frenchman had a point. It would be easier to figure out a way to escape Pin and his men under cover of darkness in the tunnel than risk his life throwing a punch at the traitor now.

"Do you both have working flashlights?" Pin asked the two men.

Samuel and Basile switched on their lights and illuminated him with the beams.

"Excellent. Good luck, the pair of you. I hope you survive this. I've enjoyed your company thus far. It would give me no pleasure to see anything bad happen to you."

Samuel rolled his eyes and he and Basile moved off into the darkness.

THIRTY-EIGHT

Samuel snuck his hand into his pocket and tapped the button to switch on his Bluetooth V transmitter, hoping that its low-frequency radio waves would give it much greater range than older Bluetooth systems, and somehow get a signal to someone outside.

Samuel and Basile hugged the wall as they edged their way down the tunnel, trying to present the smallest possible target to any archers that might be lurking in the darkness. Keeping their flashlights low, they did their best to avoid broadcasting their location to any guards who might be lying in wait. Samuel's scalp prickled, his heart beating faster as he braced himself for the inevitable arrow to come out of nowhere. "Can you see anything, Basile?" he whispered.

"Not a thing," came the reply. "There could be an archer right in front of us and we wouldn't know."

Basile risked flooding the distant darkness with his beam, unable to stand that thought any longer.

"No one there," he confirmed. "But this is madness, Samuel. What are we doing? Walk into armed men ahead of us or retreat back to armed men behind us. Pick your poison. Either way, we're dead."

"Never give up hope," Samuel advised. "It ain't over until the fat lady sings and I don't hear any music just yet." He tapped at his earpiece, trying to get a signal. "Dammit," he cursed. "I was hoping that I might be able to get out an SOS, but it looks like we're too deep underground to be able to call for backup."

"*Merde!*" Basile swore. "Why didn't you call anyone earlier?"

"By the time it was obvious that something wasn't right, Pin was watching me like a hawk," Samuel replied. "Believe me, I wanted to, but I couldn't risk him seeing what I was doing and killing us. Right now, I'm hoping that this tunnel will turn towards the surface so I can get a signal or even take us out of the caves completely."

"*Quel bordel,*" exclaimed Basile. "What a mess."

The two men continued walking, the lights denoting Pin and the soldiers' location quickly fading to black.

"So what do you make of Pin?" Basile asked. "Do you think he's with the Bruard?"

"I wouldn't be surprised," Samuel told him. "However, I'm more inclined to believe this is a solo operation. I think Pin's acting out of self-interest."

"How so?"

"We've all heard the stories about the Bruard," Samuel explained. "They're brutal and thuggish, just like Pin and his men were when they shot up the entrance chamber. However, they don't leave anything to chance. The team he brought with him isn't big enough to be certain that they could wipe out anyone we find here, given that nobody knew who or what was in here. Put it this way, he wouldn't have sent an archaeologist and an engineer down this tunnel if he had armed men to spare. Why risk us escaping into the catacombs?"

"Hmm. I wonder whether our Mr. Nam-Gi is in trouble himself? If he is associated with the Bruard, they aren't known for their mercy or willingness to spend money unless they have to. Do you think that Pin is under pressure to make this trip worthwhile?"

"I'm sure he is. His superiors wouldn't do well with failure. Which, now I think about it, may be something we can use against him... if we survive long enough."

Basile stumbled yet again, banging his knee painfully against a rock. "Gah!" he grunted through gritted teeth. He took a moment to rub his leg. "Honestly, Samuel, we should have just refused to come down this tunnel. At least they'd have given us a quick death instead of the torment of not knowing when we're going to get hit by an arrow. Let's face it, we're going to get shot sooner or later, regardless of whether we find whatever it is Pin's looking for."

"I hear you." Samuel nodded, even though Basile couldn't see him. "But we're here now, so we might as well make the best of it. Who knows? Pin may live to regret sending us to investigate. We might find something we can use as leverage against him."

"But that's what I don't understand," Basile went on. "So far, all we've seen are statues, friezes, pots, sarcophagi... All very interesting stuff, but nothing out of the ordinary and certainly nothing that would justify all this violence. Why would anyone care about this place?"

"I don't know, but I intend to find out," replied Samuel grimly. "If we get to whatever it is we're looking for first, I'm going to do my best to escape with it and get help. There's no way I intend to hand over anything to Pin if I can help it."

"What happens if-"

Basile screamed as the ground opened up beneath him. He collapsed on his back, with the wind knocked out of him, as dirt poured into him. It covered his face. Blind panic took over, and he pushed himself up to a kneeling position. The soil was still up to his waist.

"Samuel! Help me!" he spluttered.

With a sweep of his flashlight beam, Samuel saw that Basile was in a pit roughly six feet deep and eight feet across. Basile scrabbled at the dirt as Samuel reached out for him, lying on the ground with his arm dangling into the pit. As Samuel grabbed the engineer by the wrist, his flashlight rolled into the hole and went out. Samuel scrabbled about with his free hand to try and find something to brace himself with as he pulled Basile out, but there was nothing. In desperation, he reached out to hold onto Basile with both hands, trying to pull him back onto firm land, but the engineer was too heavy for him to move.

"Basile, try to climb up me," Samuel urged, feeling the sand beneath him began to slip away into the abyss.

"I'm... trying..." grunted Basile, his legs flailing as he tried in vain to get enough hold against the near-vertical sides to push himself up.

As the two men struggled to reach solid ground, neither of them noticed the man wearing a Dervish pump approaching. Light from Basile's headlight glinted from the curve of a razor sharp scimitar, which he was already raising above Samuel.

THIRTY-NINE

"Samuel!" Basile shouted. "There's someone behind you. Let me go and defend yourself!"

Samuel craned his head round and saw the hooded man. Adrenaline rushed through his body and he fought harder to pull Basile to safety.

"Don't worry about him, worry about yourself," Samuel ordered, as his foot finally found a small crevice he could use for support. Wedging his foot into it, he tried to pull Basile up, but the sudden movement caused more sand to slip into the pit.

"Either kill me or help out," Samuel barked at the approaching man. "We can always duke it out when we're all on solid ground again."

Basile closed his eyes, not wanting to see the killing blow as the man lifted his sword...

...and sheathed it, reaching down to take hold of Basile's right hand. Samuel still had his left. Working together, the two men quickly hauled the Frenchman out onto solid ground. He coughed and spluttered, trying to rub the dirt from his eyes so he could make out the mysterious stranger more easily.

Samuel picked up Basile's Maglite, pointing it in the direction of their savior, but taking care not to shine it in his eyes. "Thanks for your help," he said. "If you'll just give me a moment to get my breath back, we can have that fight if you want. Although I think it only right to warn you that I used to fence in college. I won the state championship, so it wouldn't be fair of me to fight you when I have an advantage. Why don't we forget about it altogether and call it a draw so we can go our separate ways?"

The swordsman lowered his mask, revealing a youthful Egyptian complexion, topped with a wave of thick, black hair. "I appreciate that some people use humor as a way of dealing with difficult situations, but given your predicament, I think it would make more sense if we cut the snark and got straight to business, don't you?"

Samuel nodded. "All right. My name's Samuel McCarthy and my colleague here is Basile Rossignol. I'm an archaeologist and he's an engineer specializing in ancient construction and excavation. And you are?"

"My name is Akhenaton," came the reply.

"Akhenaton?" Samuel thought for a moment. "That's ancient Egyptian, isn't it? I can't recall the meaning, although I know it was considered a powerful name."

"It is," confirmed Akhenaton. "However, its significance is something I share only with family and friends. Whilst it is blindingly obvious that you are not Bruard, you are neither family nor friend." He stood up, reaching out to help Samuel and Basile to their feet. "Are you aware of the terrors you are about to unleash upon the world if the Bruard gets their dirty hands on what is contained within these chambers?"

Samuel shook his head, brushing away the sand clinging to his clothes. "I still haven't figured out what exactly is this place. All I've had to go on is an ancient map and a few cryptic scrolls. They gave enough hints that I knew that there was something here worth investigating, but I thought we were going to uncover some funerary texts, or maybe more evidence about ancient Egyptian religious practices, but nothing that would be worth all this violence. Much as I like to kid myself that archaeology is the most important scientific discipline, I'm under no illusion that any of that would really change the world."

"Don't tell me," joked Basile. "We've stumbled into the set of some horror movie and there's a hideous demon or terrible monster trapped in this catacomb waiting for us to free it."

He laughed, but Akhenaton remained stone-faced.

"This tomb does indeed contain a monster of sorts, although it is not perhaps so obvious at first glance."

Basile's laugh faded away, as Samuel glanced anxiously down the corridor as if expecting claws to swipe at him.

"What do you mean?" Samuel asked. "Either it's a monster or it's not. I'm getting really sick of all the mysterious hints and secrets. Just tell us what's here already."

"I can't." Akhenaton shook his head. "The nature of the beast is closely guarded for the protection of all. My order simply teaches that this site has to be protected at all costs, so when we received signal that the cloaking field had been breached, we came to investigate. However, it would appear that we share a common enemy, so perhaps we can work together to unravel the enigma."

"Anything's better than dangling over a death pit," Basile told him. "I'm in. What do you say, Samuel?"

"That works for me," he agreed. "However, much as I hate to break up the party, Pin is still out there waiting for us to report back. Akhenaton, is there another way out of this place? If we can get to the surface, we can call for help from the Ministry, get reinforcements to overpower Pin and his men. No offense, but swords and arrows aren't going to cut it against Pin's guns."

"I don't know," came the frustrated reply. "Nobody has been to this cave in centuries and the maps we had of the interior layout have long since been lost. At this stage, you know as much as we do about the best direction to go."

"All right," sighed Samuel. "It looks like we really are in this together. Let's get going. At the very least, I want to put some distance between us and Pin."

"At least we don't have to worry about arrows anymore," Basile pointed out as they set off. "Only death pits and blade traps."

Samuel said nothing, looking back over his shoulder. "Shh!" he ordered, straining his ears.

"What is it?" asked Akhenaton.

Samuel listened for a moment, then shook his head. "Nothing." He shone his Maglite down the tunnel. "I thought I heard footsteps behind us, but there's no one there. Come on. Let's go. We've wasted more than enough time already."

The three men hurried off deeper into the catacombs.

FORTY

"How much further do we have to go?" asked Basile, leaning against the rock wall to take a break. "These tunnels seem to go on forever and I can't remember when I last ate or drank. If I'd have known we'd be down here for so long without a break, I'd have brought supplies."

"It's the same answer you got an hour ago," Samuel snapped, stopping beside him as Akhenaton took up position opposite them to keep watch down the corridor. "None of us know. All we can do is keep moving forward. Look on the bright side. Every step we take is a step further away from Pin."

"If we keep this up, we'll walk our way into our graves," Basile grumbled. "I'd rather be shot than starve."

"For the love of Ra, stop complaining," Akhenaton pleaded. "You're making me nervous. Besides, you're wasting energy with all that talking. Focus on putting one foot in front of the other and we'll get there soon enough."

"Sorry," said Basile. "I just wasn't expecting any of this. We were supposed to come here, check out the caves, then go back to our main dig site. I wish I'd stayed back at the camp instead."

"You're not the only one," Samuel reminded him. "Let's change the subject. Where are the rest of your men, Akhenaton?"

"They fled in all directions," Akhenaton replied. "We agreed that it was best if we split up across the various tunnels to confuse Pin and his men with multiple trails. None of us knew for certain where we were heading when we chose the paths we did, but our fates are in the hands of the gods. We are here in their service."

"So you don't know whether we could be heading towards the central inner sanctum of the catacombs or walking straight into a death trap?" Samuel clarified.

"No," Akhenaton shrugged. "All I know is that I will end up where I am supposed to be. All the members of my order have sworn an oath to give our lives to protect the secrets of St. Augustine. If that means that I die in the tunnels, then so be it. I will have died doing my duty."

"St. Augustine?" Samuel did a double take. "Do you mean St. Augustine of Hippo? What does he have to do with this place?"

Akhenaton pushed himself away from the wall. "Come on. We should get moving. We have no idea what your friends are doing or if they've decided to come after us. It's not safe to stay here."

He made to move on, but Samuel grabbed his arm. "Stop jerking us around," he demanded. "We've been open and honest with you. You can tell we're not with the Bruard. If you tell us what's going on here, we can help you. Otherwise, we might as well just step aside and let Pin have his way."

Akhenaton thought for a moment then nodded. "All right. I'll tell you what I do know. Are you familiar with my book, *On the Trinity?*"

Samuel and Basile shook their heads.

"I am not surprised. It is very specialist and not a beginner's text. It takes a certain level of education to be able to appreciate and understand my theories."

Samuel decided against mentioning his multiple degrees and two doctorates. If Akhenaton needed to kid himself that he was the most intelligent man in the world in order to keep assisting them, that was just fine with Samuel.

"My book was a treatise on various ancient philosophies and aimed at deconstructing them to put them into a contemporary context given our modern scientific understandings," Akhenaton told them. "The passage that has the most relevance to our current situation concerns my rebuttal to the Pythagorean theory of deathless souls. In it I wrote:

For we must not acquiesce in their story, who assert the Samian Pythagoras recollected some things... which he experienced when he was previously here in another body; and others, that they experienced something of the same sort in their minds: but it may be conjectured that these were untrue recollections, such as we commonly experience in sleep, when we fancy we remember, as though we had done it or seen it, what we never did or saw at all; and that the minds of these persons, even though awake, were affected in this way at the suggestion of malignant and deceitful spirits, whose care it is to confirm or to sow some false belief concerning the changes of souls, in order to deceive men.

Samuel and Basile exchanged looks.

"All right," Basile said. "You got me. I haven't got a clue what any of that meant. Do you want to put it into English?"

"In essence, it discusses the concept of déjà vu," Akhenaton explained. "That strange sensation when you feel that you've already lived through a situation, experiencing memories that one logically knows you should not. Pythagoras' explanation for the phenomenon was to claim that souls were deathless and experienced memories from earlier lives. Although a situation might not be exactly the same as previously encountered, it will retain enough similarities to give the feeling that you have been there before."

"*Formidable!*" exclaimed Basile. "But what has that got to do with our current predicament?"

Akhenaton shook his head. "I've said too much already. Suffice to say that there is evidence of St. Augustine being challenged by a contemporary to visit this tomb so that he could experience this phenomenon under unique conditions. Whatever happened had such an impact on the saint that he broke his vow of silence to write about those experiences, leaving his notes in a secret library. The key to that library is hidden somewhere in this network."

He started walking again. Basile sighed as he pulled himself to his feet, struggling to put one foot in front of the other, as he fantasized about a nice, cold beer.

"What do you think?" Basile asked Samuel under his breath as Akhenaton strode ahead. "This is all getting too weird for me. I'm just an engineer. All this hocus pocus nonsense seems utterly irrelevant."

"Yeah," Samuel agreed. "It's pretty clear that Akhenaton believes in his order and that he thinks there's something mystical about this place. I'm sure we'll find *something* here. The quality of the remains we've seen so far strongly suggest that. But that's all there is to it. Pin and his men are going to want to sell them off to the highest bidder. It's cold, hard cash that's motivating them. Nothing else."

"We've found it!" announced Akhenaton. There was a tone of unmistakable reverence in his voice as Samuel and Basile came to join him.

"Is that-?" asked Basile, marveling at the door in front of them.

"That's St. Augustine," Akhenaton confirmed, pointing to a figure decorating the door. "This is a sign. We're on the right track. Behind this door lies everything you're looking for. We have a chance to secure the secret and save it from Pin and his men."

Basile indicated regularly-spaced holes pointing towards the door from three sides. "Unless, of course, the door is booby trapped and will kill us when we open it."

FORTY-ONE

Samuel pulled on a pair of latex gloves, lightly running his hands over the carving. "The detail is incredible," he breathed. "This is one of the most magnificent examples of Roman carving I've ever seen. These tunnels happen to provide perfect conditions to preserve it. I hope that Pin doesn't get this far into the network. I can imagine the kind of desecration he and his men would do."

"Although if they went in first, we could get them to trigger any traps," Basile quipped. "It's hard for me to tell whether this door is rigged or not. I'd need more equipment, better lighting, support staff... We're risking certain death if we go through here without preparation, you do realize that?"

"No kidding," remarked Samuel.

"Your friend is correct," confirmed Akhenaton. "Records show that ancient members of my order went out of their way to protect the sites under our care. They would build redundant treasure rooms designed to tempt the greedy, false doors to fool the unwary. Any thieves wishing to steal our secrets and sell them on would meet a grisly end in one of our traps."

"But you don't have any records of whether this room is a fake or not?" asked Samuel.

"I already told you, no." Akhenaton shook his head. "Any maps of the network were destroyed to preserve the security of the site. Although there would have been guards posted here originally who knew the tunnel system inside and out, as the caves faded into obscurity, we relied on the automated security systems to protect this place while we focused on more urgent matters. There is no one left alive who can say for certain whether this door is real or not."

"We don't have much of a choice but to move forward," Samuel decided. "We've been walking forever and I don't know about you, but I don't fancy explaining to Pin that we didn't go through a door because we were scared. He's not exactly the sympathetic type. If we go back, we'll be heading straight into a trap."

"If the room beyond this door doesn't have an exit, we'll be just as stuck," Basile pointed out.

"So our choices are limited then," observed Samuel. "All right. Let's look at what we do know about this door. Maybe it will help you disarm any traps, Basile."

"Okay," agreed Basile.

"Let's start with the carving," Samuel began. "We already know that St. Augustine was associated with this site and there are certain symbols that would support the theory that this is an engraving of him, such as the book in his hands and the hops decorating his headdress, images associated with the saint. Among other things, he's the patron saint of brewers because he liked to party before he converted and went on to become one of the greatest saints ever to have lived. He was alive during the early years of the Greek Ptolemaic period, so it is possible that he visited this site as Akhenaton described and had such an impact on the builders of this tomb that they decided to immortalize him here."

"But wouldn't that mean that he'd have to have come here after the entry room was constructed?" asked Basile. "I mean, if they wanted to honor him, why not do so earlier in the site? Why not put a statue of him in the entry room with the sarcophagi or include him in the mosaics in the tunnels where he would be seen by any visitors, not hide him all the way down here?"

"I'm not sure." Samuel frowned. "Akhenaton, do you have any ideas?"

"According to the lore of my order, when Egypt was defeated by Alexander the Great, a small cult of Seshat continued to meet in secret to study the subconscious, and astrology, keeping records of their dreams to analyze them in accordance with what they knew of the heavens. Over time, they noticed certain oddities within their dreams, oddities that allowed them to penetrate the mysteries and learn the secrets of the universe. I was told that these secrets were only ever taught to one outsider, which was St. Augustine, chosen because of his pious and enlightened nature. He was researching déjà vu and the deathless soul theory, so one presumes that whatever they told him, it was related to that. Since my order prefers to keep its secrets well-hidden, it's no surprise that St. Augustine's carving was created in such an out of the way place."

"How large is your order exactly?" Samuel asked.

"I cannot say," Akhenaton replied. "As a secret society, our numbers are not common knowledge. However, my cell alone has perhaps four hundred members, divided into several dozen smaller families."

Basile let out a long, low whistle. "Four hundred in one cell? That's impressive."

"Indeed." Akhenaton approached the door and shone his torch over the inscription carved above the saint's head. "Samuel, look at this. Am I right in thinking that these hieroglyphs describe a riddle of some kind?"

Samuel stepped closer, examining the door where Akhenaton indicated. "It could be," he nodded.

"And over here," Akhenaton continued. "These slats seem to be made out of a different material to the rest of the wall. I'm wondering whether you could possibly carve hieroglyphs into them, the answers to the riddle."

"And open the door without triggering the trap," Basile finished triumphantly. "Looks like this is your area of expertise Samuel, not mine. You're a world leader in Egyptology."

"But this was set up by Akhenaton's order," Samuel countered. "Surely he's the best person to answer the questions?"

Akhenaton shook his head. "I might be well versed in the legends of my order, but these questions are beyond my understandings. They seem to reference aspects of ancient Egyptian culture that I know nothing about. I think this is your problem to solve, Samuel, almost as though it were written for you."

"All right." Samuel nodded. "Shine the light so that I can translate the inscriptions and we'll see if between us we can open the door."

Akhenaton held the torch steady as Samuel translated the first question.

"*The First of the Twenty-First,*" he read.

"Twenty-first what?" asked Basile. "Century? Amendment?"

"You need to think Egyptian, remember?" Samuel reminded him. "The most plausible answer would be that this is talking about the 21st Dynasty."

"I told you this was your wheelhouse," beamed Basile. "I wouldn't ever have thought of that. So if it's referencing the dynasty, what would be the first?"

"The first Emperor," Samuel guessed. "His name was Hedjkheperre Setepenre Smendes."

"You're carving that," remarked Basile, handing Samuel a Swiss army knife to use.

"Be careful that you only carve on the relevant slat," advised Akhenaton as Samuel steadied himself, ready to write out the Emperor's name.

"My ancient Egyptian handwriting isn't the best," he said, as he began to carefully cut into the wood. "Hopefully it's good enough to pass muster."

"Well, we're not dead yet," remarked Basile, as Samuel finished the first answer. "It can't be that bad. What's the next clue?"

"The Eternal House," Samuel read. "That one's easy. It can only be 'mastaba.' It's a mud-brick tomb, the name of which translates to 'house for eternity.'"

He began to carve into the next space, as Basile laughed. "These are all so easy," he observed. "At this rate, we'll be through in no time. I thought the ancients wanted to make it difficult to get through this door?"

"You spoke too soon," warned Samuel. "The next clue has me stumped. All it says is 2014a."

The three men looked at each other blankly.

"What on earth could that mean?" asked Basile. "If it had an AD at the end of it, that would suggest that it's talking about the year 2014, but if that were the case, it would make no sense."

"But..." Samuel's mind raced as he an idea began to fall into place. "In 2014 BC, the pharaoh was Mentuhotep II and he featured prominently in the mosaics earlier. So it could in theory be referring to him."

"How would that work?" frowned Basile. "They didn't have any sense of AD or BC back then, so they wouldn't have used the Gregorian calendar for this puzzle. I think you're barking up the wrong tree."

"I agree, it doesn't make any sense." Samuel took a matchbox-sized device from his pocket. "This is a carbon dating device. Although it isn't as accurate as the more sophisticated machines back at the camp, it should give us a sense of when this door was constructed and whether we're on the right track."

He knelt down and took a scraping from the door in an inconspicuous section at the bottom. He placed the rock fragments into a little door in the top of the device, which he then snapped shut. He swiped a command on one of the unit's faces.

"It'll just take a few moments to work its magic," he told the other two, "and then we'll know when the door was built to within a hundred years or so."

"Assuming the number does refer to 2014 BC, what would the 'a' mean?" asked Basile. "And how on earth could they possibly know about the change in the calendar centuries before it happened? I still think we're going down a dead end with this one."

Akhenaton sighed. "It's not that unbelievable," he told them. "If we're standing outside the correct treasure chamber, then my order believes that inside this room lies some kind of mechanism that allows individuals to access dreams and accurately foresee the future. Perhaps they used a modern date as a sign to tell us that they knew what was coming."

"*C'est absurde,*" Basile huffed. "That's preposterous. In fact, I'd go so far as to say that that's the most ridiculous thing I've ever heard. How can you seriously think that ancient Egyptians wrote a riddle based on the modern calendar?"

"I would never have considered it if Samuel hadn't brought up the potential confusion between BC and AD," replied Akhenaton. "But the more I think about it, the more it makes sense."

"And... we have a winner!" Samuel announced, looking at the readout on the device. "According to this, the door was built sometime around 600 BC. So whatever the answer to the riddle is, the question was definitely carved on this door long before the Gregorian calendar came in."

"Which means that it can't have anything to do with the date, so we're back to square one," sighed Basile.

"Or..." Akhenaton paced up and down as he gathered his thoughts. "Maybe it has everything to do with the date. Think about it. As Samuel pointed out, we've seen carvings of Mentuhotep II, who ruled in 2014 BC. That could be a clue that we're talking about a leader, but the leader in 2014 AD, which would be Abel Fattah el-Sisi."

"*Tu es fâché!*" Basile threw up his arms in frustration. "You're mad! You can't possibly think that that's the right answer."

Samuel and Akhenaton exchanged excited glances. "What's the worst that can happen?" asked Samuel as he turned to the door and started to carve.

"We all die horrible, painful deaths?" replied Basile, stepping out of the way of the door, just in case.

"Abdel... Fattah... el-Sisi..."

Samuel held his breath as he finished the inscription, stepping back and wincing as he braced himself for deadly missiles to come flying out of the holes in the door.

CLICK!

The door slowly swung open, a warm, bright light flooding out into the dark corridor. The three men crowded forward, putting their arms up to shield their eyes from the sudden brilliance, desperate to see what was inside the chamber.

"*Mon dieu*," Basile breathed.

FORTY-TWO

The colors created by the setting sun's rays were breathtakingly beautiful, but no one on the helicopter noticed, too caught up in their thoughts to care.

"Right. I'm taking a break," Josh announced, touching the console to activate the autopilot. "Have you had any joy in getting hold of Samuel, Shafira?"

"I've been trying ever since we took off, but I haven't been able to get through," Shafira replied, pressing the button on the comms device to send a message yet again. "What if Samuel and Basile have been taken prisoner by the Bruard and they've confiscated their comms gear?"

"Can your radio send signals deep underground?" asked Waleed. "Before you go assuming the worst, isn't it more likely that the cave they are exploring goes far below the surface and they're simply out of range?"

"He's got a point," Josh agreed. "That radio doesn't have the capacity to penetrate thick layers of rock. Most likely Samuel's waxing lyrical over some vase he's dug up and isn't anywhere near his radio. Anyway, we'll be there within an hour, so I'm going to get some rest, just in case we're about to walk into a nest of vipers."

"Wouldn't it make more sense to go back to Cairo and get back up from the Ministry or even the military?" Waleed asked. "They'd want to know if there are Bruard agents here. Shouldn't we be going towards the city rather than away from it?"

Josh looked at Shafira pointedly. "I've been asking the same question."

Shafira blushed. "I did try to get help," she pointed out. "The police wouldn't listen to me, especially when the man I saw murdered showed up at work, fit and well. We don't have the time it would take to persuade them that the Bruard are behind all this, especially since I don't have any proof. Director Haisam did too good a job of discrediting me for me to be able to rely on the authorities. Besides, I have no idea who else is working with him. He mentioned having a friend in the police force. What if the person I go to for help is another Bruard agent? No, we have to warn Samuel and get real evidence of what's going on. Then we can go back to Cairo for support."

"That makes sense." Waleed nodded slowly. "However, why is it that I get the feeling that there's another motive behind this? Correct me if I'm wrong, but aren't you a merely an office clerk? Are you sure you aren't simply using this as an excuse to get some excitement in your life?"

"I love my job!" Shafira protested.

"Shafira?" Josh raised an eyebrow.

"Alright, maybe not love," Shafira amended. "But I do enjoy my work. It's very rewarding. Even if they do pile too much on me."

"But how many times have I heard you complain that you want to be more hands on?" Josh reminded her. "How many times have you said that Yusuf has all the fun while you have to be the good girl so as not to disappoint your parents? Are you sure that Waleed doesn't have a point?"

"Fine! I want more adventure in my life." Shafira threw up her hands in exasperation. "Is that so bad?"

"It is if you're leading us into a deadly trap just because you're sick of paperwork," Josh huffed. "Sheesh, Shafira. You're getting to be as selfish as your brother." He shook his head.

"I'm sorry, Josh." Tears pricked at Shafira's eyes, but she fought to hold them back, not wanting to appear weak. "But I promise you, this isn't all about me. I'm worried about Samuel McCarthy. He's your friend. Don't you want to make sure he's safe?"

"Of course I do."

"Then focus on that. It will all turn out fine in the end, I promise."

Waleed laughed bitterly. "Much as I appreciate the touching sentimentality, you should never make promises you can't keep, my friend. When it comes to the Bruard, things *never* turn out fine."

"What do you mean?" Josh asked.

Waleed shrugged evasively. "Just what I've read in the papers. Everyone knows that the Bruard are evil."

Josh studied him, slowly shaking his head. "I don't think so. You've dealt with them, haven't you?"

"I wouldn't exactly say dealt with," Waleed admitted. "I've certainly never been a member of the organization."

"So what is your experience with the Bruard?" Shafira pressed.

Waleed sighed. "I must stress that I'm not proud of my behavior. In my defense, I was desperate for money at the time, having gotten myself into trouble with some rather unsavory characters."

"Why am I seeing a pattern here?" Josh muttered.

"I am not a bad man," Waleed began. "But I am what you might call an opportunist. I thought I could get away with it, but..."

"Wait a minute," Josh interrupted. "Are you telling me that you attempted to steal from the Bruard? You must have balls of steel!"

"'Steal' is such an ugly word," smiled Waleed. "I wouldn't go quite that far. Let's just say that I was a little creative with the truth in an attempt to perform a public service and strike a blow against the Bruard."

"Public service, my ass!" snorted Josh. "Don't try and pretend that whatever little scam you had going on was altruistic."

Waleed shrugged non-committedly. "I managed to deceive them for a week before they realized that the 'secrets' I was selling to them were nothing but a product of my imagination. I had thought that I'd have more time before they checked their veracity, but unfortunately for me, they were more efficient than I expected. I managed to get away before they questioned me, but I knew that it was only a matter of time before they caught up with me."

"What happened?" asked Shafira.

"I wish I had some impressive scars to show you," smiled Waleed sadly. "I wish that I could tell you that they had taken their pound of flesh before setting me free, but what happened was far, far worse. They kidnapped my wife and daughter and told me that I had a choice: surrender myself to face their justice or receive a video of their deaths. I was assured that they would not die quickly or easily."

"Your poor family!" gasped Shafira. "That must have been terrifying. Have they... recovered?"

Waleed paused, choosing his words carefully, his gaze fixed on the desert below. "It's hard to say if you can ever really fully recover from what they went through." Shafira patted his arm to show her support. Josh narrowed his eyes, subtly shaking his head, a movement Waleed noted.

"I suppose none of us would ever know what we would do in such a situation," Josh remarked. "I'd like to think I'd put my family first, but I can only imagine what Bruard justice would be like."

FORTY-THREE

Basile gazed around him, open-mouthed, as Samuel slowly walked along the bookshelves lining the walls, examining the manuscripts as he tried to take it all in. Akhenaton picked up a vase as large as a wastebasket, its gold trim gleaming, carefully turning it round to see the pattern painted across the middle, a sleeping figure curled around the base, their dreams morphing into war.

The room was illuminated by an unseen source, the light reflecting off the gold and gems edging the shelves to give the illusion that they were bathed in sunshine mixed with an infinite kaleidoscope on tiny rainbows from the prism-like clear jewels. Seshat and Moneta gazed benevolently down on them, two larger than life statues mounted on either side of the room.

"Good God!" Samuel breathed, his eyes wide with wonder. "This is beyond a king's ransom... and the archaeological value... it's inestimable."

"*Oui*. Have you seen these friezes, Samuel?" Basile asked, pointing to three steps leading up to a dais surrounded by paintings. "Do you recognize the events depicted in them?"

Samuel crossed to stand by his friend, frowning at what he saw.

"That's weird," he remarked. "There's the construction of the pyramids. That seems to be an image of Tutankhamun. And that's Cleopatra."

"What's weird about that?" Basile shrugged. "That all sounds like basic Egyptian history."

"That's not the strange part," Samuel explained. "Look over there. Does that man look familiar to you?"

Basile squinted at the picture Samuel was pointing at. A man with dark hair and a neat, black moustache was standing in front of a large army, their arms raised in salute to him. "No!" he gasped. "That can't be Hitler. That *can't* be Hitler."

"Even the style is different to traditional Egyptian iconography," said Samuel. "It's as though they came forward in time, saw the way that we portrayed people, and used it to represent Hitler."

"But how could they possibly have known?" Basile moved forward to the picture, still doubting his eyes.

"Exactly." Samuel stood by his friend, as they marveled at images of planes, the frightening mushroom cloud over Hiroshima, and Napoleon shooting at the sphinx.

"Perhaps someone came in here over the centuries and added the images as a record of what's been happening?" Basile suggested.

"That's easily tested. We can do some preliminary carbon dating and see how old the paint is. It'll mean taking a small sample from the image, though."

"No need," Akhenaton broke in. "If anyone had been in these catacombs, my order would know about it. Nobody's been here for centuries."

Basile and Akhenaton began to discuss possible explanations for the paintings, but Samuel was distracted when he caught sight of a pillar towards the back of the room. Resting on top of it was headgear unlike any he'd ever seen before. Shaped like a small, hemispherical papal cap, it had blue and gold stripes across it in the style of Pharaonic headdresses. As he drew closer, he noticed Greek letters inscribed around the top of the pillar.

"Come and have a look at this, Basile," he beckoned. "I've never seen anything like it."

The engineer hurried over to join him.

"See that Greek lettering?" Samuel asked. "Yet another mystery to add to the pile we have to solve."

"I knew that the Greek and Egyptians were friendly, but I had no idea they were close before the Roman conquest," Basile remarked. "So far, everything has been either Egyptian or Roman. Why is there Greek lettering here of all places?"

"There must be an explanation for it somewhere in this room." He knelt down next to the pillar to get a closer look, admiring the intricate patterns of gems set into the stonework. Meanwhile, Samuel picked up a scroll lying on a shelf near the pillar. He untied the cord wrapped around it, and opened the parchment.

"*Last night's dream was the most disturbing so far,*" he translated from the ancient Egyptian. "*I saw the chamber, left unattended for centuries, broken open by three who proved themselves worthy. They were fascinated by the paintings, distracted by the cap, determined to rescue our sacred knowledge from the tormentors...*"

Samuel looked up. "Akhenaton, have you seen this? Who do you suppose would be meant by the tormentors? The Bruard? Akhenaton, no!"

He rushed forward, just in time to grab hold of Akhenaton's arm as he raised his scimitar to destroy the headdress.

"What are you doing?" Samuel cried. "That's a priceless artifact."

"You are right," Akhenaton agreed. "This is St. Augustine's secret. It is possibly the most powerful and important relic on the planet, which is why it must be destroyed so that the Bruard can never use it. The world has survived just fine without it for the past few centuries. We may not survive if the Bruard get hold of it."

"What do you mean by St. Augustine's secret?" asked Samuel. "It's just a headdress. What threat could it possibly pose?"

"I do not know the exact details," came the reply, "but there is a passage in one of our sacred texts that states 'St. Augustine provided the key and a cap was formed that can alter minds so the implausible seems plausible and lies become fact.'"

"What does that mean?" Samuel frowned. "Is it some sort of mind control device?"

"Something like that," Akhenaton confirmed. "I must confess that I do not fully understand the extent of its powers, but I know that it has the ability to shape reality. That much is fact. Surely you can appreciate how dangerous that would be if the Bruard were to take possession of it? We must destroy it. It's the only way to save the world from them. "

He lifted up his sword again, but Samuel pushed him away from the pillar.

"I'm sorry, Akhenaton. I can't let you do that. We'll find a way to keep the headdress away from the Bruard. I can't stand back and watch you destroy it."

"Get out of my way," ordered Akhenaton. "I don't want to hurt you, but I've sworn an oath to my order and I *will* protect St. Augustine's secret. The only way is to destroy it."

Seeing the resolve on Akhenaton's face, Samuel hurled himself at the other man, trying to wrench the sword out of his grasp. The two men grappled, but Samuel was no match for the highly trained guard. Adrenaline coursed through him as he fought to save the relic, lending him extra strength, and he had almost managed to take the scimitar when Akhenaton made a sudden, swift movement, knocking Samuel's feet out from under him.

"Stay down," Akhenaton advised. "You must not interfere in-"

THUNK!

"Sorry," Basile said, as he hit Akhenaton over the head with a golden scepter he'd found on a nearby shelf. Akhenaton fell to the ground unconscious, as Basile stepped over his prone body and went to help Samuel up.

"Thanks, Basile," said Samuel. "If you hadn't have intervened, who knows what Akhenaton would have done? I know that he thinks he's acting on behalf of his order, but whatever they believe is irrelevant. We need to study everything in this room, unravel St. Augustine's secret and share it with the world."

"I knew I could trust you to do the right thing," came a malevolent voice from the door. Samuel whirled round to see Pin, framed by the blackness of the passage beyond, clapping sarcastically. "Although you're mistaken about one thing," the Bruard agent continued. "The artifacts here do not belong to the world. They are the property of the Bruard, mine to retrieve. My masters will be extremely pleased with me when I return with St. Augustine's secret."

"I won't let you," growled Samuel, lunging for Akhenaton's sword.

"Uh-uh-uh." Pin tutted and cocked his gun. "I really don't think you want to do anything stupid, not when you've come so far. Step away from the sword Mr. McCarthy, if you want to live."

Gord came to stand next to his boss. "Why haven't you shot them already?" he demanded. "We don't want to leave any loose ends."

"I gave my word to these two gentlemen that I would not shoot them unless absolutely necessary," Pin replied. "I will not dishonor the Bruard by telling falsehoods. Of course, that doesn't mean that there aren't other ways of dealing with those who are surplus to requirement. Now secure the headdress so we can get out of this hellhole."

Gord hurried to collect the headdress, while Pin kept his gun trained on Samuel and Basile.

"What do you possibly hope to gain by this?" asked Samuel. "There are plenty of more valuable artifacts around. If you want money, why not take gems or gold? This room is full of treasure. It's got to be worth half a billion at least. I can't imagine that you'll get much for that headdress. No one will believe that it's anything other than a funny looking hat."

"To be fair, my original plan had been to strip this tomb of everything and sell it on the black market to fill the Bruard's coffers. While I may yet return to do that, from what your unconscious friend was saying, this headdress is all we need. If it really can control weak minds, it will allow the Bruard dynasty to rule the world, as is our destiny and all without unnecessary bloodshed. People will be begging us to rule them."

"You'd better hope that that headdress can reach out to every mind on the planet, because only worldwide brainwashing could achieve that," remarked Samuel.

"Not quite, but close enough."

As Gord left with the headdress tucked under his arm, Pin gestured with his gun for Samuel and Basile to stand at the back of the room, furthest from the door.

"Pleasant as our conversation has been, the time has come for me to say *adieu* to you both," Pin told them.

"I swear to you, Pin, as a man of archaeology, I'll follow you to the ends of the earth if need be to recover St. Augustine's secret," Samuel warned.

"I have no doubt that you would," chuckled Pin, "but there's one small problem. You'll have to find a way out of here first. This chamber is now your *eternal* chamber. Set the explosives!"

Pin retreated, keeping his gun trained on Samuel and Basile, as his men quickly slapped bowl-sized explosive charges around the stone door frame. They pushed a button in the center of each, beginning the countdown.

"Farewell, McCarthy," called Pin. "See you in another lifetime!"

Pin and his men beat a hasty retreat. Samuel and Basile looked at each other, their faces masks of panic, as they turned and ran away from the door. The blast knocked them to the ground, as the rock face around the entrance crumbled. Golden artifacts and shards of smashed vases rained down on the pair from shelves high above.

When the dust settled, the only entrance was buried beneath a mountain of rubble.

FORTY-FOUR

Pin ran his hands over the headdress, trembling with excitement. "Such a simple thing, yet so important. This will change the world for the better."

"It doesn't look like it could change the world," Gord remarked.

"To the casual observer, it wouldn't," Pin informed him. "But, trust me. This is what we've been looking for, the final piece in the puzzle that will make all our dreams come true. Now, we need to get back to the aircraft as quickly as possible. The sooner I can present this to the Bruard, the sooner I will receive the recognition I so justly deserve."

Pin and his men hurried through the catacombs, their progress much faster now they knew where they were going and how to avoid the traps. At last, they reached the waiting craft. Its outboard cargo pods had been filled by the soldiers, with the contents of the crates from the desert striders.

Pin looked at Gord quizzically.

"Waste not, want not," the guard shrugged. "While I'm sure your hat is very valuable, I thought it best if we took things with a more obvious worth, just in case."

"Yes, well, I want to get out of this desert and away from the miscreants I've been forced to deal with. Samuel McCarthy may be an educated peasant, but he is still a peasant nevertheless. It's a pity, really. He could have been so useful to the Bruard had he only been willing to see the light. Now he will rot away in that cave, soon to be forgotten."

"Fetch my soap," he ordered the nearest soldier. Immediately, he put down the crate he was carrying and rushed to retrieve Pin's anti-bac soap. Pin held his hands out so that the soldier could pour soap liberally all over them, visibly relaxing as he wiped away any trace of contamination from interactions with non-Bruard.

The sound of a helicopter high overhead caught Pin's attention. He looked up to see the craft, just before it disappeared from view.

"Do you want me to send a team to see if the helicopter is landing anywhere nearby?" Gord offered.

"No need." Pin shook his head. "The cloaking field will have concealed our position. They'll be long gone before we head out. Keep your focus on getting St. Augustine's secret to its rightful home."

"I still don't get it," Gord told him. "How can something that only affects minds one at a time be of any help? Even if that headdress does everything it's supposed to do, it's still not going to be much use when it comes to controlling billions of people."

"I can see how you might think that we've gone to a lot of trouble for nothing," Pin agreed, "but I have no doubt that there will be a way to enhance the relic's abilities, expanding its control over déjà vu and memory. It might seem like a long shot to you, but we took a big risk in stealing this device and I'm going to make sure it was worth all our while."

"So what exactly is the secret to this device?" asked Gord. "It just looks like a hat to me."

"I'm not entirely sure," Pin confessed. "But, as you say, it's just a hat and it was designed by backward people of long ago. It won't be difficult to decipher."

"So you're going to take it straight to Korea to present to the Bruard leaders?"

"Not yet," Pin said. "I want to figure out how to activate the secret to confirm that it was worth all the trouble we've gone to. This headdress has cost me a cover identity, not to mention time and resources. Right now, I'll take it to my living quarters to experiment with it." He raised his voice to address the troops. "Wrap it up! We're leaving. Now!"

He shuddered as one of the soldiers brushed past him. Pin was in desperate need of a bath to purify himself after so long surrounded by the unclean.

Soldiers fired shots into the engines of the desert striders, rendering them unusable in case Samuel managed to break free, before piling into the VTOL. Its engines whined to life, and it rose up out of a sandstorm of its own making, leaving Samuel and Basile to rot in the catacombs.

FORTY-FIVE

Akhenaton lay comatose in the middle of the floor as Basile frantically rushed around the room, ignoring archaeological protocol as he dug through scrolls and other artifacts in search of a way out. By contrast, Samuel sat cross legged in the middle of the room, calmly reading through the pile of scrolls surrounding him.

"*Aidez moi*, Samuel," urged Basile. "Help me and stop wasting time! Reading isn't going to get us out of this place. There must be another exit in this room. We have to find it."

"*Au contraire*, my hot headed friend," smiled Samuel. "Reading is exactly how we're going to get out of here."

"What do you mean?"

"Listen to this." He picked up a scroll and started reading. "*The traitor who is not quite a traitor approached the leader with a small metal rod in hand. He meant to smite the leader, but he underestimated the man's power. Soon, the hunter was the prey, in a reversal of fortune, as it has ever been through the ages. Yet, the traitor learned that true victory does not come from the physical realm. His head contained information that he attempted to use to barter for his free-*

dom. *The leader faced a terrible dilemma, so he left the traitor under guard while he determined the best way forward.*"

"I don't understand." Basile frowned. "Reminds me of a Biblical parable. What does it mean?"

"Don't you see?" said Samuel excitedly. "That's a perfect description of what happened with Waleed."

"It's a coincidence." Basile's voice wavered.

"I don't think so," Samuel said. "Think about it. Remember what Akhenaton told us about his order and their beliefs? Then think about what Pin said about using the headdress to control the world. I think St. Augustine's secret is the ability to predict the future or tap into future knowledge somehow. Who knows? Maybe it even influences the future, somehow allowing the wearer to come up with visions like this one and write it to change what will happen. They say that the simple act of observation changes that which is being watched. Perhaps in seeing what's supposed to happen, the device actually enables you to change it. I haven't yet figured out the details, but the more I read, the more it makes sense."

"None of this makes sense," Basile sighed, temporarily giving up his search for an escape and flopping to the ground next to Samuel. "How could a headdress do any of that?"

"I don't know the science behind it," Samuel confessed. "Without the headdress, I don't think I'd be able to figure it out. But I do think it has something to do with dreams. Maybe the dream state enables some form of time travel?"

"So the headdress controls dreams?" theorized Basile.

"That's one possibility," Samuel agreed. "I'm even wondering if the headdress can take that control a step further to reprogram thoughts. It could be a way to force people to your way of thinking against their will, which would be just the kind of thing the Bruard would want. It'd explain why they're so desperate to get their hands on it. At the same time, I can't imagine that a government would care that much about an object that could only affect one person at a time."

"Oh, Samuel. So close and yet so far."

Samuel and Basile whirled round as Akhenaton groaned, clutching his head as he pulled himself up to a seated position.

"You might as well tell us everything you know," Samuel said, indicating the blocked exit. "We're going to be spending a lot of time together."

"Very well," sighed Akhenaton. "According to my order, St. Augustine's secret is a conduit that allows the mind to heighten its memory abilities, allowing it to influence other people's memories. In effect, it proves Pythagoras' deathless soul theory by enabling a user to temporarily leave their mind and enter the minds of others. Ordinarily, this could only be done to one person at a time, but we believe that someone 'of the blood' is attuned to the artifact, which could potentially allow them to use it on a wider scale. I'm sure you don't need me to tell you how dangerous that would be if the Bruard figure out how to use it."

"Of the blood?" Basile frowned. "What do you mean? An ancestor?"

"That is the most likely translation," Akhenaton confirmed. "However, we have been unsuccessful in determining whether the blood in question refers to St. Augustine's bloodline, the bloodline of one of the artisans involved in building the catacombs, those constructing the device, or even the gods themselves."

"Gods?" scoffed Basile.

"All our Pharaohs were gods." Akhenaton glared at him. "Since we have lost the device, we should consider tracing those of the blood, so we can forestall its widespread use."

"It'll be like looking for a needle in a haystack," Samuel pointed out. "Given how many generations have been born since the creation of St. Augustine's secret, there could be millions of people who can trace their ancestry to whoever your order is referring to. The Bruard will stop at nothing to find someone who can utilize the device to its full potential." Samuel's heart dropped. "I am so sorry, Akhenaton.

You were right. We should have destroyed it rather than let Pin take it. If the Bruard manage to master its power, it really could be the end of the world."

"You can't seriously believe that all this superstitious nonsense is true?" exclaimed Basile. "I thought better of you, Samuel. I thought you were a man of science."

"It doesn't matter what I believe," Samuel pointed out. "Pin clearly thought it was true. It was important enough for him to bury us rather than risk losing the device."

"Thanks for reminding me," moped Basile. "There's no way out. We can wax philosophical for as long as you like. It won't get us out of here."

"Wait a moment..." Samuel pawed through the scrolls, looking for one he'd read earlier. "Listen to this. *In order to receive words from angels, a specific ritual needs to be carried out. The petitioner must first prepare himself for communication with the metal rod that can increase the power of the mind, allowing the petitioner to give and speak thought over distance.*"

"This is nonsense," Basile sneered, as Samuel skimmed through the rest of the text. "We should be looking for a way out, dig our way out if need be. I'm sure that if I had enough time, I could find a way to tunnel through the rock fall." He started to move towards the door, but Samuel told him to stop.

"Think about it," he said. "I'm wearing the metal rod." Samuel tapped at his Bluetooth V. "It isn't as crazy as it sounds. I reckon that if I perform the ritual, it might show us a way out of here." He held up a hand to stop Basile interrupting. "It was a ritual that opened up the cave in the first place, remember? The ritual detailed in this scroll is very straightforward. What harm could it do to try? If it doesn't work, then we can attempt to dig our way out, okay?"

Basile paused for a moment. "Okay," he finally agreed.

Samuel stood up, scroll in hand. "All right. It says that I need to stand under Moneta's gaze." He went to take up position beneath the statue of Moneta on one side of the room. "First I must walk away, signifying that I am unafraid of my thoughts and am willing to share them." He moved forward three paces. "Next I must turn and face the dais and performance obeisance on each of the three steps." Awkwardly, he moved from step to step, bowing as he did so. "Now follow the stars." He frowned. "What does that mean? We can't see the sky in here."

"There." Akhenaton pointed to one of the paintings depicting an airplane. "There are stars in that picture. The Big Dipper. Follow the direction it's facing."

Samuel did as Akhenaton suggested, coming to a stop in front of the wall.

"Now what?" he asked, as nothing happened.

"I told you this was a waste of time," Basile grumbled.

Suddenly a burst of static came through Samuel's Bluetooth. "Samuel McCarthy? Are you there? Come in, Samuel McCarthy." Shafira's voice came through the earpiece.

"This is Samuel," he whooped in reply. "And you must be an angel!"

"What do you mean?" asked Shafira.

"Never mind," Samuel laughed. "Let's just say that I'm very pleased to hear from you."

"Where are you?"

"We're trapped underground. We faced off with some bad guys, and they blew up the entrance to the chamber we're in. I don't think we're very deep below the earth. We didn't have to go down any major slopes to reach this point."

"Are the bad guys still around? I'm guessing you don't know from in there..."

"We don't, but that's not the immediate problem. It's a largish chamber, but the air in here is finite."

"Are you injured?"

"Thankfully, no. We got off lightly that way. If you can track my location from my signal, you should find we're no more than fifty yards beneath the earth. There may be some way to get us out."

"We'll do whatever we can," Shafira promised.

"Thank you–I'm sorry. I don't know your name."

"I'm Shafira Khouri," came the reply. "From the Ministry of State for Antiquities."

"Well, Shafira, today you're my guardian angel."

FORTY-SIX

Shafira could barely contain her excitement, as she hung up the comms device.

"I've made contact with McCarthy," she announced, as Josh swung round, looking for a place to land that was out of sight of Pin and his men. "He's alive and he's somewhere near the surface. He's going to stay where he is so we can track him using our equipment. Although from what he told me, he doesn't have much choice: he's trapped in a cave."

"Do you think that has anything to do with the soldiers we saw gathering around the cave entrance?" asked Waleed.

"Most likely," Shafira agreed. "Thank goodness Josh knew where the cloaking device ended. We'd never have known they were there if he hadn't flown low enough to get inside its range. Do you think they spotted us?"

"Yes," Josh confirmed. "That's the downside with getting close enough to penetrate the camouflage."

"If they did, they don't seem to care," Waleed told them. "Look. They're leaving."

Josh and Shafira looked out in the direction Waleed was facing.

The VTOL began to rise vertically on a column of engine thrust, and then gain forward speed, away from the helicopter.

"Good," Shafira nodded. "Josh, are you any good with the onboard tracking equipment? We'll need to trace Samuel's signal if we're going to dig them out."

"Not my department." Josh shook his head. "I can use a radio and repair one if it's not too far gone, but tracking was always my passenger's department. I wasn't expecting this to be a rescue mission."

"Don't worry, my friends," Waleed broke in. "Thanks to a checkered career, I have a particular set of skills..."

Josh and Shafira rolled their eyes at each other.

"No, no," Waleed assured them. "There've been occasion where I've needed to splice through signals in order to obtain vital information. I am sure that I can find Samuel."

"Is there anything you can't do, Waleed?" asked Shafira.

"Not a lot," he grinned. "I've never stayed in jail for more than a week at a time, but I always learned a lot with every visit."

The rolling desert sands came up to meet the helicopter, as Josh brought them in to land. Once the swirling sand from the rotor wash began to fall back to earth, Josh climbed out and went to retrieve the tracking equipment from an external storage locker toward the rear of the aircraft.

"Anything I can do to help?" Josh asked as he brought the equipment over to Waleed.

"Yes," came the reply. "You can take this handset and walk in that direction." He pointed towards the cave entrance. "When I give the word, switch it on. I'll send a signal to your device and Samuel's. I should be able to triangulate the responses to tell us where he is, give or take a couple hundred feet."

Josh did as he was told, heading towards the cave opening.

"Turn it on," called Waleed.

Josh twisted the knob on the top of the handset, which crackled until Waleed sent out a high frequency signal.

"All right. Move over there," Waleed instructed, waving to the west.

Josh strode in that direction, as Waleed sent out another signal.

"That way now," Waleed ordered, making Josh move again.

"I've got him!" Waleed crowed. "He's here." He walked around the hillside, coming to a halt at a nondescript slope. "He was right. He's not too far below ground. The only problem is that I'm not sure if we can get to him. So near and yet so far."

"Samuel, can you hear me?" Shafira spoke into her comms device.

"Loud and clear," came the reply.

"We've pinpointed your location," she told him. "We're going to mark the site, and then figure out a way to get you out. Don't go anywhere!"

"Not much chance of that," laughed Samuel. "We're well and truly trapped. We haven't got any supplies, and I can't remember the last time I had a drink. Much as it goes against my archaeologist's soul to risk the artifacts and gems down here, I'd much rather you blew a hole in the hillside and dropped down a ladder."

"Samuel, we're going to do our best to save you *and* the relics. Stay online. We need to figure out how we're going to get to you. We'll be with you soon, I promise."

"Only precise drilling will preserve whatever's left down here, and there isn't time to get that kind of gear out here," Samuel said.

Shafira turned to Josh and Waleed. "Any ideas about how to blast through a mountain?"

"What about if we used some of the helicopter fuel?" suggested Waleed. "We can use that to create an explosion."

Josh shook his head. "It won't be powerful enough. Besides, we haven't got much fuel to spare. You really thought kerosene can get through fifty yards of rock? I thought you had the skills of a special ops agent!"

"Well…" Waleed mumbled, embarrassed.

The three of them thought for a moment, at a loss for what to do.

"Hang on." Josh snapped his fingers. "You mentioned an explosion."

"That's right," Shafira nodded.

"Which means that whoever trapped Samuel must have used explosives. Maybe they've left some behind and we can use them to free McCarthy. It's got to be worth a try, right?"

FORTY-SEVEN

Samuel stood in the position he'd been directed to by the angel ritual, terrified to move an inch in case he lost his signal again, yet unable to wipe the grin off his face.

"The cavalry are coming?" asked Basile.

"Looks that way," Samuel confirmed. "Though an estimated fifty yards of rock isn't an insignificant barrier."

"So we just twiddle our thumbs while we wait and hope there's enough air in this cavern to keep us alive?" Basile sighed. "I think next time you have a top secret mission, I'll pass."

"According to my order, a man should always follow his duty, even if it leads him into danger," Akhenaton informed him.

"Your order seems to have a lot to say for itself," Basile observed. "Yet I've never heard about it. I would have thought I would at least have heard rumors of something so wise and powerful. Are you sure you're not just making up stories?"

"Oh, my order is very real," Akhenaton assured him. "As are our legends."

"How can you be so sure? Why don't you tell us more about it so we can all judge for ourselves?" Basile prompted.

"I don't think so," Akhenaton refused. "I told you. I am only allowed to reveal the existence of my order to immediate family. You are certainly not that. I have told you everything you need to know. I cannot, *will not* tell you anymore."

"Come on, Akhenaton," Basile protested. "We've bled together, for Christ's sake. That should mean something."

"I'm sure it meant a lot when you hit me over the head with a scepter," sneered Akhenaton. "Is that really the action of a friend?"

"What was I supposed to do?" asked Basile. "You were about to-"

"Cut it out, you two," barked Samuel. "Shafira's trying to tell me something."

"Samuel? Are you there?" Her voice crackled over the comms.

"Still here, Shafira. We're not going anywhere without you."

"We've found some explosives near the cave entrance," she told him. "But, there's not very much. We're going to need the support of an expert to make sure we don't waste it. This is a one shot deal. Is there an engineer in the house?"

"Basile, this is your department," announced Samuel, as he explained what Shafira had told him.

"All right, Shafira," said Basile, taking over. "Do you have any means of drilling a hole in the rock face? Anything that will let you create a space for the explosives?"

"No," she replied. "Not that I noticed, anyway. We went through all the crates the soldiers left behind and I didn't see any drills or dremels. Do you want me to check again?"

"We may not have the time." Basile sucked air through his teeth as he considered their options. "Okay... Is there any kind of crevice you can see that's on top of our location, any natural fissure you could pack explosives into?"

"Wait a minute."

The three trapped men held their breath as they waited for Shafira to get back to them.

"Found one!" came the triumphant cry. "If I dig it out, I can create a hole right next to where your radio signal is coming from. I should be able to make it big enough to hold all the explosives. What's the next step?"

"Pack the explosives into the hole," Basile instructed.

"How much should I use?"

"What kind of explosives do you have?"

"I have absolutely no idea," Shafira confessed.

Samuel and Basile exchanged a glance. "Dammit," Basile said. "In that case, I can't really advise. If you use too much, you could kill us. If you don't use enough, you may just bury us. Without being able to carry out a site assessment, it's impossible for me to say."

"Uhh..." Shafira dithered.

"What does the material look like?" asked Basile, impatiently.

"It's in sticks, which say 'C4' on them."

"So, it is a plastic explosive. How many sticks are there?"

"Just a minute... twelve."

"And the depth of the crevice?"

"Um... maybe six feet."

Basile sighed. "Even a dozen sticks of C4 isn't going to do it. Are you *sure* there's no more?"

"I'm positive."

"Okay. You'll just have to use it all, and we'll hope for a miracle."

"Will do."

There was radio silence as Shafira, Josh and Waleed packed explosives into the crevice she'd found.

"Are you sure that telling them to use all of it is the right thing to do?" Samuel asked anxiously. "What if the explosion destroys this cave and everything in it? Who knows what ancient wisdom will be lost?"

Basile shook his head. "A dozen sticks sounds like a lot, until you think about the amount of rock that has to be blasted. And given that they can't drill a twenty-foot bore hole to place them... The only hope is that there's a hidden vertical fissure that will blow apart with a little help."

"It's better to be a living poor man than a dead rich man," intoned

Akhenaton.

"Is that one of your order's aphorisms?" asked Basile.

"No, just common sense," Akhenaton replied.

"You're prejudiced," Samuel accused. "You've already tried to destroy the headdress. I'm sure you'd be very happy if this cave system was buried forever."

"I would not lose sleep over it," Akhenaton admitted. "But then, my order understands the importance of the mind. You were born with everything you need. All of this-" He gestured to the treasures all around them. "It is just a prop, a tool that may make life easier, but it is far from essential. What matters is that we escape with our lives. Anything else is a bonus."

"Okay, that's done," Shafira's voice came over the radio, interrupting the argument. "What do we do now?"

"You need to set the detonator. If you've found fuse wire, thread that into the hole, but make sure you use enough to give yourself time to take cover."

"I found what looks like a time delay detonator," Shafira confirmed.

"Excellent. Set it for, say, ten minutes, and then get yourselves and your helicopter out of there."

"Is there anything else we need to do before we start the timer?"

"Ah, yes, there is. Backfill the hole to secure the explosives. You need as much weight on there as you can possibly get, to direct the blast downward, else it won't do a thing."

"All right. I think I saw some sandbags in one of the desert striders. I'll see what we can do. Meanwhile, I suggest you find somewhere safe to take cover. We'll have you out of there soon... hopefully." *I'm not a rock blasting or search and rescue expert, so the chances are damn near zero,* Shafira thought.

"Thanks, Shafira," said Samuel, taking over the comms device again. "We'll probably lose the signal once I move from this spot, so I'll sign off for now. I owe you dinner for this, though. Think about your favorite restaurant, and we'll go there once we're back in Cairo."

"I'm going to hold you to that," Shafira replied. She signed off, as the three trapped men looked at each other with renewed hope.

"This is it, guys," said Samuel. "With any luck, we'll be free in a few minutes. If not... it's been a pleasure working with you both."

"And you, *mon ami*," replied Basile, shaking his friend's hand.

"We can take shelter behind the statue of Seshat," suggested Akhenaton. "It seems strangely appropriate somehow, seeking protection from the goddess who guarded knowledge and wisdom. May the goddess watch over us. Our lives are in Her hands."

The three men crouched down next to the statue, the hand of the goddess raised over their heads as if in blessing. They waited anxiously, in the brace position as though riding a doomed airplane.

"Are you sure you told her-" began Akhenaton, but hell's thunder stole the words from his mouth. The three men shrunk even tighter, as rubble rained down on them. Sam could only think of the priceless antiquities being buried, as he began to choke on dust. He yanked a handkerchief from his pocket, and put it over his nose and mouth as a filter. The others, wide-eyed with fear, scrambled desperately to find items they could use for the same purpose. Basile frantically unlaced his right boot and yanked his sock off, hurriedly stretching the gray material over his mouth. Akhenaton pulled his arm from the sleeve of his robe, and wrapped the loose fabric around his face.

The dust cloud suddenly lit up with a blinding glare, as light from the noonday sun pierced the roof of the cavern.

"How are we meant to get up there?" wailed Basile, his eyes watering from the dust, as he craned his neck around the status to survey their vertical escape route. "They might as well have saved the explosives and tried to blast their way through the tunnels."

"Jesus, Basile, look on the bright side: they actually blasted a shaft through without killing us!" Samuel spat, his words muffled. "Frenchmen!"

Basile muttered something under his breath. Freedom was close enough to taste, yet so far away.

"Look around," Samuel ordered, as they got up, and began to

climb precariously up the scree that filled the now unrecognizable chamber. "Maybe we can pile up some of the larger artifacts—there are some higher ones that aren't buried—and build a way up to the opening. Basile, can you see anything we might be able to use? If there was ever a time to be creative with your engineering skills, this is it."

There was a rumbling sound, and a large boulder fell from the ceiling, narrowly missing Akhenaton as he jumped out of the way. "Whatever your solution, you better come up with it fast," he warned. "It looks like this whole place is going to collapse on top of us."

Glancing about, Basile went over to the delicately-carved plinth that the headdress had been resting on. Grabbing the plinth with both hands, he strained at it, trying to drag it towards the middle of the room. "Help me," he grunted. "If we can get this closer to the hole, we can use it as the base for a makeshift ladder. It seems sturdy enough to act as the support."

Samuel made to rush to his side, but a shower of debris rained down, cutting him off as he was about to go up the steps.

"I don't think we have time to build anything," cried Akhenaton. "If we're going to escape this place, we need to do it *now*."

"Much as it goes against everything I believe in to treat relics so badly, we're going to have to climb the statue of Moneta," Samuel decided. "It's close enough to the hole that I might be able to reach it if I jump. If I can wedge myself in there, I have some rope in my utility belt. I can pull you up."

"And if you miss?" asked Basile. "It's a long way to fall. If you break a bone, it's going to be almost impossible for us to get you out of here–if the fall doesn't kill you."

As if to emphasize his point, another rock fell from the ceiling, as an ominous cracking sound split the air.

"Debate's over," Samuel barked. "Basile, Akhenaton. MOVE!"

The two men needed no further urging, as they scrambled over to the statue of Moneta, rubble now crashing down at an alarming rate.

"Give me a boost," ordered Samuel. Basile didn't argue, kneeling down and clasping his hands together to give Samuel a foothold.

"One... two... three!"

Basile lifted Samuel up as he reached out for the statue's right hand. Grabbing it around the elbow, he swung his legs up, deftly scrambling round so that he was sitting on her arm, before calling down to the other two.

"I'm going to climb higher," he told them. "Help each other up while I see if I can reach the escape hole from her other arm. Not waiting to see if they followed his instructions, Samuel reached out, using the folds in the robe over the goddess' breast to support him as he scrambled high.

"I'm so sorry," he whispered to the status, as he edged around her face to her other shoulder so that he could shimmy up the arm that was extended towards the ceiling. Despite not believing in the ancient gods, there was something sacrilegious about using Moneta's image as a climbing frame.

Reaching her hand, his progress was halted by the torch she was holding. For a moment he debated with himself as to whether he should try to balance on it.

"Don't even think about it," warned Basile, as he followed his friend up the statue. "I can see from here that it won't support your weight. If you're going to reach the shaft you're going to have to go from there."

Samuel used the torch for support as he pulled himself up to standing. Just as he was about to reach out for the hole, the ground shook beneath them. Samuel fell back. Clenching his thighs together, he managed to stop himself falling, ending up dangling upside down.

"Stay there," called Basile. "I'm coming for you."

But it was Akhenaton who deftly climbed round to the side of the statue where Samuel was, using the creases in the statue's robe to support him as he wedged himself into position and reached up to Samuel. He stood on one foot and pushed up against his lower back, giving the archaeologist had enough momentum to pull himself back up onto the statue's arm.

"How did you do that?" marveled Basile as Samuel stood up on the statue's arm again, trying to reach the bottom of the shaft.

"My order trains us in more than myth and legend," Akhenaton told him.

"Maybe one day you'll consider me friend enough to teach me that trick," Basile replied, as Samuel reached out to the hole.

"It's no good," he called back. "I'm going to have to stand on the torch and jump."

"You can't!" warned Basile. "It'll break and you'll fall."

"I'll just have to time it right." Samuel looked down and gave Basile a smile in farewell before launching himself up onto the torch.

Just as Basile had predicted, it crumbled, crashing to the ground to shatter into a thousand pieces...

...as Samuel leapt, and caught hold of a jagged rock protruding from the side of the vertical shaft.

Bracing himself against the edge of the hole, Samuel kicked up, catching another rock further up, until he'd managed to wedge himself into the opening. He rested for a minute, his chest heaving as he gulped down air. Samuel coughed, as he swallowed more of the thick dust that still hung in the air. "It's a tight fit," he called down, "and it's getting tighter by the second. The wall of the shaft's moving. If we don't get out of here now, we'll all be buried alive."

He fumbled with his utility belt, trying to find the thick cord that was tightly coiled within one of the pouches. Pulling it out as quickly as he could, he dropped the rope and started to swing it, hoping it would gain enough momentum to get within reach of his friends.

"Catch hold of this," he called out. "I've managed to brace myself inside the shaft using my legs, so I should be able to take your weight, but I don't know how long I'm going to stay here. There's a lot of falling debris, so the rocks I'm using to stay in place might not be secure for long."

"I can't catch the rope," Basile yelled. "You need to get it closer to me."

Samuel shifted his hand further down the rope, teetering danger-ously close to falling, as he strained to make the arch of the rope's momentum wider and wider.

"I got it!" crowed Basile. "Can you pull both me and Akhenaton up?"

"I'm not Superman," Samuel yelled back down. "I can barely hold on as it is. Get up here and hurry. I don't plan on leaving either of you behind."

He pushed his feet out against the tunnel wall and gripped at jagged rocks on either side. He grimaced, and blood started dripping from his fingers, as Basile jumped away from the statue and started to pull himself up the rope.

"*Merci beaucoup*," the Frenchman said, as he clambered over Samuel, and wedged himself in the shaft. He quickly untied the rope from around his waist and threw it back down for Akhenaton to use.

Once again, Samuel began to swing the rope so that Akhenaton could reach it.

"Hurry, Samuel!" Akhenaton urged. "The statue is starting to crumble! It was never meant to be climbed."

"Ugghh!" Samuel grunted, sweating with strain and pain as the other man leaped out and grabbed the rope. There was a loud crash as the statue of Moneta started to collapse. Samuel's arms and legs shook, as Akhenaton climbed up the rope, as agile as a monkey.

At last, Akhenaton was in the shaft. He squeezed past Samuel, bracing himself against the narrow opening as he followed Basile up towards the light.

"Come on, Samuel," he called over his shoulder. "We haven't got much time. The entire cave system is collapsing."

"I'm trying," Samuel protested, as he urged his aching limbs to do his bidding. However, the effort of taking the weight of the others had taken its toll and he was running out of energy. Despite his best efforts, he could feel himself losing his grip, his hands starting to slip as the rocks began to cut into his palms.

FORTY-EIGHT

"Go on without me," Samuel urged through gritted teeth, seeing Akhenaton stop to wait for him. "Save yourselves! Somebody needs to get out of this place alive so you can warn the rest of the world of the Bruard's plan."

Akhenaton shook his head. "There's no way I'm leaving you behind," he said. "Give me your hand. Let me carry you, as you carried me."

Samuel's shoulder sent shooting pains through his body in protest at the movement, but the threatening clatter of falling rocks renewed his strength. Frantically, the three men scrabbled upward, as hand and foot holds began to give way.

"We're not going to make it," cried Basile, ducking as a suitcase-sized boulder bounced past. "The entire system is collapsing in on itself. This is goodbye!"

"No, it's not," urged Akhenaton. "We're saved. Look!"

Basile and Samuel risked glancing up. The sky grew dark as Josh's helicopter came into view, blocking the sun. The machine edged lower. The men could see Shafira's anxious face, as she attempted to guide a dangling rope into the shaft. She was trying to shout something, but her voice was drowned out by the thwap-thwap of the rotor blades.

The three men didn't need to be told twice. Clutching at the rope with both hands, they closed their eyes and lowered their heads. Samuel prayed that no more rocks would come tumbling from above as the rotor wash blew around inside the hole. Josh raised the machine higher, pulling them up, as the shaft disintegrated around them. Akhenaton, the last man out, cleared the hole just in time, as the hillside collapsed in on itself, burying St. Augustine's secret chamber forever.

"Nooo!" Waleed cried, gaping down at the treasure he would never hold.

Josh switched on the autopilot to hold the helicopter in a steady hover, as he made his way back to the door to help Shafira winch the three adventurers aboard. Samuel, Basile, and Akhenaton collapsed gratefully into the helicopter, tired, aching, and bruised but alive.

"Samuel McCarthy, I presume," smiled Shafira, holding out a hand for him to shake. She bit back the rest of the remark that almost left her lips. It would be most unprofessional of her to tell the famous archaeologist that the pictures she'd seen of him didn't do any justice to his looks. Even covered in dust and debris, there was a rugged handsomeness to the man.

Samuel nodded. "And you must be my guardian angel from the Ministry. You have no idea how pleased I am to see you." He took her hand and shook it firmly, lingering perhaps a second longer than necessary.

"What happened?" Shafira asked. "Did you uncover the secret to the camouflage technology and the other mysteries surrounding this site? How did you end up trapped underground? We saw a VTOL take off. Don't tell me you encountered the Bruard and survived!"

"All right, I won't tell you that," Samuel grinned. "However, I would strongly advise that you sit down and brace yourself before I fill you in on what's been going on. We've got one hell of a puzzle to solve, before it's too late."

AUTHOR'S NOTE

If you liked *The Eternal Chamber*, you'll love *The Knights of the Spring Dream*:

An ancient relic holds the key to cataclysmic power, and world domination. The race is on to see who gets it first.

Samuel McCarthy, lead archeologist of a six-person team, must find it first, to keep it out of the hands of the deadly, unstoppable Bruard dynasty.

Senior Bruard soldier, Pin Nam-Gi, continues to track the team after nearly burying them alive. His vicious determination to get to the ancient papal cap is relentless. Stopping him seems a distant fantasy.

The Knights of the Spring Dream, a secret order shrouded in the desert sands, protects the ancient relics of St. Augustine. They are Samuel's only option. He must seek out Fatima, the head of the Order, and gain her assistance before the ruthless enemy can reach her.

Will Samuel get there first, or will the power of the Bruard prove once and for all that might makes right?

Click here get it now.

CLAIM YOUR FREE SHORT STORY

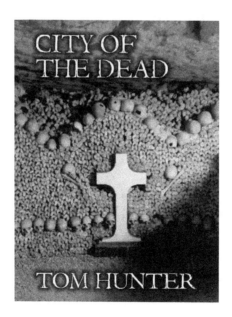

It's a tomb for six million people...

The catacombs beneath Paris aren't somewhere that Mitchell, a desperate gambler, ever saw himself going...

He's in debt to Jimmy "the Ratchet" for $600,000. Mitchell knows Jimmy's debtors don't have a prayer... until Jimmy gives him a mission that will erase most of his debt if completed.

He must go deep into the deathly blackness of the catacombs to retrieve something.

Will Mitchell make it out alive, or will his bones join the groaning masses already entombed there?

CLICK HERE TO CLAIM YOUR COPY OF *CITY OF THE DEAD*

MAY I PLEASE ASK...

Independently published books like this one are very difficult to market without reader reviews. Plus, other readers rely on them to see if the book matches their tastes. It doesn't have to be long or involved. One or two sentences saying what you liked, or didn't like, is enough.

If you're willing to leave a review, please click here. Either way, thanks for reading my work!

CPSIA information can be obtained
at www.ICGtesting.com
Printed in the USA
LVHW11s0520101018
593087LV00001B/133/P